White Desert

White Desert

Colin D. Peel

ROBERT HALE · LONDON

© Colin D. Peel 2001
First published in Great Britain 2001

ISBN 0 7090 6909 X

Robert Hale Limited
Clerkenwell House
Clerkenwell Green
London EC1R 0HT

2 4 6 8 10 9 7 5 3 1

Typeset by
Derek Doyle & Associates, Liverpool.
Printed in Great Britain by
St Edmundsbury Press, Bury St Edmunds, Suffolk.
Bound by Woolnough Bookbinding Limited.

Oh! that the desert were my dwelling-place,
With one fair spirit for my minister,
That I might all forget the human race,
And, hating no one, love but only her.

Byron

Chapter 1

SOMETIMES, at the end of a warm afternoon when the lake was unusually still, Ryder would stop rowing and let the dinghy drift, unwilling to disturb the surface any more than he had to, and not much caring whether he'd reached a good fishing spot.

This evening he wasn't even inclined to drop a line over the side, preferring instead to sit where he was and watch the midges start swarming above the bow.

Now that the weather had improved, and the temperature was rising, up here among the lakes the midges were part of everyday life. There were countless millions of them, their numbers multiplying daily along with the mosquitos – confirmation that summer had finally arrived, and a sure sign that the annual explosion of Québec's insect population was well underway.

Today, the first of the dragonflies were about too, one perching on the gunwale so close to him that he had to resist the impulse to reach out and touch it. A second later it was gone, darting away in the fading light, flying low across the water towards the rushes at the narrow end of the lake.

If Ryder hadn't watched it go, he would not have been looking south. And if he hadn't been looking south, he would never have seen the dust.

It was being kicked up by a vehicle travelling west through the forest on the dirt road from Minerve. The trees made it impossible to see what kind of vehicle it was, but he didn't need to see it. The dust was enough, a warning of possible danger – of a threat that Ryder had almost convinced himself might never come.

Quickly swinging the dinghy round, he began to row again, pulling hard on the oars while he tried to estimate how long it would take him to reach the cabin where he'd have a chance of buying time.

He began counting under his breath, glancing over his shoulder at the end of each ten strokes to assess his progress.

It was a wasted effort. He was less than a quarter of the way to the jetty when he realized he had miscalculated badly.

The car or pick-up had increased speed, and its dust cloud told him that it had already turned on to the track leading to the cabin. Worse still, by rowing towards the shore, Ryder knew he'd made things simpler for his visitors. He was not only in easy range, but unable to do a damn thing about it – a pessimistic scenario, he thought, particularly if someone had just taken the wrong road from Minerve.

Or was this really where everything would end; not in a dark alley or in an orchestrated car crash, but, of all places, on a quiet, unspoiled Canadian lake with only midges and dragonflies for witnesses?

Ryder didn't know. Nor for some reason did it seem to matter very much. He was calm, annoyed with himself for being careless, but unafraid, considering whether or not it would be worth trying his luck in the water, or whether to reverse direction and head back out to the centre of the lake where he'd be a smaller target.

In the end he decided to do nothing, conscious of a dryness in his mouth, but still calm, ready for his first glimpse of the car and prepared to act once he had a better idea of what he was up against.

It wasn't a car; it was a four-wheel-drive Ford Explorer, a green one, slowing now it had left the trees and skidding to a halt in the little clearing alongside the jetty.

A young woman got out. She was dressed in jeans, wearing a light-coloured leather jacket and carrying a shoulder bag. She didn't look like someone the PAF would send to do the job, but over the years, Ryder had met plenty of PAF recruits who had appeared to be equally presentable.

'Hello there.' She waved to him.

Ryder stayed where he was, resting his oars on the water, his attention focused half on the girl and half on the trees behind the Ford.

'Excuse me.' She waved again. 'Can I talk to you?'

Gradually he began to ease the dinghy forwards, rowing it stern-first until he reached the end of the jetty. By now he was almost certain she was alone. He was also fairly sure that she wasn't communicating with anyone in the trees, and apart from a slight awkwardness in the way she was standing, he could detect nothing threatening in her manner – an indication, perhaps, that he'd misjudged the situation.

After disembarking at the jetty he walked to meet her, an oar balanced carefully on each shoulder.

'I'm sorry to be a nuisance.' She smiled pleasantly. 'I'm looking for someone called Chris Ryder. Is that you?'

Ryder shook his head.

'Oh.' Her expression changed. 'I must be in the wrong place, then.'

He said nothing, less concerned than he had been, but remaining cautious and maintaining his concentration. She was a European or an American in her early twenties, slightly built with attractive, dark-brown eyes and a good figure. Unless she was bait for a trap, who she was, and what the hell she wanted, he couldn't imagine.

'This is Lake Lesage though, isn't it?' she said.

'You're at the bottom end of it.'

'But you're not Chris Ryder?'

'I've already told you.' He tightened his grip on the oars as she reached for something in her bag.

She produced a folded map which she studied briefly. 'I suppose I'll have to try the north road,' she said. 'Perhaps I'll have better luck there.'

She wasn't going anywhere, he thought, at least not yet. Allowing her to leave without discovering why she'd come was not an option. Someone had sent her, but if it wasn't the PAF, who was it?

Evidently anxious to move on, she gave him a tight smile to say goodbye before returning the map to her bag.

Ryder had forgotten the rules. When she withdrew her hand, this time there was a gun in it.

'I know who you are,' she said. 'Put down the oars.'

He did what he was told, moving slowly, his eyes never leaving hers, already knowing she was an amateur. She might have been smart enough to catch him off guard, but she was standing too close, and her gun gave her away – a short-barrelled .357 Magnum revolver that would just about knock her over if she ever had the strength to fire it double action with one finger.

'Do you know who I am?' she said.

'No.' Ryder's mouth was dry. again.

'I'm Isabel Corrales.'

He should have been surprised. But he wasn't. Instead there was an inevitability about this, another reminder of his foolishness in imagining that there could ever be such a thing as a fresh start. He said nothing, weighing up the odds while he waited to learn how long she intended to prolong matters.

'Did you think my family would forget?' She moved the gun slightly. 'Or didn't it matter to you?'

If she'd asked the questions less directly, he might have considered offering an excuse or an explanation. But excuses and explanations weren't going to help when the truth was as thin as it was implausible.

'Are you sure I'm who you think I am?' he said.

Using her free hand, she removed an envelope from her bag. 'Let's see, shall we?' She threw the envelope at his feet. 'Take a look. Then tell me you didn't kill my father.'

The envelope contained photographs, all of his first assignment in Colombia. Five showed him assembling the machine-pistol in his Medellín hotel room, the other three provided an unpleasantly graphic record of Pablo Corrales dying in the street. Ryder had been confronted with the photos before, but for a different purpose, and in rather different circumstances.

'Did you get these from the PAF?' he asked. 'Did they send you?'

'No one sent me, Mr Ryder. I'm here by myself to do what my family should have done seven years ago.' She pulled back the hammer. 'Is there anything you want to say to me?'

Ryder couldn't think of anything that was likely to change her mind. Although she was having trouble keeping her nerve, now she'd cocked the gun and was holding it in both hands, his edge had gone, and only experience was going to make the difference.

Over the last few minutes, shadows from the jetty had started stretching out across the lake to merge with the reflections of the treetops. Ryder had seen the effect before – an elongated, criss-cross pattern of dark lines that seemed to overlay the images of the aspens as though he was looking at a painting in a mirror. It was very beautiful and very peaceful, he thought, a picture that was as good as any to hold on to if he was going to be too slow.

'Well?' Her hands were shaking.

He delayed his answer, hoping for the return of a half-remembered skill. The trick was patience – waiting for the moment when it would suddenly kick in. He could almost sense it coming – the ability to freeze the picture in his mind until it seemed that time itself was standing still.

His other senses were becoming sharper too. He could smell pine resin and the perfume she was wearing. And he could hear himself breathing and see her knuckles whitening as she increased her grip on the gun.

'What do you want to know?' he said.

'I want to know why?'

'No you don't. You haven't come all this way to find out why. You don't care why, and you're not about to believe anything I tell you. You've already decided what you want to do, so why don't you just get on with it?'

He was as ready as he was ever going to be, but caught unawares by the unexpected appearance of a red dot on his shirt.

Had the hidden gunman been behind him, or been more careful with the laser, Ryder would have died where he stood.

As it was, he was barely fast enough. An instant before he heard the crack of a rifle, he launched himself at the girl. Simultaneously, as if in slow motion, he saw her jerk the trigger.

11

How either of the bullets missed him, he never knew. He knew only that he was still alive, and that a combination of his tackle and the recoil from her gun had somehow kept her alive as well.

But she hadn't given up. She was fighting him, endeavouring to regain her balance when another shot from the sniper zipped past Ryder's hip.

By the slimmest of margins, again he had escaped. This time the girl was not so lucky.

He heard the bullet smack into her, heard her scream and felt her crumpling beneath him.

Instinct and adrenalin took over. Before Ryder knew what he was doing, he'd kicked the gun away, picked her up as though she was a child and started out for the cabin on an eighty-yard, heart-stopping run that would have been dangerous even without her weight to slow him down.

She was slippery with blood, still struggling and swearing at him in Spanish until he shut her up by yelling at her.

She still made it hard, lying awkwardly over his shoulder and grabbing at him whenever he attempted to weave.

Two more shots came from the trees, the first ricocheting off the ground between his feet, the second brushing his arm while he was on the cabin steps trying to wrench open the door with one hand and maintain his grip on the girl's feet with the other.

Once inside he dropped her unceremoniously on the floor before slamming the door and heading straight for the bedroom to fetch his rifle. As well as being out of breath, he was cursing his stupidity, wondering why in God's name he'd bothered with her when she could just as easily be the decoy he'd thought she was.

She was sitting, propped up against the wall, eyes filled with fear, her hands pressed flat to the floor on each side of her.

'Who's out there with the gun?' He risked a quick look out of the window before he started feeding cartridges into a spare magazine.

'I don't know.'

'Give me a reason to believe you.'

12

'I don't have to give you anything.' She winced in pain. 'Why didn't you leave me?'

'Go back outside if you want; I'm not going to stop you.'

'I can't. My leg won't hold me up.'

Ryder knelt down to inspect the wound. The entry point was high up on her left thigh and, judging by the amount of blood on the floor, he guessed the bullet had gone right through.

To discover if there was an exit wound, he slipped his hand beneath her.

'*Váyase.*' She spat at him and pushed his arm away.

'Suit yourself. Bleed to death for all I care.' Ryder was endeavouring to think, unwilling to believe that the gunman was alone and trying to convince himself that this would be as good a time as any to cut his losses.

'Why are you looking at me like that?' She stared at him. 'It's because we're not safe in here, isn't it?'

'Depends if your friend in the forest has called for backup.'

'I don't know who it is. I've told you. Why won't you believe me?'

'Why do you think?' Ryder said. 'This is all a coincidence, is it?'

'Yes, I mean, no. I can't explain. . . .' Her voice tailed off.

The explanation was straightforward, he thought, but volunteering it would let her off the hook. 'You set me up,' he said.

'How does that work when I'm the one who's been shot?'

He ignored the remark, still unsure of what he was going to do. Two years ago he wouldn't have contemplated taking her with him, but this was now, and this wasn't exactly Somalia or Yugoslavia. Which meant he had to make up his mind about her – and do it pretty damn quickly.

'Look,' he said. 'No one's after you. You just got in the way. If you'll unwind a bit, I'll do what I can for your leg, then I'll arrange for someone to come and collect you as soon as I get out on the main highway.'

'No.' She attempted unsuccessfully to stand up.

Instead of helping her, Ryder watched her face, trying to decide how frightened she was at the prospect of being abandoned.

'Please,' she said. 'You can't leave me.'

'Have you forgotten what you came here to do? Why the hell would I want to take you anywhere?'

'I don't know.' Her eyes had clouded over, and she'd started biting her lip.

It was a lousy test, Ryder thought. He had no idea whether she was scared witless or in so much pain that she couldn't keep up the pretence.

'OK,' he said. 'Go to the bedroom and find something clean to use as a bandage. Wind it round pressure pads on both sides of your leg. Wind it real tight.'

'What are you going to do?'

He had no opportunity to answer her. No sooner had she finished speaking than the window exploded beside the door.

Ryder had been expecting it. What he hadn't expected was the noise that accompanied the crash of breaking glass – not the sharp crack of a rifle, but the instantly recognizable clamour of an AK47, a warning, if he needed one, of what was likely to be in store if he put off making his decision for very long.

'Now!' he shouted. 'Go on.'

Although the cabin was constructed of seasoned, rough-sawn logs, a round from a Kalashnikov could easily penetrate the joints between them. Ryder knew it, and so did whoever had fired at the window. It had either been an exploratory burst to discover whether Ryder intended to fight, or a means of establishing the range before the assault began in earnest.

What form the attack would take was only one of the unknowns: that it would come was all he could be certain of – more certain than he was about the girl. Had the PAF simply used her to find him, hoping she'd finish the job and take the blame? Or was it still conceivable that she was one of theirs?

She'd returned from the bedroom, her face drawn, her fingers red and sticky.

'Now what?' she asked quietly.

'We wait.'

'Because it'll be dark soon?'

'Right.' Using a piece of broken glass as a mirror, Ryder

angled it above his head in an attempt to determine what, if anything, was happening outside.

There was nothing to see. With the daylight all but gone, the
lake and its surroundings were barely discernible against the
sombre background of the forest.

'Can you walk at all?' he asked.

'I haven't tried.' She paused. 'Well, not properly.'

'What about swimming?'

'I don't know. Why?'

He chambered a round in the rifle. 'There's a rug under the
table. Underneath that there's a trapdoor. See if you can get it
open.'

For a moment he thought she was going to argue, but a light
flickering through the broken window was sufficient inducement
to make her hurry. She crawled away, leaving Ryder to decide on
the wisdom of responding with a couple of quick shots. Slow them
down, or provoke them, he wondered? Buy a few more minutes,
or persuade them to go for overkill if they had the firepower?

Unable to make up his mind without more information, he
waited for the light to probe elsewhere along the wall then risked
another look.

Apart from the light itself there was no more to see than
before. The beam was coming from somewhere near the jetty, a
high-intensity, white beam that was being used methodically to
scan the outside of the cabin.

'It's done,' she called.

He went to check, keeping low and tipping the table on to its
side to provide a shield between the trapdoor and the wall.

'OK,' he said. 'Now listen. Under the floor there's a crawl
space and a sort of shallow trench. When I tell you, get yourself
into the trench and out of the way. If you stay under the hatch,
I'm going to wind up on top of you. Do you understand?'

She nodded. 'Won't it be better if you go first?'

'I need to knock out that light. We don't want anyone seeing
us underneath the cabin if we can help it.'

'Oh.' She seemed withdrawn, sitting on the floor with her
arms wrapped round herself as though she was cold.

Until now, Ryder hadn't considered how much blood she might have lost – a serious mistake if she was going to run out of steam before they reached the water, and a good reason for him to get on with things.

He went back to the window where he chose a gap between two pieces of broken glass to rest his rifle.

The origin of the light was about ninety yards away, a bright spot in the darkness that would have been an easy target if it was stationary. But its owner was being careful, switching it off at random intervals and moving from one position to another. Unless there were half-a-dozen men with half-a-dozen bloody lights, Ryder thought, in which case the trench had better be deep enough.

'Off you go.' He issued his instruction without turning round. 'Tap on the floor as soon as you're clear.'

Less confident than he had been, he found he was breathing too quickly to hold the rifle steady. He made himself relax, centring his sights on the light while he listened for her signal.

A second after it came, the light went out, leaving him exposed at the window with no target.

He predicted when and where the beam would next reappear, moving his sights to the left in anticipation.

His prediction was good. When the light came on he was ready for it and able to squeeze off three shots in quick succession.

How effective they'd been was difficult to tell. The light had been extinguished at once, but whether or not he'd hit it was anyone's guess. He waited for something to happen – for some shouting, for the flicker of another light, for the AK47 to open up again – for any indication that his shots had not been wasted.

There was nothing. So silent and so dark were the lakeside and the forest that long before he heard the whooshing sound, Ryder had dropped his rifle and was bolting for the trapdoor.

He went through headfirst, narrowly missing the figure of the girl, hitting the ground too late to shout a warning.

Accompanied by a vivid burst of orange flame, the blast was severe, splintering the floor above Ryder's head and driving a length of timber end-on into the soil beside him.

Knowing he had to get her out in a hurry, but unable to stand up properly in the crawl space, he grabbed her by the wrists, intending to tow her behind him.

She was too frightened to accept his help. Breaking free, she scrabbled along by herself, using her elbows and her one good leg until they both emerged from beneath what remained of the cabin.

The whole building was starting to burn, set alight by the rocket-propelled grenade that should have killed them both. Ryder's bet had been for a swift reaction; what he hadn't bargained on was one so violent.

He prevented her from sitting up. 'We're not out of this yet,' he said. 'Can you crawl another fifty yards?'

'I can go on all fours.' She was wide-eyed, close to panic.

'They may have someone waiting for us. If we don't keep our heads down they'll be able to see us because of the flames.'

'Fifty yards to where?'

He pointed towards the edge of the lake. 'Those rushes. You can just pick them out over there. Then you'll have to swim.'

'All right.' She began to move off, but stopped. 'This is crazy,' she said. 'I don't understand what's happening.'

'You don't have to. Get going. I'll be along in a minute.' He gave her a head start, being careful not to let his imagination run away with him now that the flames were casting shadows everywhere he looked.

If another sniper was nearby, locating him would be impossible, Ryder decided. So the girl would have to take her chances. She was making good progress, but with the fire burning more and more fiercely, the whole area was being lit up by it, and the trench he'd laboured long and hard to dig might have just as well not been there. He could see her easily: and if he could see her, so could someone else. But she was already nearing the rushes, slithering into them until she was suddenly lost from sight.

Electing not to bother with the trench, Ryder relied on shadows and the cover of some trees on a risky dash to join her.

She was lying on her stomach, waiting for him in the water at the lakeside. 'Someone's here,' she whispered. 'I heard them. I saw something move too.'

'Where?' He crouched beside her.

'There.' She pointed ahead.

He told her to stay put, then, with some misgivings, back-tracked, heading for a group of scrubby trees and tangled vegetation in order to make his approach from the lake rather than the shore.

At the boundary of the cover he paused to listen, inching forwards only when he was certain it was safe to do so. Six feet into the rushes he was confronted, not by an assailant, but by a pair of startled ducks that paddled off into the shadows, quacking but making no attempt to fly.

The encounter had done nothing to help his nerves. Discovering that the girl was not where he'd left her made it worse. He found her twenty feet away, out in the open, looking for him.

'For Christ's sake.' Ryder pushed her down face-first into the mud. 'What's the matter with you?'

'I didn't think you were coming back. What happened?'

'Just a couple of ducks.'

'Oh.' She wiped away the mud. 'Why hasn't there been more shooting? Why have they stopped?'

'They think we're still in the cabin. There's only one door and they'll know there aren't any windows in the back.' He tried to read her expression. 'Are you OK?'

'If I say I'm not, you'll leave me, won't you? You didn't even expect me to get this far – that's why you made me go on ahead – because you hoped I'd get shot.'

Ryder had heard enough. There wasn't time for this, and she was irritating him. 'Listen,' he said. 'If you haven't figured it out yet, I don't give a fuck what you believe. If you want to carry on sticking your head up until you get shot, go right ahead. If you want me to get you to a doctor, just shut up and do what you're told. You're already more trouble than you're worth. Don't push your luck.'

'I don't trust you.' She hesitated. 'What happens if I can't swim? I'm getting dizzy.'

'If you can't swim, you'll have to trust me, won't you?'

She glanced at him but made no effort to answer.

Ryder changed his plan. 'OK,' he said. 'You stay here until you hear the sound of an outboard motor, but the minute you do, you have to swim or hop out into deeper water – up to your waist at least. Can you do that?'

'Have you got a boat – a proper one?'

'It's round the corner, hidden in the swamp, but I can only get to it from the lake – by swimming up an estuary. You'll be better off here anyway. You've probably got too much muck in your leg already.'

'How long will you be?'

'Give me five minutes.'

Ryder's estimate was to prove optimistic. It took him little enough time to reach the boat and remove the canopy of branches, but by then he'd decided against starting the motor, realizing that the fire at the cabin had provided an opportunity he'd overlooked.

He used oars instead, keeping close to shore once he was clear of the estuary, hoping she might have set off early when there had been no sound to alert her.

She was thirty feet out from the rushes, floating on her back and clearly relieved to see him.

With some difficulty he hauled her on board then made a place for her on one of the seats. 'Did you hear any more ducks?' he said.

'No.' She spat out some water. 'Is the motor dead?'

'We're not going to use it yet.' Ryder was studying the cabin. Except for a section of the rear wall, the whole building was engulfed in flame. The roof was gone, and the veranda was in the process of collapsing inwards. Only the stone chimney remained untouched, surrounded on all sides by piles of burning embers and clouds of sparks. It was a pretty damn good fire, he thought, but was it good enough?

He began to row again, still in comparatively shallow water, slipping the boat in and out of reeds and rushes until they were further away from the flames, and he was able to use the deeper shadows of the shoreline aspens.

No more shots came from the trees. Nor was there a second burst from the Kalashnikov or another grenade from the launcher. But whether their escape had been detected, Ryder could not be sure.

He concentrated on the job in hand, endeavouring to put some distance between himself and the fire in a boat that had not been designed for rowing. Unlike the dinghy, the rowlocks were poorly positioned, and the hull was heavy and sluggish, making it difficult for him to make much headway.

After persisting for nearly a quarter of an hour, he gave up. Behind them now, the fire had all but burned itself out, leaving a glow that was no more than a dull speck of light against an otherwise dark curtain of trees and hills. Even the smoke which had drifted north to fan out over the lake was detectable only by its smell.

'Are we going to be all right?' she asked.

'Maybe.' Because this was only the second time she'd spoken since he'd plucked her from the water, Ryder was worrying about the dizziness she'd mentioned. 'How's the leg?'

'A bit numb.'

'Soon as we've got you in the car I'll take a look at it.'

'What car?'

'We're not going to get far by boat,' he said. 'This is a pretty small lake. It's only four miles long.'

'If you didn't know I was trying to find you, why would you have this boat and a car hidden somewhere? Who else is after you?'

'Long story.' He stowed the oars then went to attend to the motor, switching on the fuel and the ignition before he pulled hard on the starter cord.

The motor burst into life at once, pushing up the bow as the hull began to gather speed and flatten out on the water.

For Ryder, the speed was as welcome as the night wind in his face. After struggling to make progress with the oars, there was a feeling of exhilaration in being able to move more swiftly – particularly so now that events had ended not in the disaster he'd feared, but reasonably well, or as well as he could have expected them to end.

By the time they neared the north shore of the lake, the moon was rising over the hills, not yet casting much light, but allowing him to navigate a course to some mud flats beside a small, grassy plateau he'd visited before. He beached the boat there, tying it to a log that was half-lying in the water before he helped the girl get out.

She was shivering in her wet clothes, refusing to be co-operative when he offered to carry her, despite her being unable to stand without assistance.

'You don't learn, do you?' Ryder picked her up anyway. 'The car's only over there by that stump.'

She said nothing, keeping her face turned away until he stood her down on one foot beside the Plymouth and told her to wait while he opened the door.

Waiting was not her strong point. Before he could stop her, she clambered into the back seat by herself.

'You don't have to check my leg,' she said. 'It's stopped bleeding.'

'You only think it has.' Ryder tried to see the bandage in the moonlight. 'You've probably left a pint of blood in the boat and another pint behind in the lake. Why not let me have a look?'

'Because I don't want you to. I don't like you touching me. I don't even like you being near me.'

Ryder got behind the wheel and slammed the door shut. 'You've got a half-inch hole through your thigh,' he said. 'If you're not in shock already, you're sure as hell going to be, so you'd better listen while you can still think straight. These are the choices: I can find you a doctor in St-Jovite or Ste-Agathe, or I'll take you with me to Montréal.'

'How far's Montréal?'

'Probably too far. A good three hours away.'

'Why would you want to take me to Montréal? Why would you want to take me anywhere? That's what you said before.'

Ryder had long since stopped wondering why he was doing this. But whatever the reason, it wasn't guilt, he told himself. What had happened tonight was simply the result of her naïvety and his carelessness, and because once he'd been committed he

21

could hardly have left her behind for the PAF to clean up.

He started the car, removing his Colt from the glove compartment and placing the gun beside him on the seat for insurance before he switched on the headlights. Then he took a final look at his passenger and told her to hold on to something for the bumpy drive along the track.

The pot-holed dirt road out to Nominigue wasn't much smoother, but it was straighter, and once he hit the asphalt on the Bellerive Station section he was able to make up time, swinging south on to Highway 11 shortly before midnight.

Encouraged by what had so far turned out to be an incident-free journey, instead of carrying on to St-Jovite he decided to stop early, pulling in to a small car-park on the outskirts of Labelle.

The girl was not in good shape. She was still shivering, lying on the seat and resisting only half-heartedly when he put a hand round her wrist to take her pulse.

'Well?' She sat up.

'You'll live. Do we find a doctor?'

'No. We're too close to the lake. I want to be away from here – as far away as I can get.'

'No one's after you. Didn't you hear what I said?'

'You said you'd take me to Montréal.'

'Only if we do a deal.'

'Like what?' She compressed her lips.

'I put a decent dressing on your leg, and you swallow a handful of tetracycline pills.' He paused. 'If things get tough I can give you a syringe of morphine you can use yourself – sealed packet, sterile needle guaranteed. How about it?'

'Stop patronizing me. Tonight doesn't make any difference to anything. If you think that helping me is some sort of trade-off for what you did in Medellín you're not just wrong, you're stupid. Helping me isn't going to help you. But you already know that, don't you? I can tell.'

'You're too strung out to tell the time,' Ryder said. 'Save your breath.' Glad that she'd come to her senses, he went to get his first-aid kit, as much impressed by her ability to handle the pain as he was by her uncompromising hostility. Despite the expensive clothes, the Rolex and her almost perfect English, in her case, what you saw was not what you got, he thought. The well-bred, well-educated Colombian girl sitting in his car had searched him out for one reason only, and it would be as well to remember how little she'd flinched once she'd decided to pull the trigger of her gun.

It was an hour and a half later, while he was travelling in the fast lane of the superhighway into St-Jérôme that he began to realize how important she would be to the success of his new-found plan. Whichever way he looked at it, the conclusion was the same: without the co-operation of Isabel Corrales, or more luck than he deserved, sooner or later, no matter where in the world he chose to go, what had happened tonight would be repeated over and over again until the PAF had finally fulfilled their promise to him.

Chapter 2

RYDER had been putting off the visit. Twice in the last four days he'd been on the point of going to the hospital, and twice he'd changed his mind at the last moment. This morning, because his most recent phone call had given him the impression that she could be discharged as early as tomorrow, he seemed to have been left with little choice but to make the effort and discover whether or not he had a problem.

How he'd be received was impossible to guess. Although she'd apparently taken his advice and continued to use the false name under which she'd been admitted, that was no indication that her attitude had softened. It would depend on how he played his hand, Ryder thought, or maybe on how grateful she'd be to get her passport back.

He'd retrieved it along with her bag two days ago when he'd made his return trip to the lakeside to inspect her Ford and to have a look over the burnt-out remains of the cabin, but, based on her past performance, she was likely to regard her passport as being of less value than an opportunity to be as rude and obstructive as she possibly could.

Telling himself that she might just have had a change of heart, he left the motel at 9.30, driving slowly towards Pointe Claire, only heading back through Lachine and continuing on into the city once he was certain that the road was free of any suspicious vehicles.

There was nowhere to park inside the hospital grounds, and the adjacent streets were equally jammed with cars. As a result, it

25

was nearly eleven o'clock by the time he'd locked up the Plymouth, walked back the five blocks to the visitors' lobby and found out what ward she was in.

He took the elevator to the fourth floor, conscious of a smell that was the same as every hospital he'd ever been in. As well as making him uncomfortable, the atmosphere was doing nothing to persuade him that this had ever been a good idea.

'Can I help you?' A staff nurse at reception smiled at him, repeating her question in French when Ryder was slow to answer.

'I'm sorry,' he said. 'I'm looking for Maria Serrano.'

'Are you a friend or a member of the family?'

'Friend. Is it OK if I go through?'

'Miss Serrano's in a private ward.' She picked up her phone. 'May I have your name, please?'

'Say it's John. Tell her I've brought her bag and the stuff she left at the lake.' He waited while his message was relayed.

'I'm afraid Miss Serrano doesn't want to see anyone right now.' The nurse was apologetic. 'If you'd like to leave her things with me, I can give them to her for you.'

Ryder dropped the bag on to the counter, more annoyed than he was disappointed, angry with himself for wasting time when he should have known better. 'If she can't figure out what's in the matchbox, tell her to use her imagination,' he said. 'And tell her I hope her leg's OK.'

'My leg's fine – if it's any of your business.'

Ryder recognized her voice. She'd come through some swing doors behind him, her mouth already set in a firm line.

'What do you want?' she said.

Either because his first impressions of her had been cut short, or because his last recollection had been of an injured, frightened young woman smothered in mud and blood, Ryder found himself staring at her without anything meaningful to say.

She was barefoot, wearing a sleeveless, white blouse and a black, knee-length skirt pulled in at her waist by a red belt. She was also wearing tiny, gold ear-rings and had a thin gold bracelet around her left wrist. Although there was nothing ostentatious or especially provocative about her clothes or her jewellery, in the

starched, austere environment of the hospital, it was difficult not
to be distracted by the way she looked. Everything about her was
distracting – so much so that Ryder was temporarily taken aback.

'Well?' she said.

'I brought your stuff.' He collected his thoughts. 'I need to
talk to you.'

'Go on, then, talk.'

'Not here. Is there somewhere we can go?'

She reached past him to collect her bag, then limped away,
deliberately letting one of the doors swing back into his face as
he followed her.

Ryder was careful not to react, accompanying her along a corridor until she stopped outside what he guessed was her door.

This time she stood aside, allowing him to enter a room that
was at least twice the size of the one in his motel.

Except for the presence of a bed and a steel-topped trolley by
the window, it was hard to imagine anywhere that could less
resemble a hospital room. Besides being fully carpeted, it was
furnished with an expensive, three-piece suite, two mahogany
coffee tables, and the walls were hung with several impressionist
paintings. In one corner, a state-of-the-art, flat-screen television
was flanked by a CD player and a computer work station complete with printer. But it was the flowers that caught Ryder's
attention most – spray after spray of them, some still cellophane-
wrapped, standing in vases on the tables, others lined up along
the windowsill with even more scattered haphazardly on the floor
around the furniture.

'Who's paying for this?' he asked.

'I phoned my uncle in Colombia.' She closed the door behind
her. 'I don't think that's any of your business either, do you?'

'Did you tell your uncle what happened?'

'Are you worried he might send someone else – someone
more professional who won't mess things up like I did?'

The possibility had occurred to Ryder. 'Look,' he said, 'I
haven't come to carry on where we left off. If you don't want to
hear anything I have to say, that's fine with me. I've got plenty of
other things to do.'

'Why did you go back up to the lake?' She sat down on the bed. 'Did you want to search through my bag to find out if I was who I said I was?'

'No. I wanted to have a look at your car. I phoned the rental outfit for you and told them where they could pick it up, but they said you'd already been in touch. The keys are in your purse.'

'Along with a matchbox.'

'Someone planted bugs in your nice Ford Explorer – two miniature radio transmitters – one under the dashboard, and one inside the rear door. They're in the matchbox.'

'What about my gun?' She swung her legs. 'Did you find that too?'

'It's in the lake. I dropped it off the end of the jetty for you. Are we going to talk, or not?'

'Depends what you want to talk about. I can guess, though. You see, my uncle told me a lot of things I didn't know before.'

'Such as?'

'Stuff about my father – about the Corrales cocaine cartel, about what my father was doing before you murdered him.'

Ryder sat down in one of the chairs. 'Was it your uncle who sent you to Québec?' he said.

She put on an artificial smile. 'I don't think you've rehearsed this very well. I come from a respectable Catholic family, Mr Ryder. They'd hardly have sent someone like me, would they? No one knew what I was doing. If I'd told my uncle or my aunt, they'd have done anything to stop me.' She paused. 'I was the one who was set up, not you. I was supposed to take the blame for killing you, wasn't I?'

'Sure you were. If things had gone to plan, you'd have been arrested before you got to the airport. You set yourself up. You had a good motive for hunting me down; you've been carrying a gun in a foreign country, and you must have asked a lot of people a lot of questions to have traced me to the lake.'

'You weren't hard to find.' She swung her legs again. 'The man in Colombia who mailed me the photos said you were somewhere in Québec. I just used money. I'm good at it. You shouldn't have given your real name to the post office in Mont-Laurier.'

Ryder had been searching for the right opening, but despite her attitude being marginally less aggressive, it hardly seemed worth trying to bring her round. 'When are you being discharged?' he said.

'Soon.' She looked at him. 'Tomorrow morning. So you'd better ask me what you want to ask me now, hadn't you?'

'How about a favour?'

'I don't owe you anything. You didn't save my life the other night. Those men weren't after me; you told me they weren't, remember?'

'OK.' He stood up. 'Have a nice trip back to South America. Your passport's in your bag, but it might be an idea to carry on pretending you're Maria Serrano while you're still in Canada.'

'To be safe?'

'Right.'

'That's not the reason.' She walked over to the door to stop him leaving. 'You're lying. You want everyone to believe we both died in the fire. That's why you went back to the lake – to see how much of the cabin was left.'

'Look,' Ryder said, 'all I was going to do is ask if you'd keep away from the phone when you get home – just for a couple of weeks.' He stopped talking, reluctant to continue because of the expression on her face.

'Is that all?' she said.

'Except that if anyone comes around looking for you, maybe your uncle and your friends could say that, as far as they know, you're still somewhere up in Canada.'

'I'm supposed to give you time to disappear, am I?' She leaned back against the door. 'So those people can't find you again?'

'Will you do it?'

'Why should I?'

He had no reason to give her – only an excuse that she would be as unwilling to accept as he was to volunteer it. 'If you don't want to help, it's OK,' he said.

'Perhaps I should tell the PAF where you are.' She toyed with her bracelet for a moment. 'That was the name you said, wasn't it?'

'You don't know the first thing about the PAF.'

'I can find out. I've already started.'

Ryder was tiring of her games. 'You're out of your depth,' he said. 'Go home and forget you met me.'

'I might do what you want if you tell me what I want to know. Was it the PAF who paid you to kill my father?'

'Ask your uncle or your mother.'

'My mother died two years ago.' She moved away from the door. 'And my uncle says he's never heard of the PAF. He's mad at me for getting mixed up in things he thinks I don't under-stand – things he won't talk about over the phone.' She paused. 'So I want answers from you.'

'In return for giving me some breathing space?'

'Perhaps.' She brushed past him and walked over to sit at the computer. 'Come and look.'

Ryder picked his way through the flowers and went to stand behind her, aware of the fresh smell of her hair while she punched buttons on the keyboard to bring the screen to life. Displayed on it was a file she had created:

Maria Serrano: File 01.

**National and International Organizations
and Publications:**

      Philadelphia Asian Forum (USA)

      Photo And Film (US magazine)

      Professional Association of Firefighters (UK)

      Pictorial Atlas of Finland (annual publication)

      Personal Address File (Internet site for celebrities)

      Performing Arts Faculty (University of Idaho USA)

      Peace Aid Foundation (Geneva)

      Pittsburg Actors Federation (USA)

      Politicians Against Freemasonry (France and UK)

      Princes And Fairies (US children's board game)

Ryder read the list over her shoulder, surprised at what she'd been able to find.

'Well?' She spoke with her back to him.

He said nothing.

'What about these?' She pushed another button to bring up a second file.

This one was a good deal more extensive. The screen was filled with the names of companies that embodied the initials PAF. There were hundreds, from all over the world, over half of them in foreign languages.

Ryder decided to take his chances with her. 'Go back to your first file,' he said.

'There's only one name that makes any sense.' She placed a finger on the screen. 'You don't mean the Peace Aid Foundation, do you?' She swivelled round on the chair. 'You're not serious.'

'I thought we were being serious.'

'I don't believe you. It's a charity of some kind. They've got their own Internet web site. I checked.'

'They've got seventeen of the bloody things,' Ryder said 'In seventeen different countries.'

Turning back to her keyboard she clicked up a description of the Peace Aid Foundation and began to read aloud. 'Non-governmental, non-profit, humanitarian, international aid organization,' she said. 'Founded in 1994 after the Gulf War and the Rwandan refugee crisis. Dedicated to the establishment of human rights, peace and democracy in all countries destabilized by civil war, political or military upheaval. Active projects in Iraq, Sudan, Ethiopia, Somalia, Rwanda, Angola, Bosnia and Kosovo. Offices in Geneva, London, Paris and New York.'

Ryder prevented her from continuing. 'I've already told you,' he said. 'You're out of your depth.'

'It gives a list of directors.'

'I know.' He reached forward and switched off the computer. 'You won't get anything off their web sites. It's all crap.'

She stood up and went to stand at the window. 'Why would an international aid organization want you dead?'

'I used to work for them. And because I know what their agenda is.'

'Were you working for the PAF when you killed my father?'

'Yes.'

'Have you killed other people?'

'Yes.'

She looked at him unblinkingly, her face expressionless. 'How many people? Where?'

'Does it matter?'

'Was it someone from the PAF who gave me those photos of you?'

'They were using you,' Ryder said. 'They take photos of everyone.'

'What do you mean, everyone?'

'Other recruits. People like me. It's their insurance.'

She was still staring at him, clearly doubting what he'd said.

He was uncertain of whether to go on, but inclined to do so now that she seemed more willing to listen. 'Do you want to hear the whole thing?' he said.

She shrugged. 'Do you know it took the doctors two hours to clean all the mud out of my leg. They thought the bone was chipped, but it wasn't.'

'Does it still hurt?'

'Mm. At night mostly.' She returned to sit on the bed again.

'Will you tell me something?' Ryder said.

'What?'

'How old were you when your father died?'

'He didn't just die: you shot him.' She stopped herself and paused for a moment. 'I was fifteen – away at a private school in California. I didn't know what had happened until my mother arrived. She had to catch a plane from Bogotá. Why?'

Ryder's question had been a mistake. Now she'd answered it, he couldn't bring himself to offer the reason for asking her. To avoid explaining he made himself comfortable on the computer chair and endeavoured to drag his mind back to the beginning. 'Let me tell you about the PAF,' he said. 'You're not going to like it, but you might as well hear the truth. The Peace Aid Foundation sucks up money from all over the world – from private donations, government grants, from multinationals and from a whole bunch of other places. They claim to hand it out mostly to developing or war-torn countries for things like health, education, birth control and landmine clearance. Their charter says they're committed to improving conditions so people can recover from civil unrest or famine or invasion. That's the official story.'

'But not the real one?'

'They run parallel projects out of their headquarters in Geneva. After the Gulf War the PAF set up a special covert division to achieve their objectives in a different way. They decided on a fresh approach – one that's cheaper and a lot more effective. Instead of arranging air-lifts of food and paying aid workers to get their legs blown off in minefields, they figured it'd be smarter to target the people who are responsible for the problems: military leaders, crooked politicians, war-lords, tyrants, dictators – anyone the PAF thinks is a troublemaker.'

She interrupted him. 'Assassinate them?'

'By whatever means. Half the governments in the West have pretty much the same idea, but they won't admit it. The politicians say it either violates some precious part of their constitution or it's against their moral principles. What they mean is that it's too politically risky even if they had the nerve to do something. The PAF don't have the problem because the PAF don't have any principles, and because they're only accountable to themselves.'

'So they send out hired assassins. Is that what you're saying?'

'They've got half a dozen – maybe more by now. The first four came from the *Alfa* and the *Vympel* groups of the ex-Soviet Spetsnaz organization. They're counter-terrorist and sabotage experts. Then the PAF hired an American explosives specialist; then they approached me.' Ryder was watching her face. 'I'd just spent three years in the British SAS, so was exactly what they wanted.'

'And because you're a trained killer it was a good career move?'

'I thought I believed in what they were doing. Taking out one guy to save the lives of hundreds of thousands of people isn't wrong. I had another reason, too.'

'What?'

'It's not important.' Ryder leaned back in the chair. 'Have you got the idea?'

She nodded. 'And it was the PAF who sent you to Colombia?'

'Your father was running a drug cartel out of Cali that had started flooding Europe with cheap cocaine. He was in competition with the Medellín family, taking all their business away from them and exporting more cocaine than they'd ever dreamed of. Europe was awash with the stuff.'

'So you shot him – shot him dead – someone you'd never met who'd never done you any harm. You murdered him because the PAF told you to.'

'I know how it sounds,' Ryder said. 'I don't expect you to understand.'

'Don't you dare patronize me. I'll decide what I understand and what I don't.' She frowned. 'Where else did they send you?'

'I had an assignment in Somalia in '96, one in Bosnia and the last one in Serbia in '99. Then I quit.'

'Well, isn't that a surprise?' Her voice was scathing. 'I am supposed to be surprised, aren't I?'

'Save your breath,' Ryder said. 'I've heard it all before.'

'You don't know what I was going to say.'

'Yes I do. Bad guy does bad things, gets a conscience, turns his life around and lives happily ever after. It doesn't work like that.'

'Why tell me? Why should I care how it works?' She was tight-lipped, and her face had lost some of its colour.

'You're going to hear the rest of it anyway,' Ryder grunted. 'Eighteen months ago, a friend of mine woke up to what else the PAF are doing. If you want a lead on what that is, run a computer check on the business interests of those important, well-connected directors. Start with Sir Richard Ballantine in the UK. Then try Senator George Latimer in the States, and someone called Gerard Poitou in France. You'll find they're not just involved with forestry, agricultural machinery and pharmaceuticals: they're running guns, munitions, tanks and supplying half of Africa and the Middle East with arms. The whole of the PAF is a front. They don't recruit people like me to help make the world a better place: they're in business for themselves. They choose targets that'll provide them with the biggest pay-off. I was-n't sent to kill your father to stop the flow of cocaine into Europe. I was sent because the PAF had done a deal with the Medellín cartel.'

'So now I'm supposed to believe you really did develop a con-science after all.' She made no attempt to keep the sarcasm from her voice. 'And you had to act out a cliché by leaving. What a shame.'

Ryder ignored the remark. 'Two of us told the PAF they could stick their assignments,' he said. 'They've been after us ever since.'

'Because you know what they're doing?'

'We can't prove anything worthwhile, but we're still a threat to them, or they think we are. They get jumpy when people pull out.'

She went to get her bag and took out the envelope of pho-tographs. 'Were these supposed to be evidence against you in case you ever decided to leave?'

'Or evidence to give to someone like you. It's an easier way for the PAF to fix a problem.'

'It would've been if they hadn't shot me. I don't see why they did that. If I was set up to do what they wanted me to do, why put those radio transmitters in my car, and why follow me to the lake?'

'Fall-back,' Ryder said. 'To make sure you didn't foul up. The sniper either figured you were taking too long, or he decided I'd get your gun away from you before you could pull the trigger. Either way the PAF messed it up.'

'Unless they believe you died in the fire.' She paused. 'That's what you want them to think, isn't it?'

Which brought her back to the beginning of their conversa-tion, Ryder thought.

'Have they tried to kill you before?' she asked.

'Eleven months ago in Mexico, and in a car accident two months after that in London.' Almost without realizing it, Ryder found himself studying her again, endeavouring for the third or fourth time to discover what it was that made her so disconcertingly attractive. 'Do we have a deal, or not?' he asked.

'For your breathing space?'

'Two weeks.'

'I need to talk to my uncle first. He hasn't been telling me everything.' She met his eyes. 'Nor have you.'

'Two weeks; yes or no?'

'I'm booked out on a flight from Dorval tomorrow afternoon. I'll make up my mind when I get home.' She gave him the same tight, artificial smile. 'So you won't know one way or the other. That'll make things more exciting for you.'

'Yeah, it will. Thanks for nothing.' He stood up and went to the door. 'Next time you go hunting for someone, I'd do some checking beforehand if I were you.' He paused with his hand on the doorknob. 'I hope your leg gets better.'

'You won't know that either, will you?' She remained where she was, standing among the flowers with her arms folded and with her back to the window. 'Goodbye Mr Ryder.'

He let himself out, wishing he hadn't wasted half a day, wondering why he'd ever considered trusting her. But it was more than the lack of trust that was bothering him, he realized: it was something less easy to define – not just the peculiar attraction she seemed to exert, but the disturbing ability she had to remind him of all the lost opportunities and of all the squandered years.

Making a conscious effort to forget about her altogether, he took the elevator to the ground floor, then walked back slowly to his car in the sunshine, his thoughts no longer of the past, but on what the hell he was going to do now.

In different circumstances, or perhaps if he'd been less preoccupied, Ryder would have noticed a Mercedes and a black Peugot that followed him discreetly along the street – two cars that were still behind him eleven miles later when he pulled into the car-park of his motel.

Chapter 3

ALEXEI Andronov Volodya was a large man, so large that he seemed to be occupying more space in the motel room than any two ordinary people would have done. He was lying on the sofa with a leg draped over the back of it, and with his other foot resting precariously on the floor between a half-full glass of whisky, an ashtray and several empty bottles. It was a position he'd taken up earlier in the evening before he'd started drinking, and before Ryder had thought to steer him into a chair where the Russian would have been able to help himself from the mini-bar instead of blocking the access to it.

'So she had a pretty mouth, good legs and big tits.' Alexei lit another cigarette.

'I didn't say so.' Ryder grinned at him. 'Your imagination's running away with you.'

'No, no. You have explained. From you I have learned the colour of her hair; you have said what it is she wears at the lake and in the hospital, and I even hear about some ear-rings. If she did not have big tits, by now you would have forgotten how she looks, I think.'

'She had a .357 Magnum. I haven't forgotten that.'

'You believe she will try again?'

'I didn't ask her. Probably not.'

'Ah.' The Russian searched for his glass. 'Then you have only her uncle and her brothers to worry about. Perhaps they will pay someone.'

'They're more likely to give the PAF a hand,' Ryder said. 'I

37

should've kept my mouth shut. If I'd never mentioned them she wouldn't have started digging around on her computer.'

'I think now she has seen what kind of man you are she will understand why it was necessary for you to avenge the death of your sister.'

'She didn't know about Grace.'

'You cannot believe such a thing; it is not possible.'

'Yes, it is,' Ryder said. 'As far as I can make out, her family kept her pretty much in the dark about who her father was and what he did for a living.'

'So when you tell her she had a butcher for a father and how because of him your sister's body is pulled in pieces from the Cacua river in Colombia, what then did this girl have to say to you?'

'I never got around to that; I only told her about the PAF.'

Either unable to absorb the improbability of the information, or too drunk to reply, Alexei stopped with his drink halfway to his lips.

'It wouldn't have made any difference,' Ryder said.

'Chris, you are my good friend, but you have been out of the business for too long, I think.'

'Yeah.' Ryder poured himself a Scotch from a fresh bottle. 'When Grace was kidnapped and killed, Isabel Corrales was only fifteen years old,' he said. 'What the hell would a fifteen year old understand about a war between a couple of rabid drug cartels? She was away at school in California when it happened.'

'You excuse her innocence because it is written that a daughter shall not be visited by the sins of her father – or because you have gone soft in the head?'

'She hasn't stayed innocent,' Ryder said. 'She'd been on the phone to her uncle, and she was trying to get information out of me all the time I was at the hospital. Isabel Corrales didn't need me to tell her she'd opened a can of worms.'

Alexei lit another cigarette. 'You think she will learn the truth from her uncle now?'

'She'll get it one way or the other – either from him or from somewhere else.'

'Then we must hope you are safe. But in case you are not, as I have said, it is better you come with me to Angola.'

Ryder had already rejected the suggestion once. 'Why make it easy for the PAF?' he said. 'If they can find me, they can find you. If we're in the same place they get us both at the same time.'

'The job in Angola is good. We will make much money there.'

'Working for some mad terrorist outfit in the jungle? I don't think so.'

'We stay in the city – in Luanda where the women are very nice.'

Ryder grinned. 'With good legs and big tits?'

'By tomorrow I shall see.' The Russian stubbed out his cigarette and drained his glass. 'But not if I remain here drinking your whisky. Soon you will please drive me to the airport or call a taxi?'

'The motel runs a transit bus every fifteen minutes. It'll take you right to the terminal.' Ryder paused, searching for the right words. 'Thanks for coming.'

'Ah.' Alexei spread his hands. 'It is nothing. When I receive your fax it is a chance for me to visit you on my journey to Africa.'

'You're going the long way round.' Ryder smiled at him. 'I could've met you in London.'

'If Moscow is not a good place for me to be, then London is not a good place for you. It is where the PAF will look next.'

'Screw them.' Ryder didn't care. 'I want to get home. It was getting kind of boring living up at the lake. I'll take my chances.'

'You have no further business here in Canada?'

'Couple of things. I've got an insurance claim to file for the guy I rented the cabin from, and there's a company making thermal imaging equipment in Ottawa who are looking for someone to help them set up a European factory. I thought I might give them a call.'

Taking care not to step on the ashtray or knock over any of the bottles, Alexei rolled off the sofa, struggled to his feet and began searching for his jacket.

Ryder handed it to him. 'Are we still going to use the Luxembourg address?' he said.

'For as long as it is safe I will continue to check there for your voice mail and, at the same number, I shall leave my messages for you. In the meantime, please forgive me for asking if you have sufficient funds.'

'I'm fine.' Ryder said.

'Only if you are sure. From the business I finish in Italy, I have done very well. You understand that for myself I require currency only to purchase good guns and some light aircraft in Angola?'

'Yeah, I understand. If I need anything I'll let you know.'

'Then I shall go to find a bar at the airport.' Alexei consulted his watch. 'It is good for two friends to meet each other again like this, I think. One day when the PAF have stopped all their silliness we will drink together at my home on the river, and I shall be able to show you something of my country.'

Because this was the nearest the big Russian ever got to being sentimental, Ryder knew Alexei was ready to leave. He also knew that the remark about the PAF had been more of a warning than an invitation for him to spend some time in Russia. Alexei's doubts about the future were no different from his own, Ryder thought, which meant it was always going to be safer for them to go their separate ways – to each find places where, for a few more months, there would be time to forget the events that had brought them together here as friends this afternoon, and, with any luck, an opportunity to forget the confused and convoluted reasons for their friendship.

Alexei's departure had left a vacuum. As a consequence, Ryder's evening had been largely wasted. He'd been busy enough, choosing to ignore the mess on the floor in favour of sitting down to undertake some forward planning. The idea had been commendable, but despite his best efforts, his execution of it had been a failure.

After considering his options, at one point even resorting to writing them down on a sheet of paper that had become unreadable because of changes and doodles, he was no further ahead than when he'd begun. The only change he hadn't made was to his destination. Nine months was too long to be away and he was conscious of the need for surroundings that were more familiar, and where perhaps, if he was careful, there would be a better chance of him resuming a normal life.

At the top of the list was the name of the Ottawa company that he proposed calling in the morning. Beneath the name were phone numbers of airlines who had direct flights from Montréal to London and reminders about returning his rental car and the need to dispose of his gun – notes that said nothing about next week or next month except for three addresses that he'd crossed out because what friends he had left in England were people the PAF could trace too easily.

He didn't want a plan, Ryder realized. He didn't want to think about the future at all.

After tearing up the sheet of paper and checking the window catches and the front door, he switched off the lights then lay down on the bed, waiting to discover how bad tonight's crop of dreams were going to be.

He was never to find out. No sooner had he closed his eyes than Ryder knew someone was outside.

There was no noise, no flicker of light, no footsteps, not even the sound of a hand trying the lock – only a sense of clear and immediate danger.

A gentle knock on the door was followed by the sound of a voice. 'Christopher, it's me, Alexei. Are you there?'

Because Alexei would have no more used the name Christopher than he would ever have whispered or employed anything other than his fist to hammer on the door, Ryder didn't think twice.

'Hang on,' he said. 'I'm just coming.'

It took him only a moment to retrieve a length of cord and his Colt from beneath his pillow and to remove the safety chain from the door. In another ten seconds he'd slipped a loop of cord around the handle of the door bolt and retreated to the kitchenette, his heart thumping, gun in one hand, the end of the cord ready in the other.

'Did you miss your flight or something?' Ryder called.

For an answer, what sounded like a cough was accompanied by

a dull thud as though the man was using his shoulder in an attempt to force an entry.

Ryder made it easy for him. Gun levelled, with the wrist of his gun hand steadied firmly against the wall, he yanked on the cord.

He heard the bolt slip back, but for what seemed like an eternity the door remained shut, eventually swinging open very slowly through an angle of less than forty-five degrees.

No one was standing there. Instead, illuminated in the light from the car-park, the figure of a man lay slumped across the sill.

Although one of his legs was still kicking, and his lungs were not yet empty, there was no doubt that he was dead. Nor was there any mystery about how he had died. Even from the kitchenette Ryder could see the tiny red-rimmed hole in the centre of his forehead. But who the hell he was, and who the hell had killed him were different questions altogether.

Gripping the Colt in both hands, Ryder stayed where he was, unable to stop the sweat from running into his eyes while he held his breath and waited to find out what was going to happen next.

'Mr Ryder, you will not shoot me, please.'

The new voice was deeper, but equally unfamiliar.

'Empty hands,' Ryder called. 'Move too fast and you're dead.'

The man was cautious, appearing from nowhere to stand in the shadow of the door while Ryder tried to identify him. The stranger was small and wiry with long hair, dressed in jeans, a denim jacket and wearing western boots.

'Who the hell are you?' Ryder said.

'I am Rodrigo Santos. It is necessary for me to speak with you.'

'Gun,' Ryder said. 'By the muzzle and drop it on the floor. If you're carrying more than one, or if you've got a knife on you, I'll need them too.'

'I have only this.' From his jacket pocket Santos withdrew a small, silenced automatic which he placed on the shoulders of the body at his feet. 'While someone can see there is a dead man here, it is not good for us to talk like this,' he said.

'You've got two seconds.' Ryder stepped out of the kitchenette. 'If you don't get that damn gun on the floor and kick it over to me I'm going to blow your head off.'

'I am sorry.' Santos was visibly nervous, using the toe of his shoe to dislodge the gun before sliding it across the carpet. 'You will permit me to shut the door?' he said.

'No.' Ryder picked up the automatic. It was a .25 Iver Johnson pocket pistol, especially modified to accept a silencer that was nearly twice the length of the gun itself – a special purpose weapon with only one possible use.

'Please,' Santos said, 'you will listen to what I have to say.'

Ryder wasn't ready to listen. 'If that guy's lying on a gun you'd better find it,' he said.

He watched while Santos manhandled the body and located a 9mm Browning.

'OK,' Ryder said. 'Kick it over here, then bring him inside.'

The small man did what he was told, waiting for new instructions after he'd made sufficient room to close the door.

'Sit.' Ryder switched on the light. 'On the floor, away from the wall.'

'We will talk now?'

'Not we, you.' Ryder held up the Iver Johnson by its trigger guard. 'Do you make your living with this?'

'For some jobs it is very clean and very quick. Such a little bullet has energy only to enter the skull, but not to come out the other side. So for many times it goes round inside like a spoon in a grapefruit.'

Ryder could imagine. 'How much are the PAF paying you?' he said.

'You speak of something of which I know nothing.'

'What about your friend here?' Ryder pointed at the body.

Santos spread his hands. 'I can say only that I am certain he comes to kill you. So, while he stands outside your door with his gun, I have shot him once in the head.'

'Why?'

'For Señor Corrales. It is his wish for you to be safe. Why else?'

If the statement had been even slightly ambiguous, Ryder could have asked for clarification. But with no possible way of misinterpreting it, he was disconcerted, unprepared for an answer he had least expected.

'You are surprised?' Santos enquired.

'Yeah, I'm surprised.'

'I shall explain. First you must know that when Señor Corrales receives at his home a phone call from his niece to say what she has done here in Canada, he is very angry with her. But later, after he learns more by the e-mail and the telephone, he becomes worried, so I am sent to make sure that until Señorita Corrales returns to Colombia there will be no problems for her.'

'That doesn't explain anything,' Ryder said.

'I have not yet finished. Since learning it was you who brought her to the hospital, Señor Corrales has done much thinking and now believes there is some good business you can do with him. For this reason I have a letter which I must give to you, and I am told to see that you also suffer from no accident.'

Ryder was thinking back, endeavouring to remember everywhere he'd been over the last few days. 'Have you been watching me?' he said.

'A little – more after you have visited the hospital where a car follows you on your return to here – a black Peugot which, if you look, you will find outside in the car-park.'

By now Ryder was starting to appreciate how truly negligent he'd been. The dead man was almost certainly a PAF field agent, but this time someone had been on his tail – a minder from the Corrales family who, if he'd been instructed to act differently, would have had no more compunction about killing Ryder than he'd had about putting a bullet into the brain of the stranger on the floor. The thought was unnerving, so much so that, in order to concentrate on the present, Ryder had to stop himself from going over all of the mistakes he'd made.

'The driver of the black car is not careful enough,' Santos said. 'At four hospitals he has asked for information on an Englishman and a girl who he thinks may have been burned in a fire, and sometimes he has questions about a young woman with a bullet in her. He waits for you to visit Señorita Corrales, I think.'

'And you tailed him?'

Santos shrugged. 'It is my job.'

'Did you see my Russian friend leave the motel today?'

'He is not followed. The man stays here to watch you. You recognize him perhaps? He is the one who attacks you at the lake?'

'Probably.' Ryder paused. 'What's this about a letter?'

'Before I give it to you it is necessary for you to realize that Señor Corrales is not involved with the cocaine like his brother in the old days.'

'What do you know about the old days?'

'I have learned how and why it is your sister dies in Medellín. But Señor Corrales himself has never been in the business of drugs. He was not in any way responsible for your sister's death. Always he has been dealing only with metals – in many places of the world.'

Ryder couldn't imagine any member of the Corrales family having interests that would be even remotely legal. 'What kind of metals?' he said.

'Silver and tin, sometimes gold.' Santos slid a sealed envelope across the floor. 'This will answer your questions.'

The envelope contained an open, first-class airline ticket to Bogotá, a bank draft for US$10,000 and an undated letter, handwritten on expensive notepaper:

Dear Mr Ryder

It is ironical after so many years and after so much bad blood that I now find myself in your debt for saving the life of my niece during her recent, ill-advised and foolish trip to Canada.

You have my word that her behaviour was based on ignorance of what has gone before - a mistake for which I must take the blame. For reasons you might understand, as her guardians, my wife and I have tried to keep certain truths from her while she was growing up - particularly those concerning the excesses of her father which in the past have caused pain and suffering to many people like yourself.

In addition to thanking you for what you have done, I have another motive for writing you this

45

letter, one that relates to a business opportunity in which we may perhaps be of some assistance to each other. To exploit this opportunity I have need of your expertise, and in return I wish to help you with the complications you have described to my niece.

Because the matter is commercially sensitive, forgive me if I say only that it involves the recovery of a valuable metal in South America - a project that, I believe, could be of significant benefit to us both.

Should you be interested in discussing this, I would be most pleased to offer you the hospitality of my home in Cali. You need only to confirm your flight details with Mr Santos at the Olympia Hotel in Montréal, after which I will at once arrange for you to be met on your arrival at Bogotá.

In the event that you prefer not to visit, I shall, of course, respect your decision and your confidence. Whatever you decide, you have my gratitude and my very good wishes for the future.

Sincerely yours
Miguel Corrales

After reading the letter twice, Ryder put it back in the envelope along with the ticket and the bank draft, then returned it to Santos. 'Tell Mr Corrales thanks, but no thanks,' he said.

Santos let the envelope remain on his lap. 'You believe it is a trap?'

'No.' Ryder looked at him. 'You could've killed me anytime you wanted, couldn't you?'

'For what reason?'

To bring the conversation to an end, Ryder lowered his gun and handed back the little Iver Johnson to his visitor. 'Thanks for keeping an eye on me,' he said.

'I have more yet to do.' Santos slipped the automatic into his pocket. 'With your help, after I have placed the body of this man in the trunk of his Peugot, I will arrange for the car to disappear into the St Lawrence river.'

'You're not at home now,' Ryder said. 'This isn't Colombia.'

'One river is the same as another, I think.' Santos smiled. 'If you would be so kind as to drive behind me in my Mercedes, afterwards I will return you here to your motel where tonight you may sleep without the need to listen and watch the door.'

Ryder wished it was that easy. He started going through the pockets of the dead man, finding nothing except for two unopened packets of chewing gum, a handkerchief and a set of car keys.

'You'll need these.' He tossed the keys to Santos. 'You'd better bring up the car as close as you can, and have a look under the seats for me, will you?'

Chewing gum and keys were about all Ryder had expected to find on the body, but, judging by Santos' expression when he returned from the car park, the contents of the Peugot had been more interesting.

'Guns?' Ryder asked.

'Inside the trunk wrapped in a blanket there is a Chinese-made Kalashnikov, a flashlight, a launcher for the grenades and an M55 Tikka rifle with a laser sight.' Santos began dragging the body outside. 'So I may tell Señor Corrales it is this man who has shot at his niece?'

'Yeah.' Ryder was checking for lights in the adjacent units, concerned that someone would see the corpse being transferred to the car. 'Tell him he damn near didn't have a niece at all.'

'He is pleased she is safe now.' Santos stopped what he was doing for a moment. 'But he will not be so happy to hear you do not wish to accept the offer he has made.'

Which was hard, bloody luck, Ryder thought. The happiness of anyone with the name Corrales was the last thing on his mind, and it was ridiculous to contemplate doing business with the brother of someone he'd deliberately shot dead seven years ago. The irony that Miguel Corrales had mentioned in his letter wasn't because of some random linking of their lives; it had happened because the PAF had sent an executioner to Québec – a reminder that could have hardly had less irony about it.

If his analysis of the situation had been more thorough, or if he could have spent the rest of the night asleep in his room instead of helping commit a black Peugot to the dark, oily waters of the St Lawrence seaway, Ryder would have had little reason to reconsider his plans. But after being delivered back to his motel and finding that Santos had been thoughtful enough to leave the envelope behind, it was too easy to re-read the letter, and easier still to wonder how Isabel Corrales might react if he were to arrive on her doorstep one sunny afternoon as the guest of her uncle.

Over the next few hours, while he reviewed the evening's events and finished off the Scotch that Alexei had neglected to drink, twice Ryder almost convinced himself that his impressions of her were as wrong as they were dangerous. But his thoughts were more confused than normal, and by morning they had been superseded by an altogether more rational excuse for justifying a trip to South America – one he would be foolish to pass up when his alternatives were so restricted.

Two opportunities in one, Ryder decided, at the very least a chance to say hello to the abrasive Isabel again and, at the same time, a way to discover why the hell a Colombian industrialist would be willing to take on a corrupt and malevolent organization like the PAF.

Chapter 4

FOR Haxhi Markovic, 18 June, 1999 would always be a special day – the day on which some years ago, in a small, nondescript Kosovo village not far from Prizren, he had celebrated his eighteenth birthday by experiencing something he had not experienced before.

Having spent an arduous month as a member of a Serbian paramilitary group assigned to cleanse a number of villages in the southern region, the experience had been more of an awakening – an appreciation of pleasure he had not expected to enjoy outside the limits of his imagination.

The girl had been terrified when he'd found her, a pretty fifteen year old hiding in the basement of a ruined building, her mother and father already dead at the hands of his companions who had moved on to loot and burn the neighbouring houses in the street.

After tying her to a tree in her own garden, for nearly half an hour on that warm afternoon, Markovic had attempted unsuccessfully to rape her, unable to maintain an erection until he'd sodomized her with the barrel of his gun and shot her three times between the legs. Only when she refused to die and he'd clubbed her to death with his rifle had he been able to achieve the orgasm he had sought for so many years of his twisted and tortured adolescence.

The incident had been a turning point for the Serbian youth, an acknowledgement that his path would not be the path of ordinary men, and the realization that he would need to lead his life beyond the accepted conventions of society if he was to seek out the other forbidden fruits that lay ahead.

In the years that were to follow, Markovic had travelled widely, almost at once discovering what he had already learned in Kosovo – that although sexual gratification was on offer everywhere, for him it was the thrill of killing that brought fulfilment and, with it, the feelings of supremacy and complete control.

And so, to develop his skills and refine his appetite, Markovic had worked hard, selling his services to whomever would pay for them, living well in whatever country he chose and indulging himself by preying on young women who invariably paid a fatal price for returning the smile of the confident, good-looking stranger.

This morning Markovic's confidence was lower than it had been for several months. Last week's meeting in Geneva had gone well, but not well enough for him to be certain of securing the job, and, after being asked to travel here to London overnight, he was anxious to learn the result of his interview.

He tipped the taxi driver and, for a moment, stood outside the Peace Aid Foundation building, studying the green-coloured, olive branch logo on the glass doors before he went in and made his way to the second floor.

He was met there by a secretary, a heavily made-up woman wearing glasses who had thick, dark eyebrows – an indication that her pubic hair would be of a type he particularly disliked.

'Are you Mr Markovic?' she enquired.

'I have an appointment for ten forty-five.' He spoke with his back to her.

'It's through there.' She pointed to a door. 'Sir Richard's waiting for you. You can go in right away.'

Inside, at one end of a wood-panelled room that smelt faintly of cigar smoke and furniture polish, three men were seated behind a long, curved table.

One of them stood up. 'Mr Markovic,' he said. 'I'm so glad you could make it.' He waved at a solitary chair in the centre of the room. 'Please do sit. My apologies for the short notice.'

In Geneva it had been Sir Richard Ballantine who had opened

the conversation and done most of the talking, but Markovic sensed that today the Englishman was less likely to have things his own way.

'You already know Monsieur Poitou, of course,' Ballantine said. 'This other gentleman is my colleague Senator Latimer from the United States. Fortunately, he's in the UK for a few days, and therefore able to help us determine your suitability for the job.'

Markovic sat, saying nothing while he tried to decide if Latimer would prove to be as big a prick as Ballantine was. In contrast to the Englishman and the Frenchman who were in their sixties, the American was no more than forty, well dressed in an expensive suit and a silk tie, but equally disdainful, staring at Markovic as though he was something dirty that had crawled in off the street.

'Now then.' Ballantine remained on his feet. 'Since Monsieur Poitou and I spoke to you last Thursday, we've been able to go over some of the references you gave us. You seem a very busy person.'

'Being busy is easy.' Markovic folded his arms. 'Getting results is not. Are my references satisfactory?'

'Well, let's say they appear to be, shall we? We have some reservations about your motivation in a number of projects for which you provided details, but in general you're considered a viable candidate. Whether or not we proceed any further depends on you.' Ballantine lowered himself into his chair. 'First of all it's essential you understand what you've already been told – namely that the public face of the Peace Aid Foundation is one of a major humanitarian organization which cannot under any circumstances be seen to be engaging in activities of any other kind. You do appreciate that, don't you?'

As well as knowing how he was expected to reply, there had been time enough for Markovic to rehearse his lines. 'If you'd lived in my country you wouldn't ask the question,' he said. 'I lost my family to the Kosovo Liberation Army, and I have friends in Serbia who lost theirs in the NATO bombing. In northern Iraq last month I met people whose children were executed by Iraqi Republican Guards simply because their families came from

Kurdish villages. If the British and the Americans had addressed the problem of Milosevic and Saddam Hussein when they had the chance, how many innocent lives do you think could have been saved?'

'I'm sure none of us can answer that.' Poitou twirled a pencil between his fingers. 'If you feel so strongly about it, perhaps you'd care to tell us why you, yourself, were content to let things unfold in the way they did.'

'I'm Serbian and I'm one person. And I wasn't working for an organization with offices in four countries. What do you suppose I could have done?'

'Are you suggesting you would have acted differently if you'd had the resources – that in reality you don't just work for money?' Poitou inspected his pencil.

'In case you've forgotten, let me remind you of something,' Markovic said. 'I didn't approach you: you approached me. We've been over all this. I work for money like everyone else, but I've never taken on a project I didn't believe in, and I've never considered working for individuals or companies who are interested in exclusive, personal gain. It's too dangerous, I don't need the risk and I don't need a lecture from you on what I do for a living, or what the Peace Aid Foundation believes is the high ground. If I didn't understand what we're discussing, or if I thought your solutions were wrong or unworkable, we wouldn't be talking to each other.'

'Well, well.' The American, Latimer, was smiling. 'A mercenary with morals – or are you, I wonder, being a little glib? It's a bit of a stretch to imagine you sharing what you call the high ground with an organization like the PAF, don't you think?'

'I don't share anything with anyone. I make up my own mind about things.' Markovic remained composed. 'Are we going on with this, or not?'

'Possibly.' The senator cleared his throat. 'Have you been told what the job is?'

'Two men who used to work for you,' Markovic said. 'People who can make waves that might interfere with your programme.'

'They're not your ordinary, run of the mill, pissed-off ex-employees. One's an ex-Spetsnaz Russian who's a trained combat pilot, and the other was in the British SAS.'

This was new information for Markovic, a slant that not only put a different complexion on the job, but one that gave him an excuse to renegotiate his fee. 'Where are these men?' he asked.

'The Russian's either in Italy or somewhere in Africa,' Latimer said. 'Three days ago the Englishman was in Canada, but since then we understand he's bought himself a British Airways ticket to London. He used a credit card and his own name.'

'Which is either too obvious or very clever, depending on what he wants you to believe.'

'Indeed.' Latimer produced some folders. 'These are their files – photos, military records, details of their assignments for us, friends, acquaintances, sexual preferences, places where they might be found, names they've used in the past and a list of people who, for their own particular reasons, might be willing to undertake the job themselves if they're adequately informed and pointed in the right direction.'

'Like the Colombian girl was?' Markovic interrupted.

Latimer frowned. 'I wasn't aware you'd been informed about her. Do you know we've lost contact with our agent in Canada?'

'Maybe he got careless.'

'And you wouldn't?'

Markovic didn't bother to reply. During the last two or three minutes he'd been analysing the personalities of each director in turn, identifying their flaws so he could guess how they behaved in their private lives. It was a technique he used often, a means of determining the best way to manipulate them for his own purposes.

Of the three, Poitou was clearly the weakest, a fleshy, bald-headed man with thick lips and thick fingers who would almost certainly prefer to observe the sexual act between two or three other people than be a participant himself. Ballantine, although a product of the English class system, and someone who believed in his own superiority, was different but intellectually incompetent – a sterile individual with a possible liking for small boys or pornography, Markovic thought; a dry, hollow man who would couple with his wife, if he had one, only out of a misplaced sense of duty. The American alone had any spine, someone who might fight if he was cornered, although not unless the odds were heavily in his favour.

'Well?' Latimer said. 'Why should we be persuaded to employ your services?'

'I didn't come to persuade you.' Markovic smiled. 'I came because I was invited. You have your priorities; I have mine. If we can combine our interests, then we'll all be happy. If not, I'm sure you can find someone else, and there are other places I need to be.'

Intending to create a less formal atmosphere, Ballantine made the mistake of injecting some small talk. 'Your English is very good,' he said. 'Do you speak other languages, too?'

'We had schools and universities in Serbia before the NATO bombing.' Markovic kept his voice level. 'They have been rebuilt.'

'Yes, of course.' Ballantine picked up the files. 'Perhaps we should get to the point. Subject to the agreement of my fellow directors I think I can say we're prepared to proceed, but not, I'm afraid, at the price you mentioned at our previous meeting.'

'At the previous meeting I wasn't given details of the two men.' Markovic smiled again. 'The price is doubled.'

The Frenchman placed his hands palms down on the table. 'Who do you think you are?' he said coldly. 'Are you under the impression that you're the only one who can do the job?'

'My fee is fifteen hundred US dollars a day for expenses, plus fifty thousand dollars per head should I be successful within a period of three months – all funds to be deposited in an offshore bank of my nomination in a currency of my choice. In the event of failure, I expect only my per diem expenses to be paid. For this, I guarantee to provide immediate and incontrovertible evidence that the contract has been completed to your satisfaction irrespective of wherever in the world it takes place. I further guarantee that there will not be and will never be any traceable connection between myself and the Peace Aid Foundation.' Markovic paused for effect. 'If these terms are unacceptable to you, we have nothing more to discuss.'

Predictably it was Latimer who responded first. 'Mr Markovic,' he said, 'your guarantee of confidentiality is unnecessary. We arrange our own insurance.'

In spite of what sounded like acceptance of his offer, Markovic was expressionless, waiting while Ballantine wrote something on a piece of paper which he handed first to the senator and then to the Frenchman.

Poitou was still the fly in the ointment, Markovic thought, a shit-head who, even if he was capable of appreciating the risk, would always resent paying for the services of a specialist.

'Very well then.' Ballantine spoke with more authority. 'I believe we can do business on the condition that you report weekly by telephone to a private number in Bonn, and on the understanding that the foundation will take whatever steps are prudent to distance itself from any association with you and from any action you may embark upon. Are these terms agreeable to you?'

'Of course.'

'Good.' Sir Richard coughed discreetly. 'There's one more thing: we may decide to include the Colombian girl in your contract. It depends on how much we think she might have learned about the PAF.'

'I see.' Aware of a familiar tingling in his fingertips, and of a weak but unmistakable stiffening of his penis, Markovic displayed no emotion. 'Shall we go through the files?' he said.

Five and a half thousand miles away, in the scented garden of the Corrales hacienda, Ryder was enjoying an experience of a different kind.

The hacienda was beautiful enough, a gracious eighteenth-century masterpiece of sweeping arches and shady balconies, set in over three acres of grounds overlooking a valley twenty miles north east of Cali, but it was the garden that created an environment out of a fairy-tale.

In front of him, early morning sunshine was filtering through the trees, bathing a baroque stone gateway in a golden glow, while shadows across the paths and terraces were being replaced first by light and then by colour.

Adding to the sense of unreality were the trees themselves. Covered in long, silvery fronds of tillandsia that had grown to form curtains of transparent foliage, the barbas de viejo was dispersing the rays of the sun to illuminate a carpet of orchids at Ryder's feet as though the flowers were either on fire, or lit by some magical source from beneath the ground.

He had seen none of this before. Last night, because it had been well after midnight when he'd arrived, the house had been in darkness, and apart from an elderly, Spanish-speaking lady who had greeted him and shown him to his room, there had been no one to say hello, and no chance for him to inspect his surroundings.

Ryder had gone straight to bed, relieved to have finally stopped moving after a journey that had been too long. But he had slept only fitfully, ill at ease in the home of a man he'd never met, in a country which, even after seven years, was hardly the safest place in the world for him to be.

Over the last two legs of his trip he had managed to suppress most of his reservations about coming, but now he was having second thoughts, doubting the wisdom of becoming involved with what was obviously one of the wealthiest and most influential families in Colombia.

The extent of the influence was hard to miss. In Bogotá his passage through Customs and passport control had been suspiciously easy. Then there had been the flight by executive jet to the airport at Cali where, despite the lateness of the hour, he'd been offered the choice of a helicopter or a limousine for the short trip up here into the hills – not to impress him, Ryder realized, but simply because it never occurred to people as wealthy as this to operate in any other way.

Intending to obtain a better view of the valley he walked out through the gateway, feeling the sun warm on his skin while he breathed in the fresh, early morning air.

He should have stayed where he was. The fairy-tale was an illusion, destroyed by the sight of security fencing, guard dogs and armed men. Even the wrought-iron gates, which last night in the dark had appeared to be so elegant, were in the light of day spoiled by the coils of razor wire strung along their tops – an ugly reminder of the penalty for being rich in this part of the world.

The let down was short-lived. Hurrying across the courtyard towards him, the elderly housekeeper was calling his name.

'*Desayuno.*' She beckoned. 'For Señor Corrales, please.'

Ryder went to meet her, guessing that the master of the house was up and about and ready to receive his guest.

Miguel Corrales was waiting in the breakfast-room. He bore no resemblance to his late brother; instead, he was a short but distinguished-looking gentleman with greying hair, a rather leathery skin and with the same dark, brown-coloured eyes as his niece.

'Mr Ryder.' He shook hands. 'What must you think of my rudeness? I'm so sorry you weren't properly welcomed when you arrived. Isabel was supposed to stay up, but it seems she forgot my instructions.'

Or ignored them, Ryder thought. 'It's OK,' he said. 'It's my fault for turning up so late.'

'I trust you had a pleasant trip?'

'A bit long. I flew out of Kennedy, but I took a train from Montréal to Boston, then caught a bus down to New York.'

'As a precaution?'

Ryder nodded. 'I booked myself on a flight to London too.'

'After what I've heard from Santos, it's as well for you to be careful.' Corrales smiled. 'Particularly when you're not sure what you're walking into or what you're leaving behind.' He waved a hand at the breakfast table. 'If you'd care to join me, there's fresh juice, coffee, toast and cereal. If you'd prefer something cooked I can order it for you.'

Although the Colombian's English was not as faultless as that of his niece, his command of the language was nevertheless very good, spoken with an accent that was detectable only at the end of certain sentences.

'If you don't mind I'll pass on breakfast.' Ryder helped himself to orange juice. He was already less uneasy, starting to loosen up now he had a better idea of who he was dealing with.

'I realize you've only just arrived,' Corrales said, 'but I think I should acquaint you with a small problem which has arisen since you received my note. One I hope you can help resolve.'

Ryder didn't have to be told what the problem was. 'Isabel,' he said.

'I'm afraid she's not at all happy about your presence here. Because the truth about her father has been kept from her for so long, she now doubts whatever my wife and I say to her.'

'Have you explained everything?'

'As much of it as I know, including the source of her allowance and why she was misguided in making her trip to Canada.' Corrales paused. 'Mr Ryder, allow me to be frank. In case you're wondering, yes, some of what you see around you was paid for by my brother – by the sale of cocaine. I'm not proud of that, but all men have things in their past of which they are not proud. You must understand that, although my brother and I grew up together in this house, before I'd reached the age of twenty we had gone our separate ways. A certain rivalry between us continued to exist, however. So when I became unusually successful in the mining industry, to show that he could be more successful than I was, my brother Pablo started dealing in narcotics on a large scale. In five years he made more money than my family had accumulated in three generations.'

'And he went off the rails in the process?' Ryder said.

'He became dangerous, able to think of nothing except the need to break the stranglehold that rival cartels had on the world cocaine market. To achieve his ends he embarked on a campaign of terror and violence which, as you know, culminated in the kidnapping of Dolores Moncado, the daughter of one of the most powerful men in the Medellín cartel.'

'At her wedding,' Ryder said quietly. 'Where my sister was a bridesmaid.'

'According to the police reports, the Moncado girl was educated in England at the school your sister attended. Is that not correct?'

'They were friends,' Ryder said. 'That's why Grace flew to Colombia for the wedding. Grace and Dolores had always done everything together.'

'That they died together is a tragedy for which I can never be forgiven. If my wife and I had known of my brother's plans, we could perhaps have stopped him – or arranged for him to be stopped.' Corrales went to the coffee percolator, standing beside it for a second or two before he filled his cup. 'It's difficult to know how else to express my regrets,' he said. 'I have no excuses – only a certain understanding for the action you subsequently undertook.'

'Understanding that Isabel doesn't have?'

'She wishes to hear your side of the story – perhaps not such an unreasonable request.'

Ryder knew he was missing something. Awkward though it might be for Corrales to have a guest whom his niece resented and disliked, there was a deeper underlying reason for this preamble. 'Does what happened seven years ago have some bearing on this mining project of yours?' he asked.

Corrales looked over the rim of his cup. 'The past is past,' he said, 'for you, for me and for Isabel. If she can be persuaded to leave it there, and providing you and I can do business, I'm hoping for her assistance. But first she must accept the truth, unpleasant though it is.'

It sounded a bit like a lecture for a schoolgirl, Ryder thought. 'Do you want to talk about the project now?' he asked.

'I'd prefer you to speak with my niece first. Would you mind?'

Not wishing to appear rude by suggesting it would be a wasted effort, Ryder avoided the subject for the remainder of breakfast, containing his curiosity about the project while Corrales provided him with a short history of the Cali region and described how the hacienda had been acquired by his grandfather in 1899 after the War of The Thousand Days.

It was fairly interesting, but Ryder was glad when the Colombian summoned the housekeeper and asked her to find Señorita Isabel.

'My niece is a difficult young woman,' Corrales explained. 'She may have already gone out.'

'Why would I do that when we have a visitor?' Isabel entered the room unannounced, going to say good morning to her uncle and kiss him on the cheek before confronting Ryder.

'How nice to see you again.' She smiled slightly. 'I'm sorry I missed you last night.'

The smile had been as contrived as the others he remembered, but on her home territory she was more confident, issuing an unspoken challenge for him to shake hands with her.

Ryder decided not to try. 'No limp,' he said. 'Is your leg better?'

'Yes, thank you.' She let her smile slip. 'I didn't think you'd come.'

He already knew why he had. Over the last few days there had been plenty of opportunity to wonder how accurate his recollections of Isabel Corrales would turn out to be. On the train to Boston, on the bus to New York and on several occasions during the long flight to Bogotá he had all but convinced himself that his impressions of her had been coloured entirely by events.

But he'd been wrong.

She was dressed in designer jeans and a thin, silk blouse, plain, ordinary clothes that would have passed unnoticed on anyone else of her age and build. Yet, on her, for some inexplicable reason, they were anything but plain and no more ordinary than the young woman who was wearing them.

Corrales coughed politely. 'Mr Ryder,' he said, 'after you've met my wife, Isabel will show you round the house. We have some things you may care to see. I'm afraid I have correspondence to finish and phone calls to make, so perhaps we can meet again after lunch. In the meantime, if there's anything you require or anywhere you'd like to go, Isabel will be happy to make the necessary arrangements. We're pleased to have you as our guest, so you have only to ask.'

Judging by the expression on her face, Isabel was neither pleased nor happy. 'For goodness sake,' she said, 'why don't you just explain?'

'I have.' Corrales spoke disapprovingly. 'If you give Mr Ryder the chance to do so, I'm sure he'll be glad to answer the questions you have for him.'

'Oh stop it. And stop being so stuffy, too,' She turned and went to the door. 'Well, Mr Ryder, do you want the guided tour, or not?'

What Ryder wanted was information on the project, but because her uncle was evidently anxious to start with a clean slate, the tour seemed unavoidable.

After taking his leave of Corrales he joined Isabel at the door, waiting for her to lead on while he prepared himself for the interrogation.

Surprisingly, to begin with she made no mention of her father. Instead, over the next twenty minutes she made a rather too obvious effort to play the part she'd been instructed to play – either because she had nothing to gain by behaving otherwise, Ryder thought, or because in the home of her uncle, where good manners went hand in hand with good breeding, she was simply following the house rules.

Her aunt proved to be a striking and charming woman, clearly delighted to have an English-speaking visitor who, as she was at pains to point out, was not only a welcome change from the dreary Colombian businessmen who came to dinner, but someone closer to the age of her niece, and therefore likely to be better company for her.

After advising Ryder to disregard her husband's enthusiasm for new projects she drifted off to the lounge, smiling at her niece before she left and whispering something to her about being careful not to bore their European guest.

'My aunt thinks the English are the only people left in the world with any social graces.' Isabel pointed to one of more than a dozen paintings hanging in the hallway. 'Aunt Christíana was born in Cali. That's her when she was seventeen. The women of Cali, Las Caleñas, are supposed to be the most beautiful in the whole of Colombia.' She stopped speaking abruptly, embarrassed by the implications of her remark.

'Well,' Ryder said, 'if I'd known that before I could've told a friend of mine.'

'I didn't think people like you had friends.' She turned to prevent him seeing the patches of colour on her cheeks.

'He's the guy I told you about – Alexei, the one who walked away from the PAF at the same time I did.'

'Oh.' She went to stand beside a mural of pre-Colombian motifs, but instead of explaining where the mural came from or what it represented, she ignored it altogether. 'I heard about the attack at your motel in Montréal,' she said.

'That's how I got to meet your minder. Santos took care of the problem.'

'You sound like Uncle Miguel. Santos gives me the creeps. He always has done – right from when I was a little girl.' She walked off towards a glass cabinet containing a selection of pottery and three gleaming, gold miniatures. 'I suppose you think it was me who told the PAF you escaped from the fire.'

'No, I don't think it was you. They'd staked out the hospitals; I should've guessed they would.'

'This pottery's pre-Hispanic Nariño,' she said, 'but the gold comes from the Calima culture. My uncle collects it.'

Ryder could understand why. Inside the cabinet, resting on individual cushions of green velvet and illuminated by concealed lights, a gold jaguar, a gold frog and a gold eagle were amongst the most magnificent objects he'd ever seen. The animals weren't just gleaming, they were luminescent, radiating a deep, yellow glow as though each of them was surrounded by a halo.

'I'd better show you the sculpture, too,' she said. 'Uncle Miguel might want to know what you think of it. It's one by Edgar Negret.'

Standing inside the doors to the patio, the sculpture was a disappointment, reasonably imposing, but so abstract that Ryder didn't bother to ask what it was supposed to be.

As indifferent towards it as she was towards him, she volunteered nothing in the way of an interpretation, giving him only a moment to inspect it before she led him outside to the pool.

By Corrales standards the pool was unremarkable apart from a huge, mosaic picture of a puma sparkling on the bottom beneath the water. The animal was about to pounce, every detail of it fired into thousands of gold and silver ceramic tiles that made up its shape.

Ryder wasn't sure whether it was tasteless or not. He was sure, however, that this was the place Isabel had chosen to stand her ground.

Unfolding a lounger at the poolside, she stretched out on it, waiting while he found himself a chair.

'Why didn't you tell me about your sister?' she asked.

'What difference would it have made? You wouldn't have listened. According to your uncle you won't even listen to him. You don't want to hear the truth.'

'Yes, I do.' She put her hands behind her head. 'At the beginning I suppose I didn't.'

'But you do now?'

'I've heard his version; now I want yours.'

'OK,' Ryder said. 'Just so long as you remember I'm here on business, not to justify myself to you. Start an argument, and you're going to be talking to yourself. Is that clear?'

She nodded.

'I got the news about Grace over the phone,' Ryder said. 'It was sometime at the end of September – about a month after I'd been discharged from the SAS. I was in London flat-sitting for her when the police called me long-distance from Medellín.'

'To say she'd been killed?'

'Along with her friend Dolores Moncado. Bits of them had been found floating in the Cacua river the day after Dolores's wedding. They'd been shot in the head, and their bodies cut up with a chainsaw. The night before they died, your father sent a tape to the Medellín cartel saying that Dolores and Grace would be released unharmed only if the Medellíns pulled out of the European cocaine market. The police had been given a copy of the tape, the Colombian Internal Security Service had a copy too, so did one of the big newspapers.'

'If that's true someone would've done something, wouldn't they?'

'Your father had the Press sewn up, he had the police and the Security Service in his pocket and he claimed the Medellíns had forged the tape to incriminate him for something he didn't do.' Ryder paused. 'You know how things work in your country.'

'So that's your excuse for believing the police instead of my father.'

Ryder carried on without answering her. 'Six weeks after Grace's funeral I was approached by the Peace Aid Foundation. A guy called Sir Richard Ballantine came to see me. He had a whole lot of stuff from the police in Medellín saying they couldn't prove anything, but that they'd raided one of your father's warehouses and found a chainsaw. It had Grace's blood all over it and what they suspected were your father's fingerprints on the handle. The PAF had also got hold of two men who worked at the warehouse – they confirmed it was your father who killed my sister.'

'Which is what you wanted to hear.' Her voice was caustic. 'Because you'd already decided it was him.'

'I had an interview with the PAF in Geneva, and a meeting with the three directors about a week afterwards in London. You know the rest.'

'An eye for an eye,' she said. 'And you even got paid for doing it.'

'Grace was twenty-three years old. She didn't deserve to die.'

'But my father did?'

'Look,' Ryder said, 'think what the hell you like. I don't want to talk about it any more. Your uncle said he can use your help on this mining project of his, but if you and I can't stop banging our heads together we're not going to get far, are we?'

'If you believe plutonium comes out of a mine, you don't have to worry about banging your head against anything; you'd better get on the next plane home.'

Sensing that he'd missed a step, Ryder was uncertain of what to say.

'Uncle Miguel didn't really tell you it's a mining project, did he?' She was mocking him now, enjoying his discomfort.

'What plutonium?'

'Mars-96. But I don't think I'm supposed to talk about it.' She swung her legs off the lounger and stood up. 'Are there other parts of the house you'd like to see?'

'No.' Ryder looked at her. 'Are you going to tell me what Mars-96 is?'

'Ask my uncle. I didn't send you that stupid letter, he did. Now if you'll excuse me, I have more important things to do. The housekeeper will bring you anything you need. I'm sure you'll find a way to make yourself at home.'

Ryder watched her walk away, knowing she was being deliberately evasive to annoy him, and that the truth about her father would never allow either of them to properly forget the past.

His return to Colombia had been a mistake, he thought. And if he'd ever imagined that coming here could be a good idea, the mention of plutonium and the attitude of Isabel Corrales made it abundantly clear how very wrong he'd been.

Chapter 5

NOW Corrales had opened the french windows, bees were coming into the study, buzzing around the vases of cut flowers that stood on the bookcase and the desk.

The Colombian seemed unaware of them, leaning back in his chair with his fingertips pressed together. 'I'm not certain where to begin,' he said.

'Try the beginning.' Ryder smiled.

'In this instance I think not.' From a drawer of the desk Corrales took out a large black and white photograph. 'This is a picture of a Russian, three-stage Proton rocket,' he said, 'the largest launch vehicle in the world.' He gave the photo to Ryder. 'One that's powerful enough to put a six tonne payload into orbit around the planet Mars.'

'Mars-96,' Ryder said. 'Isabel mentioned it.'

'What else did she mention?'

'Plutonium.'

'Ah.' Corrales brushed away a bee. 'Then it's best if I start my story some years ago – on Saturday, 16 November, 1996 when, shortly after midnight, the Russian Mars-96 space probe was launched from the Baikonur cosmodrome in Kazakhstan. Mars-96 was the most ambitious interplanetary expedition the Russians had ever undertaken. In addition to its own multi-stage booster rockets, the probe had five sections: a five tonne spacecraft for orbiting Mars, two special landers designed to enter the Martian atmosphere and transmit data from the surface, and two penetrators to sample the soil from deep beneath the ground. You may have read about it.'

Ryder couldn't remember whether he had or not, but he had a good idea where this was leading. By assuming that Mars-96 was precisely what Corrales had just confirmed it was, in the four hours since Isabel had chosen to leak information to him, he'd been able to fill in some of the gaps for himself. As a result, before he finished his lunch on the patio, he'd concluded that the business he'd come to discuss was more wide-ranging and probably more risky than he'd first suspected.

'The Mars-96 launch was monitored by many scientists,' Corrales said. 'The Americans tracked the vehicle successfully from Kwajhalein island in the mid-Pacific, and the Russian space-tracking facility at Yevpatoriya followed its trajectory across China and onwards until it reached a parking orbit a hundred and sixty kilometres above the Earth. It wasn't until Monday the 18th that the Russians realized that the upper stage and part of the probe had separated at the very beginning of the flight. Their scientists had been tracking the wrong section of it. So had everyone else.'

Pleased that his guesses had been right so far, Ryder stopped himself from interrupting.

'I can see your mind working.' Corrales smiled. 'I'm sure I don't have to tell you that the two landers and the two penetrators carried plutonium batteries for the generation of electrical power.'

'How much plutonium?'

'Eighteen canisters containing a total of two hundred grammes or nearly half a pound of almost completely pure radioactive material. To determine where these extremely hazardous canisters might have fallen back to Earth, the US Space Command took over two weeks to analyse the infrared tracking data from their spy satellites. The first statement they issued was incorrect; the second one they believed to be more accurate. It was rather carefully worded.'

'What did it say?'

'Form your own opinion.' Corrales cleared his throat before starting to read from a sheet of paper. 'Debris surviving the heat of re-entry would have fallen over a two-hundred-mile-long portion of the Pacific Ocean, Chile and Bolivia. US Space Command is not able to estimate what portion, if any, of the Mars-96 space-craft might have survived re-entry. The Russians are in the best position to address the materials on board their spacecraft and whether any portion of the spacecraft might have survived.'

'Bureaucratic crap,' Ryder said. 'To stop any panic.'

'Of course. The Russians' attempt at diplomacy was equally facile. The head of their Space Agency, Yuriy Koptev, met with the ambassadors of Argentina, Bolivia, Chile and Peru to assure them that there was no chance of any plutonium leakage and that there was a minimum threat of radioactive contamination of the Pacific.' Corrales paused. 'So, except for the designers of the probe, everyone was happy and promptly forgot about the problem.'

'Except you,' Ryder said.

Corrales shook his head. 'You misunderstand me. Until two months ago I had never heard of Mars-96. I had little knowledge of plutonium, and even if I had known of these things I would have had no interest in them.'

'But now you do.'

'Yes, Mr Ryder, now I do. I also think you will come to share that interest with me. Are you familiar with the market for pure plutonium?'

'The black market?'

'If you like.' Corrales stared into the distance. 'As well as being one of the most dangerous substances known to man, plutonium is, of course, the major component of nuclear weapons. All over the world, terrorists and third-world governments are scrambling to accumulate as much of it as they can. You need only five kilogrammes to construct a bomb, and in the wrong hands, because it is so very poisonous, it can be scattered in small particles by conventional means to create spectacular weapons of terror. For these reasons it is worth an extraordinary amount of money.'

Ryder decided to force the pace. 'And you know where you can lay your hands on two hundred grammes of the stuff,' he said.

Corrales smiled slightly. 'I wish that was so. I do know, however, of a single canister that has been located in a remote and very desolate part of South America.'

'So you think the others are lying around in the same place somewhere.' By now Ryder was intrigued, waiting impatiently to hear the rest of it. 'How much is two hundred grammes of plutonium worth?' he asked.

'According to the research Isabel has been doing on the Internet and through the libraries, between three and five million American dollars. The price is dependent on the nationality of the buyer and on the end use for the material. Finding the right customer may be as difficult as finding the canisters.' Corrales hesitated for a second. 'Which is why I need your help and why you need mine.'

'To do what?'

'My proposal is this.' Corrales stood up from his desk and went to stand at the open windows. 'I would like to think that with my assistance and with the information I have, you will be able to employ your expertise to locate the remains of Mars-96. For my part I believe I can secure a buyer for the plutonium.' He looked at Ryder. 'One who would satisfy both our requirements.'

'Such as?'

'There are many people we could approach. The US for example, who presumably would be anxious to prevent the plutonium from falling into the wrong hands, and the Russians who, in reality, are the rightful owners of the wreckage. Then there are the governments of other countries who are eager to develop their own nuclear capability. We also have terrorists, guerrilla groups, ethnic minorities who are struggling for survival, dictators and those international organizations trading illegally on the fringes of the weapons business.'

'Jesus,' Ryder said slowly. 'The PAF.'

'From what Isabel has told me, the Peace Aid Foundation would seem to be a particularly suitable customer.'

Ryder was too busy thinking to say anything.

'I presume you wish to hear the rest of my plan?' Corrales's smile had broadened. 'We appoint an agent to offer the plutonium to the PAF at a price they cannot refuse,' he said. 'Then, after we've taken their money and recorded the transaction secretly on video tape, we wait for them to on-sell the material to a third party. As soon as they do that we supply copies of our tape to the authorities in several countries. By such means we will make a handsome profit and, at the same time, incriminate and destroy the men who have been trying to kill you.'

At face value the plan was inspired, Ryder thought, but only workable if the plutonium could really be recovered. 'How sure are you that you can find the canisters?' he said.

'With the appropriate technology – very confident indeed.' Corrales returned to his desk. 'I will underwrite all costs for the search and guarantee you ten per cent of whatever we happen to make from our efforts. What do you think?'

Ryder grinned at him. 'One canister, either from Argentina, or Bolivia, or from Chile, or Peru. Are you going to tell me where?'

'Forgive me. In my business one becomes accustomed to being cautious.'

'You want a commitment from me before you say anything more, right?'

'It would be best for both of us.' Corrales paused. 'I hope you see this as an opportunity – especially when there is nothing illegal about searching for the canisters. In my opinion the plutonium belongs to whoever finds it, and what possible harm can there be in selling to it a large, internationally responsible peace organization?'

'Why choose me?'

'Why should I not? You're familiar with the PAF; you have skills and experience which are suited to a project that will have certain complications associated with it, and I believe you to be an honourable man. You saved the life of my niece at some risk to yourself. Why would I look elsewhere?'

The answers were too slick, Ryder thought. And the project sounded too straightforward to be true. 'What kind of complications?' he asked.

'In South America there are many places where life is as cheap as a packet of cigarettes – places where travel is difficult because

71

of political unrest, or because of extreme conditions at certain times of the year. The plutonium is not sitting in someone's garden somewhere. If it was, the canisters would have been found long ago.'

Ryder was trying to read between the lines, but he wasn't trying very hard, reluctant to turn down the job when none of his other options offered anything like the same prospects. 'If I agree to this, when do you want to start?' he said.

'It will be prudent to begin as soon as we are able to procure the necessary equipment. We will require a suitable vehicle, sophisticated electronics and an aircraft of a type I hope you can recommend. We shall also need an experienced pilot.' Corrales studied a bee that had landed on his arm. 'I already have access to a guide.'

'What if I say no?'

'Even without the inducement of exposing the PAF for what they are, ten per cent of five million dollars is still five hundred thousand dollars.' Corrales watched the bee take off. 'Isabel believes you will not accept; I, on the other hand, am confident she's wrong. It is, of course, Isabel who will be your guide.'

'Forget it,' Ryder said. 'I'll make my own arrangements, thanks.'

'May I take that to mean we are to become partners?'

'Yep. You can take that to mean we are.' Despite his reservations, Ryder knew there was only one decision he could make – not just because his options were so limited, but because as things had turned out, his return to Colombia had clearly not been the mistake he'd thought it was. The continuing animosity of Isabel Corrales was a shame, but compensating for it was a project having many times the potential of anything else he'd been considering.

'May I say how pleased I am?' Corrales pushed a button on his desk. 'My niece will be surprised. I asked her to remain at home so she could join us if things went well.'

'To do what?'

'Isabel has learned much about Mars-96. She'll explain what we've discovered about the trajectory of the probe before it hit the Earth, and she can describe some of the problems you may encounter in the search for the canisters. You must understand that my niece is an intelligent and well-travelled young woman.'

Intelligent enough to have travelled all the way to Canada, Ryder thought. If Corrales could've seen her with a loaded .357 Magnum in her hand, he might want to adjust his opinion a little.

If Isabel was surprised, she was taking care not to show it. She walked in through the french windows to stand beside her uncle, glancing briefly at the photo of the Proton rocket on his desk. 'Well, well,' she said. 'So you've told Mr Ryder all about your clever project.'

'He has agreed to participate, but prefers you do not accompany him.'

'Oh.' She opened her mouth to say something, but apparently thought better of it.

'Your uncle says you've got a fair idea of the probe's trajectory,' Ryder said, 'but he hasn't said where you think it landed.'

'That's because he didn't want to put you off. You don't know what you're letting yourself in for.' She went to the bookcase and came back holding a map. 'There wasn't any conclusive evidence until one of the canisters showed up,' she said. 'Just an eyewitness account of a fireball, and a report from someone at the Catholic University in Antofagasta – that's a town on the Pacific coast of Chile.'

'And the data from the US Space Command,' Ryder said.

'We've got better information from some Russian sources. I suppose you want to know everything?'

'I'm not going to find much plutonium unless someone tells me where to look for it.' Ryder was searching for a way to break the ice, aware that Corrales would not have offered her as a guide unless she had some knowledge of the crash site.

'You can see on here.' She unfolded the map and smoothed it out on the desktop. 'The yellow line shows what we believe was the final path of the Mars-96 probe.'

The line began out in the far reaches of the Pacific, travelling north-east over the coast of Chile and finishing just inside the

Bolivian border where someone had drawn a circle with a red flow-pen.

'There's a man called John Van der Brink,' she said. 'He was an electronics specialist at the European Southern Observatory near La Serana. In November 1996, while he was camping with his wife Katrina in the mountains of southern Chile, he saw something enter the Earth's atmosphere in the middle of the night. He described it as a bright, slow-moving meteor about ten degrees above the horizon.' She slid her finger along the yellow line to a small green dot. 'That gave us the first rough coordinate.'

'Then you got a couple of others.' Ryder could see more dots, both inland and both further north.

'Mm.' She nodded. 'From Luis Barrera. He was the director of the Astronomy Institute at Antofagasta University. He spent two months collecting information from people who'd seen the streak of light, taking photographs of the terrain and calculating the route of the fireball. Just before Christmas 1996 he released a report which no one read because by then the loss of the Mars-96 mission was old news.'

Corrales interrupted her. 'The lack of interest was partially the result of where the probe was lost,' he said. 'The south-west of the Bolivian high desert Altiplano is not a place where people choose to go. It is sparsely inhabited, extremely cold and one of the most inhospitable regions in the world.'

'Have you got a copy of the report?' Ryder asked.

'Isabel has it on file in her computer. She will show you. The man Barrera was in no doubt of the trajectory. He's certain the probe broke up at an altitude of eighty kilometres while travelling at a speed of seven thousand metres per second above the Chilean coastal town of Tocopilla. It was heading for Oruro in Bolivia. The fragments, he believes, would have landed in the south-west corner of the Bolivian Altiplano.'

'Which is where you found the canister,' Ryder said. 'Where you've drawn the red circle on the map.'

'Unfortunately no.' Corrales leaned back in his chair. 'I regret it was not me who found it. My knowledge comes indirectly through a business associate. You see, Mr Ryder, over the years I have acquired interests in many countries. In all, I own seven mines in South America, two of which lie near the Bolivian town of Potosí. They produce tin, and, sometimes if I'm lucky, a little silver. Three months ago, the manager of my Potosí mines was on a hunting trip for vizcachas in the cold of the salt desert. For local knowledge he employed the services of a young native Indian who tried to sell him what the boy called a handwarmer. It was an unusually heavy, sealed container about the size of a thirty five millimetre film canister.'

'And unusually hot,' Ryder said. 'In more ways than one.'

'According to my manager, Castaña Diaz, it is warm to touch. The boy had come across it in the dust of the high plains near the Laguna Colorada which is the red lake you can see here.' Corrales placed his finger alongside the circle.

'Did Diaz realize what he'd got hold of?'

'Like me, he is a mining engineer. He guessed the canister contained a radioactive isotope of some kind, and thought perhaps it was space debris. After he'd mentioned it to me I became curious and arranged for the boy to be interviewed privately. Since then, because I regard the discovery to be important, the boy and his father have been relocated to a safer place. I have also learned of more wreckage lying in the desert. It is badly burned and melted, but displays identifiable Russian markings.'

'But no more canisters.' Half an hour ago, Ryder had been intrigued; now he was fascinated. 'Maybe they burned up during re-entry.'

'As long as my manager has not reached the same conclusion that I have, we shall learn soon enough. On the Altiplano, people live by their own rules and Diaz is not a man I would trust in a matter such as this.'

Isabel frowned at her uncle. 'You don't trust anyone,' she said. 'The plutonium doesn't belong to you any more than it belongs to Señor Diaz. And you're not telling Mr Ryder the truth: you know it'll be dangerous to search for the canisters, so why don't you just say so?'

'I'm sure he understands.'

'Radioactive danger, or something else?' Ryder asked.

'It depends,' Corrales said. 'According to Russian literature, the plutonium-238 is in the form of pellets that were formed at high temperature. Provided the canisters are intact, the radioactive hazard will be minimal.'

'Which leaves us with your tricky friend Diaz.'

'Or his compatriots.' Corrales cleared his throat again. 'The key, I believe, is swiftness. With good weather, the right people, the best equipment and with precise information we shall steal a march on anyone with similar aspirations.'

'Because you've got a better plan?'

'I think so.' Corrales used a pencil to draw a tiny rectangle on the map. 'In this area here, just south of the Laguna Colorado, there is an airstrip for servicing a remote meteorological station. I propose basing a light plane there – one which has been fitted with powerful, infrared, thermal-imaging equipment. By flying along the path of the Mars-96 probe and conducting an aerial, infrared survey of the ground, I believe it will be possible to detect any objects that are warmer than the surrounding soil.'

Ryder wasn't so sure. 'Carrying out a search pattern from the air won't work by itself,' he said. 'Even if we use the best global positioning system we can buy, it won't pinpoint the location of a canister to closer than a radius of about twenty-five metres. A Magellan NAV1000M might get us a bit nearer, but that still leaves a hell of a lot of ground to search for something that's only a couple of inches long. We'll need Geiger counters.'

'I see.' Corrales put his fingertips together. 'After so many years have passed I suppose we must assume the winds of the Altiplano will have buried the canisters in sand and salt to some depth. Obtaining Magellan GPS units should not be a problem, but I am less confident about selecting an appropriate aircraft. I've been rather hoping you could suggest one.

Ryder looked at him. 'I know someone who can – someone who could get the right plane and fly it for us too.'

'You have a contact?'

'Alexei Volodya. He dropped out of the PAF when I did. Alexei flew combat jets for the Russian Air Force before he joined the

Spetsnaz, Special Forces. He'll fly anything anywhere we want.'
Ryder paused. 'He'd do it for nothing. If Alexei thinks there's a
chance of choking off the PAF, you won't have to pay him.'

'Expenditure is of minor consequence, but I fear I am not persuaded. Forgive me for saying so, but since you will not consider
taking my niece as a guide, I am a little reluctant to accept this
Alexei you recommend when he is someone I have never met.'

'Isabel said the project could be dangerous, and you said the
Bolivian salt desert is a pretty tough place. Why would you want
me to take her there?'

'Mr Ryder, if I have overstated the unpleasantness of the
Altiplano, I'm sorry; that was not my intention. But I have not
been altogether frank with you.'

Ryder decided to make it easy for Corrales. 'You want her to
ride shotgun,' he said. 'In case I disappear with five million dollars' worth of plutonium.'

'Not at all. If that was my concern I would insist on sending
Santos with you. No, there are other considerations. Isabel's
mother was of Indian extraction. On the Altiplano the predomi-
nant languages are Quechua and Aymara. Isabel speaks them
both. She has also accompanied me many times to visit my mines
in Potosí, so she is familiar with the native people and their customs. By comparison, you have no such experience.'

The rationale was only half-plausible, Ryder thought, a cover-
up for the real reason Corrales wanted his niece to go, and an
indication of what the trade-off for recruiting Alexei was going to
be.

'Mr Ryder,' Corrales said, 'we both have much to think about.
May I propose we break off our discussion and continue with it
later? In the meantime you must enjoy yourself, so, after you've
studied the information on Isabel's computer, she'll drive you
into Cali. We have a fine city and some very old churches in the
Plaza de Caycedo. Since Isabel tells me you've admired the
Calima gold in my collection, you should visit the Museo del Oro
where there is more on display. On another day perhaps she can
take you south to Popayán which is the most beautiful colonial
city in Colombia.'

'I'm sure she's a good guide.' Ryder grinned. 'She doesn't have to prove it to me.'

'No, no. It is a courtesy. She'll be glad to.'

Ryder doubted that she was going to be as glad as her uncle thought. 'It's OK,' he said. 'If I want to go anywhere I can go by myself. I don't want to put Isabel to any trouble.'

She gathered up the map from the desk without looking at him. 'Mr Ryder doesn't appreciate my company,' she said. 'He thinks I'm more trouble than I'm worth. He told me that in Canada.'

Ryder had forgotten, but evidently she had not. 'Look,' he said, 'if you've got the time, a trip into Cali would be great. I'd like to go.'

'How very diplomatic.' She smiled slightly. 'In that case I'd better go and change, hadn't I?'

The day had been one of surprises for Ryder, but the evening was turning out to be equally unusual. Just as before, for reasons that he suspected had more to do with her uncle than herself, over the course of the afternoon Isabel had made an effort to suppress her antagonism. But unlike this morning, once they had left the house she had slowly become less brittle, and on more than one occasion had almost gone out of her way to be agreeable.

In Cali, for over an hour they had explored the city centre together. They had drunk coffee down by the river in the cool of a breeze. They had walked to the Iglesia de San Antonia, a magnificent hilltop church with a view to match, and just on dusk they had taken the elevator to the 43rd floor of La Torre de Cali, the highest building in the city where, after watching the colours of an extraordinary sunset, they had dined in a comfortable, airy restaurant on the top floor.

Throughout it all there had been little sign of the other Isabel, her eyes flashing only once when Ryder made the mistake of trespassing on to personal ground by asking how old she was and where her mother had come from. Since then, and for nearly all of the drive home, although she had answered his questions pleasantly enough, she had been quieter as if absorbed in her own thoughts.

She was continuing to be uncommunicative, standing beside a wall lamp in the lounge with a glass of wine in her hand, either waiting for Ryder to reopen the conversation or expecting him to say goodnight.

In the diffused light, her strapless evening gown was the same honey colour as her shoulders, creating the impression that she was half undressed. So good was the illusion that he'd started to wonder if she was standing there solely for his benefit.

'There's something I need to know.' He tried to assess her mood. 'You don't really want to go to Bolivia, do you?'

'I've just come home. I don't think I'm ready for another adventure.'

'Do you have a choice?'

She sipped at her drink. 'Probably not.'

'Because of your uncle?'

'You've given him the excuse he was looking for.'

'I have to take you with me if I want Alexei to pilot the plane – is that going to be the deal?'

'Sort of. It's too complicated to explain.' She went to refill her glass. 'You don't understand how Uncle Miguel operates.'

He'd been right about Alexei, but he'd been wrong about her leg. Once or twice this afternoon she seemed to have been favouring it, but now, after a day of sightseeing in town, she could no longer disguise her limp.

Perhaps because she knew he was watching her, instead of returning to the light she came to stand in front of him with a peculiar expression on her face.

'Searching for plutonium with a bad leg might be a lousy idea,' he said. 'You could use that for an excuse of your own.'

'The bullet's left a scar. I was hoping it wouldn't, but it has. Look.' Inexplicably, as though unconscious of what she was doing, she lifted her skirt waist-high to show him.

Ryder could barely keep his eyes away. For all that her white bikini briefs concealed she might as well have been wearing nothing. She knew it, and Ryder knew it. But the reason for her immodesty was unclear. To embarrass him? A test? A promise? Or to tease?

He had no idea. In the few seconds she gave him, he was able to see the puckered depression disfiguring the otherwise flawless skin of her upper thigh, but as quickly as she'd raised her skirt she dropped it again.

'I don't suppose it'll matter in Bolivia,' she said. 'The high desert's hardly the place for shorts.'

Some promise, Ryder thought. This was a message: the Corrales family had decided on the part she would play, and in case he'd overlooked the possible pay-off for taking her with him, he'd just been issued with a not-so-subtle hint.

'Is there a way you can contact your friend Alexei?' she said.

'It might take a while.'

'We'll need time to get the equipment together anyway.' She smoothed down her skirt. 'It's funny, isn't it?'

'What?'

'How all this happened.'

He wasn't certain. Reviewing how or why he'd become mixed up with her and her uncle was not a priority. Considering the implications of what she'd said and attempting to predict what might occur from here on was of more concern.

He was still concerned an hour later, long after he'd said goodnight and gone to think things through in his room. But gradually the doubts began to fade, and soon most of them seemed vague or more imagined than they were real. The recovery of the Mars-96 canisters was a project with enough positives, he told himself – a way to shaft the PAF: an opportunity to make some proper money, with the added bonus of working with Alexei.

The downside risks were harder to define, but even if the project failed, what would he have lost? Little or nothing, Ryder concluded, except perhaps the chance to discover whether Isabel would still be willing to show him how well her scar was healing.

If the notion had been less provocative he would have been able to get her out of his mind and pay more attention to his plans. But in her company over too many of the soft, warm summer days ahead in Cali, the fantasy refused to go away, and it would not be until he reached the bitter wasteland of the Bolivian Altiplano that he would come to count the cost of his foolish preoccupation with her.

Chapter 6

THE flight attendant reached in front of Markovic to collect his empty glass. 'Would you like another drink?' she asked.

'No, thank you.' He thought her breasts were nicely shaped, but he doubted that she'd be much good in bed. 'How soon before we land?'

'We should be outside the terminal around five past ten. Are you visiting Colombia on business?'

'Every six weeks. I'm a property developer.' He smiled at her. 'You know how things are in Bogotá.'

'Yes.' She nodded as though she understood before walking awkwardly away.

Markovic watched her go, then folded up his table, reclined his seat and closed his eyes, ready now to consider his next move, aware that, so far, he'd been luckier than he deserved to be.

Much as he'd expected, by the time he'd reached Montréal the trail had gone cold, and after a fruitless and expensive week during which he had failed to obtain a single list of departing passengers from any airline, he'd nearly been inclined to start again.

When the breakthrough had come, it had been more good fortune than the result of hard work – a chance encounter with a barman at the airport who'd been able to identify the Russian from a photo. After that, almost as if it had been planned, everything had fallen into place – a similar identification by the driver of the courtesy bus who'd recalled a large man he'd picked up from the Lachine motel, and the equally valuable information supplied by the motel manager who, for three $100 notes, had provided a list of the telephone calls the Englishman had made on the day he'd checked out.

The rest had been simple, so much so that at one point Markovic had wondered whether the trail he'd been following had been deliberately laid.

But it was no more false than the flight attendant's manner, he told himself. The voice mail left by Ryder at the Luxembourg number had sounded as authentic as the messages left by Volodya, and there was no reason to believe either of the men suspected how easy it had been for a stranger to access their private communications.

A sloppy system, Markovic thought, less watertight than e-mail or fax, and not even encrypted because, just like the directors of the PAF, they believed they were so fucking smart.

But from here on, things would become much harder. Now that the Englishman and the Russian were about to rendezvous somewhere, their need for the Luxembourg number had gone, and in the future, discovering where they were and what they were doing would not be a matter of luck or good fortune, but a question of how careless they were and how well they would be able to disguise their tracks.

There was another question to consider too – for Markovic, one that held more interest. Was it conceivable that the Colombian girl had become involved? And if so, in his next contact call to Bonn, would he receive instructions to include her in his contract?

To contemplate the prospect he elected to break his rule and order another drink. After all, he reasoned, an extra $50,000 would give him the choice of spending winter in the south of France, or of putting the money towards another apartment on the coast in Spain.

He pushed the button on his armrest, smiling pleasantly at the flight attendant as she hurried to offer him her services.

While Markovic was ordering his drink, in the Geneva boardroom of the Peace Aid Foundation, Sir Richard Ballantine had already finished his second glass of after-lunch port. He had also finished listening to the tape of the most recent telephone report from Bonn.

'We can use this as part of our insurance package,' he said. 'There's no mention of our names on it.'

Poitou removed the cassette from the machine. 'We hardly need more insurance,' he said. 'Markovic supplied us with sufficient information to guarantee his silence.'

'We didn't check out everything. I'm still not happy with our arrangement with him. I'm not certain he's going to the right place either. What business could Ryder possibly have in Colombia?'

'The Corrales girl perhaps.' Poitou lit a cigar. 'To prevent her from surprising him again.'

Ballantine shook his head. 'He took her to hospital in Montréal, and he went to see her there afterwards – we know he did. What I don't understand is why.'

'Do you believe there's something between them?'

'For God's sake, what could there be?' Ballantine waved away the cigar smoke. 'We gave her photos of Ryder killing her father, and Ryder won't have forgotten what happened to his sister. There can't be any two people with less in common.'

'So it's as I said: he's gone to eliminate her. Ryder won't take risks. He never has.'

'Nor has Volodya. So what the hell are they up to?'

'We have no evidence to suggest they're up to anything.' Poitou studied the ash on his cigar. 'All we have is this two-minute tape from the man Markovic.'

'Telling us that two of our ex-employees are in touch with each other, and saying it sounds as though they're joining forces. If Ryder's in Colombia, we'd damn well better assume Volodya's going to be there with him.'

'Why concern ourselves? If Markovic is right, we can expect his account to be submitted sooner than we thought. If he's wrong, he'll have to complete his assignment somewhere else. I see no reason to doubt him.'

'I'm afraid I don't share your confidence.' Ballantine went to pour himself another drink. 'The bastard's too smooth, and he's still a Serb.'

'And we're still supposed to be discussing the distribution of funds to the Kosovar refugees.'

'Indeed we are.' Ballantine raised his glass in a mock toast. 'Here's to them. If their Liberation Army continue buying their guns through us, we may even have to launch another public appeal for them.'

On another continent, far from the boardrooms of Geneva, Ryder's thoughts were not of the Kosovo Liberation Army or of the PAF, but of his assignment in Africa, where, seven years ago, sweat-stained and blistered by the sun, he'd spent a week fighting the scorpions and the thorn trees of the Somalian desert. Weighed down by his M-16 and a heavy pack, travelling alone between Mogadishu and Baidoa, he had crossed what he'd then believed to be the most unforgiving place on Earth.

He'd been wrong.

This far south, even viewed from the comparative comfort of the Jeep, the tablelands of the Bolivian high desert had become truly forbidding – a featureless expanse of nothing that appeared to be unending in whichever direction Ryder looked.

Yesterday's drive from La Paz to Oruro had provided him with some idea of what to expect, and Isabel had done her best to describe the Altiplano, but he had not imagined it would be like this.

He hadn't anticipated how low the temperature would be either. Despite being forewarned, the cold at night was not a kind he'd encountered before, a penetrating, bone-chilling cold that yesterday evening had driven them back to their hotel in Oruro after spending less than a quarter of an hour outside in the Plaza de Febrero.

The change of environment had been too swift, Ryder decided. Seventeen days had passed since he'd made the decision to come here, but fifteen of those days had been spent in the warmth of Cali where they'd used the time to contact Alexei and gather together the necessary hardware for the trip. Nor had the flight from Colombia been long enough to prepare them for a twenty-degree difference in latitude – a change from mid-summer near the equator to mid-winter in Bolivia at an altitude of over 10,000 feet.

Only the Jeep was impervious to the cold – a low mileage, two-year-old Cherokee that Corrales had arranged to purchase sight unseen, ready for them to pick up on their arrival in La Paz. It had been a good choice. The heater was efficient, the front bumper boasted a brand new winch, and the roof rack had been reinforced to handle the weight of two additional spare wheels.

The Cherokee was a tough and hardy vehicle that should have had more than sufficient room in it. Instead, it was already two-thirds full, crammed with the supplies that Isabel was buying wherever and whenever they stopped. Between cans of fuel, a portable generator and the countless boxes containing their electronic and communication equipment, she'd managed to jam enough clothing, canned food and bottled water to sustain a family for several months.

Up to now, Ryder had avoided complaining, persuading himself that the food and water would provide a barrier between the front seats and the three metal boxes at the back.

Two of the boxes contained photographic equipment – cameras and lenses to support their cover story of being an advance crew for a US television company. It was the third box that worried Ryder, a heavy, specially made, lead-lined chest for the canisters. At the moment its eighteen compartments held nothing more hazardous than rolls of 35-millimetre film, but how well the shielding might work for radioactive plutonium was a question Isabel's research had failed to answer.

For much of their journey from Oruro she'd been half-sleep, waking up in time for lunch at Challapata where she'd bought salteñas, rugby-ball-shaped pasties stuffed with beef and olives and a mysterious mixture of vegetables. Since then, except for adjusting the heater or telling him not to drive so fast, she'd been dozing, leaving Ryder to find his own way south to the desert community of Uyuni where they were supposed to be meeting the boy.

Although Ryder had yet to see anything resembling a signpost, with only one road in, and with an adjacent railway line to guide him, the chances of getting lost seemed minimal.

He waited until they were entering the outskirts of town before reaching across to wake her up.

'Are we there?' She rubbed her eyes and stretched.

'I think so. When does it get dark here?'

'I don't know.' Isabel pointed. 'Welcome to Uyuni.'

To their left, about a hundred yards away, was a vast graveyard of decaying steam locomotives. Some were in pieces, others were in the process of being cut up for scrap while the remainder looked as though at some time in the distant past they'd steamed in from the desert and expired where they'd stopped.

The sight was a warning of what to expect. Uyuni was unlike anywhere Ryder had ever been, a collection of bleak buildings huddled together against the cold and the wind in the thin air of the Altiplano, a weird, otherworldly place, as sterile and unwelcoming as the desert surrounding it.

Evening rush hour in Uyuni was a non-event. Along with several rickety trucks, a few tractors belching smoke were grinding their way through town, but except for the odd four-wheel-drive vehicle parked on the main avenue, cars were few and far between.

'What are we looking for?' Ryder asked.

'The town centre – the Plaza Arce.' Isabel consulted her map. 'The boarding-house is supposed to be on the west side facing the railway station.'

Finding somewhere to park was as easy as locating the station. Ryder swung the Jeep on to a gravel pad beside the line then switched off the ignition and got out to see what the temperature was like. 'Better put your parka on,' he said. 'Bring the map too.'

'We don't need the map.' She joined him and pointed again, this time at a single storey building across the street. 'Residencial Pisitaqui,' she said. 'Over there by the restaurant sign.'

Because Isabel had insisted on running the Jeep's heater on the high setting, the outside air temperature was something of a shock, making Ryder wish he'd put on gloves before trying to lock the doors with fingers that were already beginning to hurt.

'When were you here last?' he asked.

'I've only ever been once – when I was little. My mother brought me to a carnival or a festival called La Diablada. That means the dance of the devils. We didn't stay overnight, though. We went back to a proper hotel in Potosí.' She set off across the plaza. 'Come on, let's see if the boy's home.'

'What's his name?'

'Agudelo. His father's name's Carlos. I think that's what my uncle said.'

The Residencial Pisitaqui was a seedy, run-down establishment advertising rooms for nine bolivianos, an overnight rate so low that Ryder wondered if it was a misprint. He waited inside the lobby while Isabel spoke to an elderly woman who was sitting on the floor polishing a copper kettle.

The woman seemed preoccupied, waving her rag in the direction of a corridor before resuming her work.

'Well?' Ryder asked. 'Is the boy here?'

Isabel nodded. 'With his father. If they only speak Aymara or Quechua, let me do the talking.'

'Sure. Just remember not to tell them too much.'

'Don't you trust me?' She walked away down the corridor, keeping her back to him as she knocked on the door of the apartment.

Carlos Agudelo was a Bolivian Indian in his early forties, a tall man with long, dark hair, sunken eyes and bad teeth. He seemed unsurprised to have visitors, speaking quietly to Isabel for nearly a minute before he shook hands with Ryder and asked them to come in.

Although the apartment was tiny, it was clean and it was warm, sparsely furnished with a wooden table, two chairs and two beds.

The Bolivian was clearly ill at ease, introducing his son, José, by means of hand gestures alone.

'He's embarrassed because he doesn't speak Spanish.' Isabel explained. 'He doesn't know you're a gringo.'

The boy stepped forward. He was almost as tall as his father, but painfully thin, about nineteen years old, dressed in jeans and a woollen sweater that was several sizes too large for him. 'I have some American,' he said. 'In Challapata where I live, there is a friend who teaches me. Please you will sit.' He offered the chairs. 'You have come for the handwarmer?'

'Do you have it here?' Ryder asked.

'Of course.' Reaching under one of the beds the boy produced a six-inch length of lead pipe that had been hammered flat at each end. 'Señor Santos makes me keep it safe in this way.' He gave the pipe to Ryder. 'You can feel it is warm, yes?'

It wasn't warm. It was hot. Ryder handled it gingerly, wondering how thick the lead was. 'When did Señor Santos come to see you?' he asked.

'He visits two months ago after I have tried to sell the warmer to Señor Diaz who runs the mines in Potosí. It is Señor Santos who pays for my father and for me to move here to Uyuni where we are not known. He has said people will come to pay much money if I can show them where I find the warmer and the pieces of metal.' The boy turned to face Isabel. 'You bring this money?'

'Yes.' She smiled. 'Is it all right for you to go with us tomorrow? You might be away for a few days.'

'It is OK,' he said. 'My *auqui* will not mind.' The boy spoke to his father in Aymara, pointing first to Isabel and then to the lead pipe.

This was the first time Ryder had handled a canister of plutonium. It was also the first time he'd heard about Santos visiting Bolivia. Not that he should be surprised, he thought – particularly when the boy was the key to locating the Mars-96 wreckage. Nor would Corrales have gone ahead with the project unless he was satisfied the boy was telling the truth and could keep his mouth shut. And who better to make certain than Santos?

'You have good transport?' the boy enquired.

'Jeep Cherokee,' Ryder said. 'You'll have to squeeze in the back with the food and stuff.'

'If there is room I shall bring my rifle for the vizcachas. Then we will have fresh meat.'

'Rodents,' Isabel said. 'Like long-tailed rabbits. They live in the cactus on islands in the salt desert. Now you know why I've been buying canned food.'

'Tomorrow, on the way to the meteorological station I shall show you where it is I find the handwarmer,' the boy said. 'But before we leave, you must buy kerosene for the drip heater at the cabin. Otherwise for you it will be very cold there.'

A heated cabin sounded a good deal more civilized than trying to sleep in the Jeep, Ryder thought, especially if Isabel was going to be as cool as she had been last night in Oruro.

'Right,' he said. 'We'll pick you up here at nine o'clock in the morning.'

'You have the money for my father?'

'Sure.' Ryder took an envelope from his pocket. 'Five hundred American dollars. Three hundred for the handwarmer and another two hundred so you can both stay on in Uyuni for a while after we've gone home.' He offered the envelope to Agudelo.

'He doesn't understand.' Isabel switched to Aymara, taking the envelope and opening it to reveal the notes.

'Ah.' Agudelo nodded. '*Take chuima'hampi.*' He screwed up his face. '*Cun sañasauca'ha coffee?*'

'He'd like us to have coffee with him,' Isabel said. 'Have we got time?'

Ryder checked his watch. 'Not if we're going to contact Alexei at five o'clock. I don't think it's a smart idea to use our phone from in here. Say we don't mean to be rude, but we need to find somewhere to stay and get something to eat.'

Isabel stood up and smiled at the Bolivian, launching into another polite explanation of which Ryder recognized not a single word.

Because the goodbyes took longer than expected, it was nearly five minutes to five when they reached the Jeep to stow away the piece of pipe in the lead-lined container and search for the satellite phone.

Eventually it was Isabel who found it, lying on her stomach in the back, half-covered in clothes and cardboard boxes.

'I can feel it,' she said. 'You must have wrapped it up in a sleeping bag.'

'Drag the whole bloody lot out. I know Alexei: if we're late making the call he won't hang around.'

She extricated the phone and gave it to him. 'Can we use this from anywhere?' she asked.

'Just about – as long as there's a satellite overhead some-where.' Ryder leaned back against the door of the Jeep, fumbling to push buttons until he removed his gloves and started over again.

There was a delay, a buzzing tone, then a crackle followed by the sound of Alexei's voice.

'It's me,' Ryder said. 'Where are you?'

'Buenos Aires.'

'What the hell are you doing there?'

'You say it is important we have the best plane for the job, so I have bought the best. They are not so easy to find at a good price.'

'How long before you can get here?'

'I have today supervised the fitting of long-range underwing tanks, and I have also secured some other equipment for us. If the weather remains fine, I shall leave tomorrow morning to arrive at your airstrip in the evening your time. You must under-stand that for such a small aircraft it is a seven-hour flight, and I have not yet decided where I must refuel. If I am late, do not be concerned.'

'You need to get here in daylight,' Ryder said.

'You forget the two-hour time difference.' Alexei paused. 'Chris, the coordinates you have given me for the airstrip are cor-rect?'

'Hold on a second.' Ryder found the map and gave it to Isabel. 'Do you think the Laguna Colorado would look red from the air?'

She nodded. 'I don't see why it shouldn't – as long as the sun's still up. He can't miss it anyway. It's a fairly big lake, nearly ten miles across. The airstrip's about four miles south of it.'

'OK.' Ryder relayed the information, asking Alexei to phone at the same time tomorrow if he was going to be delayed.

'So the girl is with you?' Alexei said.

'You can say hello to her when you get here. Don't waste your batteries.' Ryder pushed the end button to terminate the call, relieved that things were more or less on schedule and pleased that there had been no unforseen complications.

'Where did he say he was?' Isabel asked.

'Argentina – Buenos Aires. He'll be at the airstrip tomorrow evening.'

'Well, that'll be nice for you, won't it?' She slammed the rear door of the Jeep with unnecessary force. 'I'm hungry. Let's find somewhere to eat.'

'Isn't it a bit early?'

'If you don't want to come with me, I'll go by myself.' Raising the hood of her parka she limped off towards the nearby group of shops and restaurants.

There were three restaurants to choose from; the El Rosedal, the Paso Dorado and one with a sign that read 16 de Julio. Isabel selected the de Julio, entering ahead of Ryder and sitting down in a booth at the far end of the room.

'Have you got a problem?' He took off his coat and laid it beside him on the seat.

'No. Have you?'

'Look,' Ryder said. 'We managed to get on OK in Cali. Now you're all scratchy again. You might not enjoy being here, but until we know whether we can find the canisters, I'm stuck with you, and you're stuck with me. You might as well get used to it.'

'I don't have to get used to anything. Do you want me to order for you?'

'Sure, whatever you like.' He decided not to bother with her, letting her speak to the waiter and waiting until they'd finished their main course of chopped llama meat and yuca before he leaned back and grinned.

'What?' She scowled at him.

'When you said I didn't know what I was letting myself in for, I figured you meant the climate.'

'I did.'

'Unwind then. All you're doing is making things tougher for yourself.'

93

'I know.' She rearranged her knife and fork on her plate. 'I don't expect you to understand.'

'Try me.'

'All right. I'll tell you why I don't enjoy being here: it's because I'm ashamed for not standing up to my aunt and uncle.'

'After they gave you your riding instructions?'

'It's not just this stupid plutonium thing. It goes right back to when my mother died. I think she realized what kind of man my father was. That's why she made Aunt Christíana and Uncle Miguel promise to bring me up in the way she wanted. She was frightened how I might turn out.'

'Did she say so?'

'No. But I know she hated all the money from the drug trafficking.'

'What's that got to do with you being ashamed of yourself?'

'Because I always seem to end up doing what I'm told.' She hesitated for a moment. 'You think I'm a spoilt, little rich girl, but it's not like that. You see, I haven't got any money of my own. It's in a trust fund. Until I'm twenty-nine all I get is a monthly allowance. I can't go anywhere or do anything unless my uncle and aunt say I can.'

'How did you get the cash to go to Canada?'

'I saved nearly six thousand American dollars, I borrowed another five and I sold some jewellery – not the jewellery my mother left me – you know, just the stuff you can buy in shops.'

'And got a hole blown in your leg for your trouble.'

'And a vacation in Bolivia.' She smiled briefly. 'If you haven't worked it out yet, Uncle Miguel's very impressed with you, Mr Ryder. He thinks you live in the real world while I'm supposed to be immature, irresponsible, self-indulgent and headstrong. You've come to Bolivia for the money, but I've been sent to get straightened out. Those are his words, not mine.'

'Three things,' Ryder said. 'Forget the money: I'm here to get the PAF off my back; I'm not interested in straightening out you or anyone else; and you can stop calling me Mr Ryder. I don't like it.'

'What a shame.' She started using the tip of her knife to delaminate a beer mat. 'If I hadn't made certain you'd bring me with you, my allowance would've been cut. But you guessed that, didn't you?'

'It wasn't hard.'

'You're not hard to read either. You're the same as all the other men I've met. I've seen how you look at me.'

'Fine,' Ryder said. 'So I'm just an ordinary guy, you're not a spoilt, little rich girl, and you and I are in Bolivia for different reasons. Now we've got that out of the way, are we going to have a shot at working together, or not?'

'You don't need me.' She put the beer mat back on the table. 'Not now you're going to have Alexei to order around.'

Ryder couldn't believe she was feeling left out. It was just her usual resentment coming to the surface again, he decided. Except that she sounded more flat than resentful – perhaps because she was already feeling lonely in an environment that was only going to get worse.

'What did you think of the boy?' he asked.

'About him being cheated, you mean? He's been given three hundred dollars for something worth a thousand times more than that.'

'You can do a fair bit with three hundred dollars in this part of the world.'

'I suppose.' She changed the subject. If I'm such bad company for you, maybe I should stay here in Uyuni.'

'How are you going to get straightened out if you do that?' He smiled at her. 'What about ordering some dessert and coffee, or are you leaving it up to me?'

'You ought to try a *chicha cochabambina*. It's a drink made from fermented maize. It'll make you sleep well.'

'Assuming we can find beds to sleep in.'

'Hotel Avienda,' she said. 'I asked the boy's father. Hot water, no cockroaches and no fleas.'

'You'd better make the best of it then. If you're expecting a five star met station you might be disappointed.'

'I wasn't even expecting to be in Bolivia. If I hadn't met you, I wouldn't be.' She glanced at him across the table. 'It's as though I'm being punished.'

'For what?'

'You don't have to make me say it. You know what – because of my father – for what he did to your sister.'

Chapter 7

THE road was deteriorating. For most of the 150 mile journey down through Alota, Cascada and more recently across what the boy had called the Valle de Rocas, the surface had been passable. But now they were even further south it was becoming more rutted, dustier and rougher by the mile.

Potholes were the worst problem. They were scattered across the road in groups, some sending bone-jarring shocks through the Jeep's suspension if Ryder saw them too late, while others were either impossible to avoid or barely negotiable at any speed because of their depth.

But all around, compensating for the road conditions, was a landscape of haunting beauty, an immense, almost treeless wilderness of glaring plains, lonely mirages, scrubby, windswept basins and dry, eroded badlands. So empty was the high salt desert of the Altiplano that Ryder had long ago given up trying to come to terms with it. The whole region was too wild, an ethereal part of the world to which no one could relate because people did not belong in a place like this.

Seated beside him, Isabel seemed similarly overawed. Unlike yesterday when she'd continuously fallen asleep on the drive from Oruro to Uyuni, on this, the last leg of their trip, she'd remained wide awake, occasionally talking to the boy in the back, but mostly staring at the unfolding scenery as though she too was intimidated by its eeriness.

The boy himself was unmoved, lying on a pile of clothing,

apparently as insensitive to the environment as he was unwilling to answer Ryder's questions about the Mars-96 wreckage he was taking them to see.

'I'm freezing.' Isabel leaned forwards to adjust the temperature control lever.

'I've told you,' Ryder said. 'If you keep turning up the heat, you'll never get acclimatized. We have to get used to the cold. Starting tomorrow we're going to be working outside most of the time.'

'You will stay cold for many days,' the boy said. 'For those who visit from the Amazon low country, it is four weeks before they stop shivering.'

'Why the hell would anyone come here?' Ryder couldn't think of a reason.

'Some are miners. Some smuggle cocaine into Chile or Argentina, but other men are from the CNPZ. You have heard of it?'

'No.'

'It is the Nestor Paz Zamora Commission – guerrillas who fight the government in my country. They hide in the Cordillera mountains where they will not be discovered.' The boy pointed at an outcrop of bleached rock beside the road. 'Soon we must turn west into the desert. Please, you will say when we have travelled a half of one kilometre more.'

After driving for six hours across the Altiplano, it was a mystery to Ryder how anyone could navigate their way around without a compass. What landmarks there were fell into three categories – large rocks, small rocks, or enormous, shallow dust bowls that for all practical purposes were indistinguishable from one another. Even the horizon was an unreliable guide, although now the clouds were clearing it was possible to pick out the dramatic shape of the solitary and rather sinister Licancábur volcano near the Chilean border. The cone seemed remarkably close, he thought, an indication that the red lake could not now be far away.

'How far into the desert do we go?' he asked the boy.

'In low gear, for less than twenty minutes. Sometimes there are patches of salt which are soft, so it is better you use the four-wheel-drive, I think.'

Ryder thought so too. Keeping an eye on the odometer he engaged the transfer case and waited for more instructions.

'It is time?' the boy queried.

'Just about. Where to?'

'You turn there in front of the *llareta*.'

Isabel translated. 'That little bush,' she said. 'Over by those pebbles.'

The boy was more alert now, either scanning the mountain range for some unseen, distant pointer, or screwing himself around in the Jeep to peer out of the dusty rear window.

If anything, the salt pan was easier to drive on than the road. The surface was smoother, pothole-free and, except for a few areas where Ryder could feel the tyres beginning to drag, he was able to stop fighting the steering wheel and spend more of his time looking around.

'How are we doing?' he asked.

'To the north a little.' The boy squinted ahead. 'You keep the sun in the corner of the windshield.'

'OK.' Ryder adjusted course, endeavouring to drive in a straight line while he tried to identify a reference point in a landscape where there weren't any.

Isabel was trying too, evidently beginning to doubt the boy's ability to recognize where he was.

'How on earth do you remember where you found the hand-warmer?' she asked.

He shrugged. 'For me it is not so hard; for other people perhaps. Please, there is something you will tell me – in case there is a scientist staying at the meteorological station, what is it we say we are doing?'

'You'll like this,' she said. 'Have you heard of Butch Cassidy and the Sundance Kid?'

The boy smiled. 'Everyone in Bolivia knows of them. In the old days, they are the bandits who robbed the Aramayo payroll at Huaca Huañusca. They die here on the Altiplano in a big gun fight at San Vincente, yes?'

Isabel nodded. 'Have you seen the movie?'

'Who has not?'

'Well, if anyone asks, we're an American TV crew who are in Bolivia to see if it's possible to make a series about what else Cassidy and the Kid got up to when they were in this part of the country.'

The boy was amused. 'I think it will be better to make such a programme in Hollywood,' he said. 'Now I see it is not the cameras but this other equipment which you will use to find more warmers.'

'If the electronics don't freeze up.' Isabel passed him a map. 'Can you show me where we are?'

'I am not so good with maps.' He returned it to her. 'In five minutes we will be there.'

His estimate was optimistic.

It was more than a quarter of an hour later when he suddenly asked Ryder to stop the Jeep.

'Where?' Isabel said. 'There's nothing here.'

'I look.' The boy climbed out, reaching back inside to collect his rifle before trudging off across the salt in an apparently random direction.

'I shouldn't have mentioned Butch Cassidy,' Isabel said. 'Now he's going to take his gun with him everywhere.' She wound down her window, shielding her eyes from the sun while she endeavoured to get her bearings.

Ryder was watching the boy. 'Do you think he has any idea where he is?' he asked.

'I don't know.' She shivered. 'It's getting colder.'

'We're up around thirteen thousand feet. Can't you feel yourself breathing harder?'

'I've been sitting still too long to feel anything.' Pushing open her door, she stepped out into a patch of fine, white dust. 'I'm going to stretch my legs. Don't go away.'

'Hang on.' Ryder had seen the boy waving to them. 'Looks like we're in luck after all. Grab a Geiger counter and a GPS unit.'

'We're not going to be that lucky – not on our first day.'

'Why not? You never know.'

She rummaged around inside, handing him the detector before slipping a Magellan unit into the pocket of her parka. 'It'll be a false alarm,' she said. 'It has to be.'

It wasn't a false alarm. Either by drawing on his experience, or by acting on some instinctive sixth sense, the boy had brought them to within eighty or ninety yards of what at first sight appeared to be a piece of fractured stainless steel. It was the size of a newspaper, severely burned, discoloured and, at some time in the past, one of the edges had melted to form an uneven row of metal beads.

Because most of the fragment was buried in the same white dust, Ryder was unable to dislodge it or even rock it from side to side.

The boy was pleased with himself. 'The warmer I find is eight hundred and fifty-two paces away,' he said, 'in a line which is thirty-seven degrees east from here.'

Ryder was suspicious. 'How do you know it was thirty-seven degrees east?' he said.

'By this.' Upending his rifle, the boy pointed to a small compass let into the butt. 'How else would I know?'

Isabel had a wide smile on her face. 'Who needs global positioning?' she said. 'Do you really think this is a piece of Mars-96?'

Ryder was fairly confident. The steel section looked as though it had been torn from a cylindrical fuel tank. It was curved in two planes, and although badly distorted, he could just about estimate the original diameter of the tank.

He switched on the Geiger counter, sweeping the pick-up head over the ground in an unsuccessful attempt to detect any sign of radioactivity above the background level.

'Let me try.' Isabel took it from him. 'You can get the GPS reading.'

He managed to retrieve the Magellan from her pocket without taking off his gloves, but decided to operate it in bare hands. Even then the exercise was difficult, the cold numbing his fingers so quickly that he was forced to take a second reading before he was satisfied with the result.

Away to the west now, where the sun was sinking fast, the sky was a strange colour, and the wind which had been blowing all

101

afternoon was beginning to drop along with the temperature.

Not a place to linger at this time of day, Ryder decided, especially with the cabin still some miles away and with Alexei due to arrive at the airstrip before nightfall. 'We'd better move,' he said. 'We've got the coordinates so we can come back another time.'

Isabel was surprised. 'Don't you want to see where the canister was?' she said.

'It's getting late, and we need to find out what shape the cabin's in.' Ryder turned to the boy. 'How far's the meteorological station?'

Instead of answering the question, the boy pointed over Ryder's shoulder.

Half a mile away, a cut-down truck was coming across the plain, travelling fast, dust billowing from its tyres, heading directly for the stationary Jeep.

A chance encounter with another vehicle was so unlikely that Ryder knew it wasn't even worth considering. In such a godforsaken place, the arrival of strangers was no more an accident than it was good news.

'Who are they?' he asked the boy.

'We will find out.'

As the truck drew closer, Ryder could see it was a rusted-out Volvo. It had no windshield, the doors and much of the body was missing, and someone had removed the top of the cab with a welding torch. Even so, despite its ramshackle appearance, its engine sounded healthy, and once it had come to a halt alongside the Jeep, he could discern fresh paint on the bonnet where a Russian SGM machine-gun was mounted.

Five men spilled out. They wore thick, fur-lined jackets over army fatigues and were armed with assault rifles, holstered automatics and grenades.

Two men remained behind to guard the Jeep. The other three approached the boy who, for reasons of his own, was already marching off to meet them.

Ryder had smelt trouble the moment he'd seen the truck. By now he could taste it, but how much trouble they were in, he wasn't sure.

Judging by Isabel's expression she too was apprehensive, but not yet as apprehensive as she should be, either waiting for him to reassure her or to do something.

'Listen to me,' he said. 'Whoever these guys are, you keep your hood up and your mouth shut. Don't look at them. I mean it. Have you got that?'

She nodded nervously. 'They're not soldiers, are they?'

'No, they're not soldiers.'

'What do they want?'

He was reluctant to guess. After one good look at Isabel, what they wanted could change at any minute, and with only the boy for backup, the odds were lousy if the situation were to take a nasty turn.

One of the men had engaged the boy in conversation, laughing when the words Butch Cassidy were mentioned, and pretending to quick-draw an imaginary six-gun from his hip.

An encouraging sign, Ryder told himself, but nothing like encouraging enough.

Still laughing, the man came over to inspect Isabel. He was unshaven with closely cropped hair and had a small scar running across his left cheek.

'So you are the girl who is to search for the little capsules,' he said.

The statement was as bland as it was telling, leaving Ryder in no doubt about the seriousness of their predicament. Nor was there much doubt about how wrong he'd been to believe in the harmlessness of the boy and his wretched father.

Being careful to move slowly, he stepped forward. 'If you want to talk, you talk to me,' he said. 'What can I do for you?'

The man ignored him, using the front sight of his rifle to hook back the hood of Isabel's parka.

Although she'd dropped the Geiger counter and become rigid, she was managing to control herself, but breathing fast and dangerously close to panic.

Ten feet away, two rifles were levelled at Ryder. The men who held them were without expression, standing motionless, too well trained to take their eyes off him. The boy, though, was

103

uneasy, shifting his weight from one foot to the other, his head lowered to avoid any eye contact at all.

The man with the scar turned his attention to Ryder, holding out a scrap of soiled paper. 'For you,' he said.

It was a map, poorly drawn, showing two roads, one of which led to the word *mina*.

Ryder was losing his battle to keep calm, praying Isabel could hold on while he tried desperately to second guess his way out of a mess that was getting more threatening by the minute. That it was the boy who'd betrayed them no longer seemed to be in question, but the reason for the map was less clear.

'You bring much equipment,' the man said. 'So I give you one week.'

'For what?'

'To deliver the capsules. After the road from Uyuni meets with the road from Chiguana you will drive north for three kilometres. There you will find the track to the old mine where, seven days from now, we shall do our business.'

'I don't think so.' Ryder kept his voice level. 'I've already got a buyer for the capsules, thanks.'

The man turned to summon his companions. 'What then will you exchange for the girl?' he said.

Ryder had been expecting the worst, but he'd never expected this. As a result, his reaction was unthinking and nearly fatal.

As he heard Isabel start screaming for his help, and as she kicked out despairingly in an attempt to free herself from the two men who were dragging her away, Ryder made his move, bringing back the edge of his left hand ready, but coming to his senses just before he began the forward sweep.

The man had his rifle trained on Ryder's chest. 'If I shoot you, the girl will show us how to operate the equipment,' he said. 'It will be a pity if she must work too hard to enjoy our company.' He smiled. 'Perhaps we shall see how many of my men she can enjoy at one time.'

Ryder gritted his teeth.'If you want to trade, you'd better listen,' he said. 'Hurt the girl and I'll cut your heart out. If you or your men even think of touching her, I'll hunt you down, I'll find you and I'll kill you. You don't want to mess with me. Do you understand?'

Some of the man's bravado disappeared. 'Talk is cheap,' he said. 'But I think you are not so tough.' He turned as if to walk away, then, without warning, lunged back with his gun, ramming the muzzle savagely into Ryder's stomach.

Only half-prepared, Ryder was too slow to escape a blow that drove him first to his knees and then face down in the dust.

Through a haze of pain, fighting for breath, he watched Isabel being thrown bodily into the truck where the boy and his companions were waiting to hold her down.

A moment later, as swiftly as the men had arrived they were gone, leaving him helpless and alone on the darkening wastes of the Altiplano with nothing but tyre tracks and her footprints to remind him of how thoroughly and of how terribly he had failed her.

Chapter 8

LONG before Ryder could see anything in the moonlight, he was alerted by the sound of the approaching plane. It was losing altitude and airspeed fast, swinging in from the south as though Alexei had already sighted the airstrip. In case he hadn't, Ryder went to the Jeep and turned on the headlights to illuminate what he could of the concrete, hoping Alexei would be able to avoid the worst of the bumps and washboard on the eastern boundary.

The plane was an old utility PC-6, a high-wing Pilatus Turbo-Porter, painted a dull beige colour without markings of any kind on either its wings or fuselage. Close to stall speed it touched down sixty feet in front of the Jeep, bouncing twice before it turned to taxi back towards him.

Now reinforcements had arrived, already Ryder was refining the details of his plan. As soon as the whistle of the turbine began to die, he went to meet his friend, telling himself not to rush things and trying to decide how best to explain what had happened and what had to be done about it.

The Russian was too busy urinating against a wheel to say hello, evidently grateful to be on the ground after his long flight and unable to shake hands until he'd finished and rezipped his fly.

'That is more comfortable,' he said. 'Except where I stop to refuel in Asunción and in Tarija I have been pissing in an empty vodka bottle. In a plane that will not exceed two hundred knots,

I think it would have been easier to piss out the window. I am sorry the journey has taken me so long.' He stopped talking abruptly, aware of the expression on Ryder's face.

'Problem,' Ryder said. 'We have to talk. You'd better come in the warm.'

At this time of year on the Altiplano, warmth was a relative term. If the temperature inside the hut was higher than the temperature outside, it was by only a few degrees. Alexei, though, appeared not to notice, clearly more concerned at the prospect of a problem than he was about the cold.

'So the girl is not here,' he said.

'No.'

'She has returned to Colombia?'

'No.' Ryder shut the door and went to check the kerosene heater. Over the half hour he'd been here he'd been struggling to adjust the wretched thing, losing his temper with it each time the flame began to die.

'Allow me.' Alexei took over, kneeling to inspect the controls before stepping back to kick the flue with his boot. 'It is necessary to dislodge the soot,' he explained. 'Now you see how the flames climb higher.'

Ryder could already feel the improvement. The heat was flooding out now, filling the space between the two bunks and the wooden work-bench which were the only furnishings in the rudimentary building.

As well as being rudimentary, the hut was filthy, thick with dust, smothered in spiders' webs and smelling strongly of rancid cooking fat, old tobacco smoke and stale urine. It was also windowless, illuminated only by the flickering light from the heater and ventilated by fixed louvres let into the south wall through which the night wind was blowing unimpeded.

'I see we are without room service.' Alexei sat down on one of the bunks and lit a cigarette. 'But I think you are not ready to eat. You have some sickness?'

'I got stuck with the sharp end of a rifle.'

'Ah. So the girl has double-crossed us. This is the complication you mention?'

'It's worse than that,' Ryder said. 'She's in trouble. We have to go and get her.'

'I should have stayed in Angola.' Alexei blew out a stream of smoke. 'When first I retrieve your message from the Luxembourg number, I wonder if you are thinking correctly. Then, later, when you talk to me about the plutonium on the telephone from Colombia, I decide you are going crazy since the girl has started opening her legs for you. But I agree to come here because you are my friend, and because I wish to believe this is an opportunity for us to sabotage the PAF. Now, after travelling halfway across the world to this nice place in Bolivia, I learn I have to help you get her back from wherever she has gone.'

'I know where,' Ryder said.

'Good. But I still do not understand this problem very well. Perhaps when you have explained I shall understand better.' Alexei smiled. 'If I can keep awake long enough to listen.'

'There isn't time to explain.'

'Chris, I have been flying for many hours. On such a cold night, you cannot expect me to help you find anyone without a reason.'

'I'll give you the reason.' Ryder went to stand with his back to the heater, endeavouring to collect his thoughts in order to present his case in the most persuasive way. He started with the journey south from Uyuni in the company of the boy, describing how the late afternoon off-road excursion had led to the location of the Mars-96 wreckage before he went on to give an account of what had happened once the truck had arrived on the scene. He left nothing out, playing down his concern for Isabel, but, at the same time, attempting to convey the need for urgency.

When he'd finished, Alexei remained silent, stretched out on the lower bunk, hands behind his head as though waiting for more information.

'They'll rape her,' Ryder said quietly. 'You know they will.'

'Of course.' The Russian raised himself on to an elbow. 'After the wars in Bosnia and Kosovo, it is the same in many countries where there is no law. So, to prevent such an occurrence, why,

109

instead of following these men, did you travel here to meet me?'

'There are five of the bastards. I figured you might give me a hand.'

'Chris, this girl is nothing to you. How can she be? Less than a month ago she has tried to kill you. You must forget her.'

'And do what instead?'

'Recover the canisters without her; you and I together.'

'Great idea,' Ryder said. 'That'll make her uncle real happy, won't it? We give Corrales five million dollars worth of plutonium and explain that as part of the deal we let his niece be raped and killed.'

'Why not keep the plutonium for ourselves?' Alexei grunted. 'Have you considered that?'

'No. It's a lousy option. The last thing I want is the Corrales family hunting me down again. You don't want it either. We've already got the PAF on our backs, and without Corrales we'd have to find our own buyer for the plutonium. You and I can hardly ask the PAF for an offer, can we?' Ryder paused. 'I wouldn't do it anyway.'

'What?'

'Double-cross Corrales. I like him.'

'But not as much as you like his niece?'

'That's got nothing to do with it. I shot her father – remember? Half the time she doesn't even want to talk to me.'

'Perhaps her judgement is better than yours.' Alexei smiled slightly. 'Now tell me, if we go to this mine, is it possible we shall face more than five men there?'

'Yeah, it's possible.'

'And we must assume the boy will be with them?'

'Right.'

Alexei struck a match on the side of the heater and lit another cigarette. 'You must forgive my questions,' he said, 'but how sure are you that it is not the boy and his father who have employed these men?'

'Pretty sure. They're not smart enough. It has to be Diaz. He's the only other person who could have guessed there are more canisters lying around out in the desert somewhere. Diaz knew about the plutonium before Corrales did. He's probably got a fair idea of what the stuff's worth.'

'You say he is the man who operates the tin mines for Corrales?'

'In Potosí. All I know is that Corrales doesn't trust him.' Ryder was losing the battle to contain his impatience. 'Look,' he said, 'we're wasting time. Are you going to help, or not?'

'You are suggesting we rescue the girl by driving to the mine tonight?'

'No. It'll take too long in the Jeep. You're going to fly us there.'

'And where do we land?'

'We'll find somewhere. There's plenty of moonlight, and plenty of hard patches on the salt-flats. I've driven over them.'

'What if they hear the noise of our engine? What if we are unlucky with our landing? What if the ground is too soft for us to take off again?'

'We'll land downwind and go in by foot. We can cut the engine and glide down, can't we?'

'In moonlight? On to a salt desert?'

'Never mind the fucking plane,' Ryder said. 'If it gets stuck, what do you care? Corrales is paying for it. We'll walk out if we have to. All you have to do is get us there.' He left the hut, returning with a cardboard box and a rifle.

Alexei eyed the rifle. 'Lever-action Winchester,' he said. 'I think we shall need more than a cowboy gun.'

'It's not a cowboy gun. It's chambered for .44 Remington Magnum. I bought it new in La Paz.'

'The men did not take it when they searched the truck?'

'Isabel had it buried under a generator and a whole bunch of fuel cans.' Ryder opened the box and took out one of the infrared thermal-imagers. 'They were more interested in the electronics.' He handed the imager to Alexei. 'Maybe this'll give us an edge.'

The Russian was not convinced. 'You assume they will not lie in wait for us,' he said. 'If they have made the girl talk they will know you were expecting the arrival of a friend.'

'Let's find out. Are you ready?'

'No.' Alexei went to extinguish the heater. 'But I am too tired to argue with you. I shall save my energy for escaping from the plane when we crash.'

Outside, although the wind was still easing, what there was of it cut through Ryder's parka as though he was wearing nothing more substantial than a shirt.

Raising his hood, he followed Alexei over to the aircraft, aware that his plan was as ill-conceived as it was dangerous, and trying not to imagine the mission ending in a fiery landing out on the Altiplano where the wreckage was unlikely to ever be discovered.

He put the thought aside, easing himself into the PC-6 and waiting while Alexei used a flashlight to search for something in the cargo-bay.

'What the hell are you doing?' Ryder said. 'Come on. Get this thing rolling.'

The Russian climbed into the cockpit seat, stowing a rifle behind a bulkhead. 'That you and I cannot travel without guns is a sickness the PAF has given to us,' he said. 'But perhaps it is good I have brought an M-16.' He gave Ryder two small pills. 'I also have these. One now and one when we land.'

'What are they?'

'Benzedrine.' Alexei swallowed what looked like a handful of them. 'Amphetamine pills. For a while at least they will keep us awake. Now, while you admire my skill as a pilot, please use the map and a GPS unit to tell me exactly where it is we are going.'

Ryder had only the vaguest of ideas. In the absence of any local knowledge, a map was of little more value than a GPS unit. All he had to pinpoint the location of the mine were his instincts and the scrap of paper that Isabel's kidnappers had given to him.

Being careful not to dwell on the possibility of ending up in the wrong place, he strapped himself in, holding his rifle on his lap, watching Alexei complete a cursory pre-flight check.

The PC-6 was underway soon enough, vibrating badly with its rivets rattling as it gathered speed. It jolted over the corrugations, weighed down by the long range, under-wing tanks, but still managing to become airborne in less than half the take-off distance Ryder was expecting it to need.

Alexei kept the throttle open, holding the plane in a steep climb for nearly a minute before he cut back the turbo-prop and allowed the PC-6 to flatten out in level flight.

'More or less due north,' Ryder said. 'See if you can follow the road. It skirts round the left side of the lake.'

The dark, flat mirror of Lake Colorada was easy to pick out. The road was not. In the moonlight, except for the outline of some hills to the north-west, everything was white, the same peculiar milky-whiteness that Ryder had been conscious of when the Jeep had emerged from the Valle de Rocas into the afternoon sun. But viewed from high altitude at night, instead of being a landscape of haunting beauty, the southern reaches of the Bolivian Altiplano were truly not of this world, a featureless desert from which all vestige of colour had been leached away.

'We can land on a road maybe,' Alexei said. 'Then our wheels will not sink so much.'

'The roads are full of bloody holes.' Ryder was endeavouring to decide where they were. 'We'll be better off on the salt-pan. There aren't that many soft patches.'

'The ground is no different from the pictures of the moon I have once seen at an exhibition in Moscow – ground where it may be easy for us to find the canisters, but not a place where anyone would wish to live.'

As things had turned out, it wasn't much of a place to visit either, Ryder thought, confirmation of the warnings from Corrales that he should never have ignored. 'There, over on your right.' He pointed. 'About two o'clock. That little lake.'

'It means we are close?'

'Yep. You'd better start heading east. We shouldn't be far from the road intersection.'

'How far?'

Ryder consulted the map. 'Five kilometres – maybe seven. It's hard to tell.'

'So, for the noise we make, we may already be too close.' Alexei reduced airspeed, banking sharply, his attention half on the altimeter and half on what surface features he could see from the cockpit windows. 'If we are not to circle, and if the track to the mine is three kilometres north of the road intersection as you have been told, it will be necessary for us to land in the next five minutes. You will look for a suitable area, please.'

'Carry on for a bit.' Ryder peered ahead. 'Do what I said: come in from the north so the wind carries our engine noise away.'

Alexei nodded, holding the turn for a few more seconds before he throttled back to allow the PC-6 to start losing altitude. 'Tighten your harness,' he said, 'and do not become concerned if we land heavily. These planes are very strong.'

Ryder was not reassured. At first sight, apart from the odd outcrop of rock, the desert seemed to be uniformly flat. But he knew it was deceptive. Shadows, he told himself, study the shadows, search for breaks or distortions that would indicate the presence of inclines or broken ground.

Even at the low speed of eighty knots, the Porter was still travelling at well over a mile a minute, making it all but impossible for Ryder to choose somewhere that was neither too close nor too remote from where he thought the mine should be.

In the end, the job was made easy for him. To his right, somewhere in the hills, there was a glimpse of what looked like a distant fire. He saw it again, for longer this time; flames and a bright spark of yellow light. It was about a mile away, visible only intermittently because the glow was being blocked by the foothills and some ridges.

Alexei had seen it too. 'I cut the power now,' he announced. 'With flaps down we will stall at fifty knots. Please say when our airspeed drops below that figure.'

A moment later, inside the cockpit everything became unnervingly quiet. For Ryder the silence was worse than the roar from the turboprop. He could hear air rushing past the fuselage, but could see nothing much in the way of detail, aware only that the plane was approaching the salt-pan at an alarming rate, at an angle that was far too steep.

He braced himself for impact, placing his hands on the instrument panel as Alexei pulled back on the stick.

The Porter responded sluggishly, moving too slowly for its nose to come up before a bone-jarring shock shook the whole

114

plane from one end to the other.

An instant before the tail wheel touched down, Ryder was certain they were going to cartwheel. But somehow the PC-6 kept going, smashing its way between unyielding clumps of *llareta* bushes and over rocks of all sizes that had appeared from nowhere. And amidst all the clattering and banging there was dust – clouds of it streaming past the wings and the now almost stationary propeller, obscuring Ryder's view until he suddenly saw what he'd feared most.

Less than thirty feet ahead was the outline of a dust-bowl.

Instead of swinging the rudder, Alexei started cursing, fighting to hold the PC-6 in a straight line while he repowered the turbine.

As if given a new lease of life, the Porter accelerated over the rim, initially gaining speed until the wheels began to drag through the layers of salt lining the bottom of the bowl. It slowed, shuddered, then on full power taxied easily up the other side, lurching back over the edge to stop in another whirlwind of dust.

'Jesus Christ.' Ryder had his teeth clenched. 'Couldn't you have found somewhere else?'

Alexei didn't answer, kicking open his door and getting out to inspect the landing gear before he went to stand at the edge of the dust-bowl. He was still there, hands in his pockets when Ryder joined him.

'So,' the Russian grunted, 'there is much flat ground, yet I chose to land in a large hole.'

'Nowhere's flat.' Ryder spat out a mouthful of dust. 'It only looks that way. Is the plane OK?'

'Of course.' The Russian squinted at him. 'Your stomach bothers you again?'

'What do you think?'

'I think you will feel better after we walk to the fire we have seen because I am sure it is where we shall find Miss Corrales. Do you not agree?'

'I'll let you know when we get there.' Over the last hour Ryder had lost confidence, still trying to convince himself that Isabel's captors were unlikely to harm her when she was their only bargaining chip, but no longer able to suppress the worst of his doubts.

Returning to the plane, he collected both rifles, picked up the thermal-imager and began stuffing his pockets with ammunition.

Alexei came to help, swinging his arms to keep warm. 'You swallow the other pill now,' he said.

'I don't need it.' Ryder handed over the M-16 and tossed a pair of binoculars at him. 'I've got enough adrenalin running through me, thanks.' He waited impatiently while Alexei took a quick GPS reading of the plane's location, then set off in what he thought was the correct direction for the road intersection, walking fast until the Russian seized his parka to make him slow down.

'Chris, listen to me.' Alexei maintained his grip, forcing Ryder to assume a more realistic pace.

'What?'

'There is something I wish to say that is better said now than when we have work to do.'

'Don't bother.' Ryder was in no mood for advice. 'I know she mightn't be there, and I know we might be too late.'

'No, no. It is something else. When on my way to Africa I stop in Montréal to visit you, I tell you then that I think you are going soft in the head. If I am right, whether you like it or not, this is a good time to remember all you have learned in the past. Do you understand me?'

The reminder was unnecessary. As a result of his own foolishness, in the space of a few weeks, so swiftly had Ryder been overtaken by events that there was no likelihood of him separating the past from the present. There was no separation. Just as one had led to the other, so the death of Pablo Corrales had brought him here tonight, where perhaps, if he was lucky, some correction could be made for what had gone before.

Or maybe not, Ryder thought. Maybe you couldn't do that. Maybe the price for buying your way out of the past was never being able to forget it. Because he found the idea depressing he concentrated instead on where he was going, keeping his eyes away from his watch, and his thoughts fixed firmly on the present.

In comparison with the twenty-minute flight from the airstrip, the hike across the salt-flats seemed to be unending. Even after they came out on to the main road to Chiguana and were able to make better speed, for Ryder, each step was taking too long and adding to his belief that they could have already overshot the access road to the mine.

He was about to voice his concern when Alexei shone his flash-light on a broken sign. It was lying face-up in the dust near some fresh tyre marks, the word *mina* still visible where years ago the letters had been burned into the wood with a hot iron.

'They are kind to show us the way with their wheels.' Alexei took the lead, restricting the beam from his flashlight with his fingers until the tyre marks disappeared at the entrance of a gravel track into the foothills. 'How far now to the mine?'

'I don't know. They didn't say.' Ryder started feeding rounds into the Winchester's magazine. 'That fire's pretty close. I can smell the smoke.'

'I also.' Alexei removed his gloves, spat on his hands and rubbed them together. 'Let us hope there will be good cover for us.'

The cover was better than they could have hoped for. The track was no more than 300 yards long, winding upwards, first between house-sized blocks of stone, then to the mouth of a small rock-strewn canyon.

'We have them trapped, I think.' Alexei stopped. 'So we must be cautious. It is never good to put men in a corner where they will fight like rats if they have no way to escape.'

'I'll see if we can get round behind them on to some higher ground,' Ryder said. 'I won't be long.'

'We shall both go.' Alexei pointed with his rifle. 'There. We can climb, where the cracks in the rock are wider.'

Despite moving slowly to avoid dislodging the multitude of stone slabs that lay balanced on the tops of every boulder, they made good time. After climbing for only a few minutes they found themselves overlooking a large, flat arena that was flanked

117

to the north by a rock-face in which the entrance to a derelict mine was clearly visible.

As though laid out for their benefit, everything else was visible too, making the thermal-imager immediately redundant. Sixty or seventy yards away, illuminated by the light of a blazing fire was what Ryder had hoped to see.

The truck was there, blocking the exit of the canyon; the men were there, and the boy was there. Isabel was with them, tied by her wrists to a rope that was secured to a rusted-out steel trolley that had once been part of the mining operation. She appeared to be unharmed, on her feet facing the fire to obtain what warmth she could from it.

'Dead men,' Alexei whispered. 'They tell you where they will be, but are too stupid to post a guard.'

'They wouldn't be expecting trouble,' Ryder said, 'not this fast.'

'They rely on their heavy armament.' The Russian swivelled round. 'You did not tell me about the machine-gun on the truck.'

'I didn't want to put you off.' Ryder was studying the campsite, endeavouring to decide how best to handle things.

To the left of the Volvo, the carcass of a roasted goat was impaled on a spit. Closer to the mine, the boy was busy gathering up pieces of splintered pit-props to put on the fire, while his companions were lounging on the ground smoking cigarettes as they passed a bottle around between them.

One of the men tossed a bone at Isabel, laughing loudly when she kicked it away from her in disgust.

'What do you think?' Alexei said.

'They've got fully-automatic rifles and grenades. I don't want her caught in the middle of anything.'

'So we wait. Soon, when they are drunk and sleepy, you will go to cut her free. I shall watch from here. At such short range, I can guarantee your safety.'

It was Isabel's safety that was worrying Ryder. One of the men kept glancing in her direction. He was unshaven like the others, wearing a dirty sweatband around his forehead and had his hair drawn back in a ponytail. Instead of drinking he was watching

Isabel, clearly more interested in her than he was in joking with his friends.

So what? Ryder told himself, men stared at her wherever she went, and he should be thankful that nothing worse was happening.

'Chris, you have not answered me,' Alexei said. 'Shall we wait?'

'Yeah.' In the absence of an alternative, Ryder couldn't think of anything else to do, particularly when his statement about Isabel being caught in crossfire had been more of an excuse than a reason for holding back.

Against the Winchester and an M-16 from a vantage point as good as this, the men and the boy would stand no chance. Ryder knew it as well as the Russian did. But Alexei, too, was holding back, equally unwilling to use excessive force because he had no stomach for it either.

With each passing minute it was becoming colder now. The chill of the night air was seeping into Ryder's shoulders through his parka, and from beneath him the rock on which he lay was sucking away his body heat. His stomach was more painful too, aching from a hollowness that had nothing to do with the bruise or the cold.

He made himself more comfortable, wondering whether the binoculars would help him identify the man with the scar – the leader, and probably the main threat if he remained sober and awake for the next few hours.

There was too much damn light, Ryder thought. And, if the boy kept throwing wood on the fire, God knows how long Isabel would have to stand there.

He was wrong. Waiting was not going to be an option.

The man with the ponytail had staggered to his feet and was approaching her.

She retreated, backing away until she was brought up short by the rope around her wrists, unable to move any further.

Reaching out, the man gripped her under the chin, twisting her towards him and kissing her roughly on the mouth.

She fought, trying to bring up her knee between his legs, breaking free long enough to spit at him, but losing her balance when he hauled hard on the rope.

When he next jerked it, she was better prepared, spinning round to kick out, but missing and nearly falling over again.

The man laughed, mimicking her attempts to resist. Then he reeled her in, pulling on the rope until she was standing defiantly to face him.

For the second time tonight, Ryder's teeth were clenched. He watched as the man stepped behind her and wound his fingers in her hair to keep her still while he unfastened her belt and pushed down her jeans to stop her from kicking.

'Chris,' Alexei spoke quietly, 'you wish me to end this?'

'No. I'll do it.' Ryder chambered a round and checked that the safety was off. The Winchester was cold and unsteady in his hands, and he was temporarily unable to slow his breathing. He was apprehensive, too, reluctant to risk a shot from a rifle he'd never fired before.

'Easy.' Alexei whispered. 'The girl will fight again.'

Provided she did, Ryder thought. Even then, with open sights, a seventy-yard shot was not a great proposition. 'I'll be going down to fetch her,' he said. 'All you have to do is make sure she's OK until I get there. You don't have to go overboard.' He paused. 'You know what I mean.'

The Russian nodded.

'Never mind the boy. He's only a kid.'

'It is better you stop talking and get ready. Look.'

Ryder hadn't stopped looking, and he was as ready as he was going to be, trying not to imagine what Isabel was going through.

She'd been pulled backwards to the trolley, rigid with fear, her wrists still tied, powerless to prevent the man from using his knife to cut away her parka from behind.

Ryder saw her make one last effort to twist herself around and saw how her head snapped back when the man wrenched on her hair. Already her parka and her sweater were in ribbons, allowing her remaining clothing to be stripped off.

Going through Ryder's head were the words of the mantra: *concentrate; expect the unexpected; think of nothing but the target; don't rush, but whatever else you do, never delay too long.*

Delaying was not an issue. In his mind he was back in Africa outside the church, sighting on the open shirt-front of the Somali war-lord who, by sensing Ryder's presence early, had somehow triggered the bomb that had taken the lives of over twenty children.

No bomb this time. And no children. Just a terrified young woman who should never have been forced to experience this kind of horror.

The man had finished undressing her. She stood naked in the flickering firelight, helpless and vulnerable, head lowered, refusing to meet the eyes of the other men who were whistling and shouting their encouragement.

Ryder's hands were steadier now. They were much steadier. And his breathing was under control. But still there was no opportunity for a clear shot.

Despairingly, for a moment he didn't think there would be one.

Instead of releasing Isabel's hair and going round to face her, the man was fumbling with his fly as though intending to penetrate her from behind.

She was saved by the increasingly enthusiastic catcalls from the man's companions.

Urged on by their shouts, he stepped aside to show them his erect penis, thrusting out his hips in an act of mock intercourse to demonstrate his virility.

The mistake was fatal.

Before he could advance on Isabel again, Ryder's bullet caught him above the breastbone, slamming him back against the trolley and turning his chest into a soup of blood and splintered ribs. He died where he stood, his body toppling sideways to lie lifeless at Isabel's feet.

Ryder had guessed the impact of the big hollow-point would be severe, but he'd underestimated the extent of the damage it would cause. He'd underestimated the Winchester's muzzle-blast as well. In the confines of the canyon the noise was deafening, still ringing in his ears when Alexei fired a warning burst from his M-16.

Ryder barely heard it. He was already on his way, slithering feet-first over boulders and rocks, tobogganing wildly on his back across the layers of loose slabs and praying he'd be able to hold on to his rifle until he reached the canyon floor.

Below him, men were abandoning the camp, two scrambling for their weapons, the boy and the other two running for the safety of the truck.

Or to man the machine-gun, Ryder wondered? Could they swing it round that far? He didn't know; nor did he know if Isabel was going to have the sense to lie flat on her stomach.

He was about to yell out at her when, above the crack of Alexei's rifle and the sound of bullets zipping past him, came the stutter of a Kalashnikov. But no sooner had it begun than it fell silent, its place taken by the roar of the truck's engine, and the voice of a man shouting instructions.

Ryder hit the ground awkwardly, nearly turning an ankle in his attempt to remain upright. But he was in one piece, moving fast enough to make himself what he hoped was a difficult target, and no more than thirty feet from Isabel.

She'd frozen, standing white-faced and spattered in blood, apparently oblivious to the danger she was in.

Ryder sprinted, weaving only once before knocking her legs out from beneath her in a headlong tackle.

The fall brought her to her senses. She struggled to free herself, using all her strength and biting into his forearm through his sleeve.

'For Christ's sake,' Ryder shook her. 'It's me.'

Although she stopped trying to get away, there was no real response until he dragged her behind the steel trolley and started wiping the blood off her face.

'You hurt me,' she mumbled. 'I can't breathe properly.'

'You'll be fine.' He untied the rope from her wrists, then wasted precious seconds wrapping his parka round her and helping her to pull up her jeans.

Through the smoke and dust, Ryder could see the Volvo moving at the canyon exit. What he couldn't see was the machine-gun or the direction in which the truck was heading.

Quickly he hauled Isabel to her feet. 'Mineshaft,' he shouted. 'Now. Go on.'

'No. Not without you.'

He didn't argue. Instead he took her by the hand. 'OK,' he said. 'We're going to run like hell. When you feel me pulling, you weave with me. If anything happens you get into the mine, and you stay there until Alexei collects you. Have you got that?'

'We don't have to. The truck's gone.'

'If it comes back we're both dead.' Ryder set off fast, hoping Alexei would guess where they were going and that none of the men had taken refuge in the mine.

There were no more shots, no sudden burst of fire from the machine-gun and, to his relief, no sign of anyone inside the mine.

Ryder crouched in the entrance, listening, trying to decide if he could hear the truck returning. He couldn't. Except for his own breathing, he couldn't hear anything at all. A bad sign, he thought.

An avalanche of rocks confirmed his suspicions. He swung the muzzle of the Winchester, aiming through the smoke at the outline of a man.

It was Alexei.

'Jesus.' Ryder lowered his gun.

The Russian stopped beside the fire, lighting a cigarette from one of the embers before he sauntered over to meet Isabel. 'So, you are the little *señorita*,' he said. 'I am pleased you are safe.' He inspected her more closely. 'Chris has told me much about you.'

She said nothing, shivering uncontrollably and drawing Ryder's parka closer around her shoulders.

'We'd better get going,' Ryder said. 'We're boxed in here.'

Alexei shook his head. 'They will not come back. They are too frightened.'

'How many got away?'

'Three men and the skinny boy. Of those who stay to fight, I am forced to shoot only one – after he tries to kill you on your way down.'

Close bloody call, Ryder thought. He'd been unaware of the danger, believing that the Kalashnikov had been firing at Alexei. 'Two dead,' he said.

'No. The man I shoot is still alive, but only just. He is over there.' Alexei waved his M-16 towards the track. 'I was going to shoot out the tyres of the truck to slow it down, but then I decide it is better if we allow them to leave unhindered.' He looked at Isabel again. 'You can walk?'

She nodded.

'She'll be all right as long as she doesn't go into shock,' Ryder said. 'We can give her a hand if she starts falling over. It's not that far to go.'

'Indeed.' Alexei gave Ryder the imager and the binoculars to carry. 'However, for a short while I shall remain here to discover who sent these men.'

'We know who: it was Diaz.'

'You only guess. For the future welfare of Miss Corrales it is necessary for us to be sure.' Alexei spat out his cigarette and stepped on it. 'You will please leave this to me. It is best you go ahead.'

Ryder avoided comment, taking Isabel's arm to help her over the pile of old railway lines in the mouth of the mine.

She rejected his assistance, clambering over them unaided and setting off unsteadily by herself.

Alexei raised his eyebrows.

'Don't worry about it,' Ryder said. 'It means she's OK. I'll see you later.' He went after her but was too late.

She'd stopped beside the trolley, standing with both feet on the rope, shivering again, staring down at the remains of the man with the ponytail. He was lying on his back, eyes open, his penis no longer erect but protruding pale and flaccid from his fly.

'Keep going,' Ryder instructed. 'You don't want to remember any of this.'

'Was it you or Alexei? I want to know who did it.'

'No, you don't.' Ryder propelled her towards the track, annoyed with himself for allowing her to revisit a scene she was better off forgetting, and anxious to get her out of a canyon which only had one exit.

For the next five minutes she accompanied him in silence, occasionally limping or bumping into him if she stumbled and only asking how much further it was to the Jeep after he'd located the wooden sign at the roadside.

'About eighty miles,' he said. 'We came by plane. The Jeep's back at the met station.'

Although he was pleased she'd asked a question, because she was clasping her hood to her face, he couldn't tell how well she was holding up. A few minutes ago, the sound of a muffled shot had startled her, but she'd said nothing. She'd been expecting it, Ryder had decided then, but now he was beginning to think it was because she'd been running on empty for some time.

His own condition wasn't much better. Without the protection of his parka, so chilling was the night wind that from his waist up he could feel nothing but the numbing ache in his stomach and a throbbing in his forearm where she'd bitten him.

Alexei had foreseen the problem. Signalling with his flashlight to avoid alarming Ryder again, he marched over to them. In addition to his M-16, he was carrying a newly acquired AK47 and a fur-lined jacket.

'For you.' He gave the jacket to Ryder. 'I have cleaned off the blood.'

'Thanks.' Ryder put it on at once, discovering that every pocket was crammed with ammunition clips and grenades.

'I have brought what I could.' Alexei explained. 'It is a precaution.'

To spare Isabel the details, Ryder chose not to ask what Alexei had learned and how willingly the information had been provided.

He shouldn't have bothered; she asked Alexei herself.

'It is as we suspected,' he said. 'Like your uncle, the man Diaz is offering much money for the canisters.'

'Oh.' She scraped a boot heel across the salt. 'Isn't that convenient? If you think there's no difference between Diaz and my uncle, I suppose that's why I can't see any difference between you and that man you've just murdered.'

'OK.' Ryder had seen this coming. 'That'll do. Let's find the plane, shall we? We don't know if Alexei can get it off the ground yet.'

'You have my guarantee.' The Russian was amused. 'I promise you I have no desire to stay in such a godforsaken place.' He put down his guns and lit another cigarette, shielding his match from the wind, and, for a moment, using it to illuminate Isabel's face. 'I do not expect your thanks,' he said. 'What I have done tonight is not for you: it is for Chris. So, if you wish to scratch like an ungrateful little cat, you must use your claws on him.'

Whether the statement had caused her to rethink was doubtful. But Ryder was past caring, too cold to worry about what the hell she thought, and too tired to wonder if she comprehended the real cost of her rescue.

It was only after they'd reached the shelter of the plane and completed a rough but uneventful take-off that he attempted to review everything that had happened and why it had happened.

He should not have tried. He could still feel the Winchester kicking against his shoulder – still hear the sound of the bullet smacking home; another set of unpleasant recollections that were best left unreviewed if he wanted to get rid of them.

Instead of remembering, he took the advice he'd given Isabel, making himself forget, sitting slumped in his seat, watching the ground drop away as the PC-6 winged south on its climb into a starlit night – a night that to Ryder now seemed as empty and lonely as any he could recall.

Chapter 9

IN this part of the high plains, dawn was a dreary and unspectacular transition from night to day, bringing with it no lift in temperature and little improvement in Ryder's mood. Wherever he looked the Altiplano was the same – as desolate and unwelcoming as it had been in the moonlight.

Only the smell was different. Overnight there had been a wind shift – a slight one, but enough to turn the air sulphurous. The fumes were drifting north, coming either from the Chalvin hot springs, or the Sol de Mañana, the big geothermal geyser that, according to Ryder's map, were a good deal closer to the airstrip than the more distant Licancábur volcano.

This morning there was no sign of the volcano. It had gone, its dark cone no longer visible on the horizon because, unlike yesterday, the horizon too had gone, replaced by a uniformly grey backdrop against which, in the early light of dawn, the sky was indistinguishable from the land, both equally sombre and both equally cheerless.

Ryder walked over to the Jeep where Alexei was sitting on the bonnet working the action of the Winchester to unload the magazine.

'For a little gun, this one hits very hard,' Alexei grunted. 'Why did you purchase it?'

'I met an old trapper when I was up in Québec. He said he'd got tired of carrying around heavy hardware, so he'd started using a .44 Magnum. He said you couldn't beat it for stopping

127

things inside of about sixty yards.' Ryder paused. 'I'm not sure how accurate it is, though. You know what lever actions are like.'

'Last night the accuracy was good.'

'No, it wasn't. That was supposed to be a shoulder shot. I wasn't trying to kill the bastard.'

Alexei held up a cartridge. 'I think a bullet of this size will kill a man if he is hit in his foot.' He grinned. 'But not at three hundred metres. You have been instructed to fetch more containers of water for Miss Corrales?'

'No. She's got plenty.'

'Since she has no shower to use, perhaps you should have stayed to pour the water over her.'

Ryder smiled. 'I don't think so.'

'She is speaking to you?'

'Sort of. She's OK – a bit shaky, but she said she slept all night – which is more than I did.'

'It was unnecessary for you to spend so many hours alone out here in the Jeep. I would have shared the watch.'

'You were more stuffed than I was.' As well as still being tired, Ryder was cold again. After returning here last night, and after they'd coaxed the drip-heater back to life and bundled Isabel into one of the bunks under a mound of blankets, for a while he'd been tempted to stay in the warmth of the hut, abandoning the idea because he knew it was too risky. He'd spent the rest of the night chewing Benzedrine pills in the Jeep, using the thermal-imager to scan for tell-tale signs of an approaching vehicle and running the Jeep's engine whenever the temperature became uncomfortably low. As a result, it wasn't until he'd got out at dawn that he'd realized how cold the night had been, and how little warmth was coming from the sun.

'That guy you shot didn't have a scar across his cheek, did he?' he asked.

'No.' Alexei shook his head. 'Why?'

'He was the one who did all the talking.'

'Ah. Then he will be the cousin of Diaz. I learn this from my interrogation. He is a member of some guerrilla group that fights against the Bolivian government.'

'The CNPZ.' Ryder said.

'You know of them?'

'The boy said they're the Nestor Paz Zamora Commission. It looks like our friend Diaz bought off the boy and then got the CNPZ to give him a hand.'

'You believe they will search for the canisters by themselves now?'

'I don't know. Either way we'd better assume they're still out there somewhere.'

'We shall find the plutonium before them.' Alexei spoke with confidence. 'They have no expertise, no aircraft and, with two of their men dead, they will not risk another confrontation with us.'

'Except we're going to lose a couple of days because of Isabel.'

'You have told her of your decision?'

'No.' Ryder glanced towards the hut. 'Not yet.'

'When I speak with her this morning, I am not certain if she is unwell or just unwilling to talk.' Alexei smiled. 'Yes, she is a very beautiful young woman, but if you will permit me to say so as your friend, I think you are pissing against a very strong wind.'

'I'm not doing anything. She's only here because her uncle sent her, and because there wasn't a hell of a lot I could do about it.'

'Of course. You have explained this to me more than once.' The Russian slipped down off the bonnet. 'So, while you go to see if she is ready, I shall see if one of the sheds behind the hut contains a toilet we can use.'

Ryder waited until he'd gone before rummaging through Isabel's things in the Jeep and selecting what he thought was appropriate clothing. Then, armed with the satellite phone, he walked back slowly to the hut.

The door was open, either to admit more light, or because she'd seen him coming through the louvres. She was wrapped in a blanket, standing over the drip-heater drying her hair.

'I brought you these.' He placed the clothes on her bunk. I wasn't sure what you'd want.'

She looked at him. 'What would you know about what I want?'

'Not a lot. How are you feeling?'

129

'Mixed up, dirty, sick. How am I supposed to feel?'

Ryder knew better than to offer an answer. The signals were all bad, and judging by her expression, things weren't about to get any easier.

'You didn't have to kill that man,' she said.

'What would you like me to say?'

'Nothing. I don't want you to say anything.' She sat down on the bunk. 'You think I'm in shock or something, but you're wrong. Nobody grows up in Colombia without knowing what violence is, and if I ever forget I've got a whole bunch of photos of my father being shot, haven't I?'

'Are we going to go back to the beginning again?'

'No. You don't understand.'

'Try me.'

'I can't.' She lowered her eyes. 'I just feel so awful – but for a really stupid reason. I think it's because of – you know – because of having to stand there with no clothes on.' Her cheeks started burning. 'I know it's crazy, but I can't help the way I feel. I can't even. . . .' She stopped abruptly, unable to continue.

Ryder was groping for the right words, disconcerted as much by her frankness as he was by her embarrassment. 'Look,' he said, 'it happens to everyone. It takes a while to get your perspective back. If you talk to people who've crashed their cars, the first thing they'll ask is if their groceries are OK.'

'You're doing it again. I don't want your platitudes. I just need some time. I'll be all right as soon as we start looking for the plutonium.'

'You're not looking for anything.' He put down the phone on the pile of clothes. 'You have to call your uncle.'

'What for?'

'Alexei's flying us to Tarija. From there you and I are going to catch the first commercial flight we can get on to La Paz. Your uncle needs to send someone to meet you.'

'So they can escort me on back to Colombia? Is that what you've decided?'

'What do you expect? There's not a single thing stopping Diaz from trying again, is there?'

'But it's OK if he does as long as I'm back home – because you and Alexei can handle those men better without me. Is that right?'

'More or less,' Ryder said. 'Your uncle's not going to be happy about you staying here, and you sure as hell don't need any more straightening out, do you?'

'No.'

'Make the call then.'

'Not until I'm dressed.' She began unwrapping the blanket from her shoulders. 'Are you going to watch like you did last night?'

He left her, closing the door of the hut behind him, wondering if she was really going to be co-operative. Although she was less withdrawn and less self-conscious, he was still suspicious, doubting that her confidence could have returned so quickly, but aware that he was just as likely to have misinterpreted her responses. Despite her ordeal, she was no more predictable this morning than she'd been at any other time, Ryder thought, which was probably reason enough to get her out of the way.

He leaned back against the door, endeavouring to reconcile the memories of his first evening with her in Cali with the images of last night – an impossible comparison between a warm evening in Colombia with a bitterly cold, dark night in Bolivia. There was another comparison too – one he'd already tried not to make and one that was equally meaningless and confusing – the contrast between her embarrassment of today and the incident in the living-room of her uncle's hacienda when she'd lifted her skirt to expose the wound in her thigh.

The Bolivian desert was not the place to dwell on such things, Ryder decided. Maybe, if he were to meet her again one day when this was over, he'd be able to discover why he couldn't stop looking at her and why, for half the time, she appeared not to mind.

He was glad when Alexei came to find him.

'Ah.' The Russian pulled up his collar. 'So you are still out in the cold.'

'What's in the sheds?' Ryder asked.

'In one: meteorological instruments for recording temperature, barometric pressure, humidity and wind speed. In the other: a coloured poster of a Bolivian girl with big tits, and a broken toilet seat over a deep hole which only a brave man would use.' Alexei smiled. 'May I assume Miss Corrales is making her phone call?'

'No. She's getting dressed.'

'No, I'm not. I've finished.' She opened the door. 'Are you having another discussion about me, or do you want to come in?'

She was wearing clean jeans and a thick, high-necked woollen sweater that had some kind of Indian motif embroidered into the front of it. Her sleeves were pulled down, but now she no longer had the towel to conceal her wrists, Ryder could see what a mess they were in. One was badly bruised, and both were swollen and raw from rope burns.

Alexei frowned. 'You need bandages,' he said. 'Then in Tarija we shall find a doctor.'

'No one's going to Tarija.' She put her hands behind her back. 'I can stop Diaz.'

Ryder had an inkling of what was coming. 'How are you going to do that?' he said.

'By doing what you asked me to do. By phoning Uncle Miguel. As soon as he hears what's happened, he'll send someone to Potosí.'

'Someone like Santos?'

'If he's at home.'

Ryder said nothing, calculating how long it would take someone to reach Potosí so he could tell her what a lousy idea it was.

Alexei didn't bother with a calculation. 'Señorita Corrales,' he said, 'it is unwise for you to remain in a place such as this.'

'You said the men who got away will be too frightened to try again. I heard you tell Ryder. All we have to do is be careful for a few days. After that we won't have to worry because my uncle will have had time to fix things.'

A gamble, Ryder thought, based on her assumption that the long arm of the Corrales family would extend this far.

'Well?' she asked him.

'Once your uncle hears about last night, he'll want you on a plane right away.'

'No, he won't. I'll only tell him what he needs to know.' She paused. 'Anyway, we shouldn't have to stay here long – not now we've got that GPS reading for the wreckage the boy showed us.'

'How do you figure that out?'

'It's obvious, isn't it? If we can find another canister – just one more – we'll have two sets of coordinates. Two are all we need.'

Ryder had been slow to appreciate what she'd been saying, but he was well ahead of her now, annoyed with himself for over-looking something so fundamental.

'Do you see?' she asked.

'Yeah.' He nodded. 'If we've got the locations of two canisters we can draw a nice straight line between two dots on our map, and that defines the re-entry path of the Mars-96 probe.'

'It's better than that: the line defines the crash corridor exactly. We won't have to rely on five-year-old sightings from Chile or those guesses by Luis Barrera at the university in Antofagasta. We'll know exactly where to look.'

'Miss Corrales is correct,' Alexei interrupted. He'd unfolded the map and was studying it in light from the heater. 'Instead of being forced to conduct a wide search pattern from the air, two sets of coordinates would permit us to fly a straight course which will save us many hours and much fuel.'

'Assuming we can find another canister,' Ryder said.

'Oh come on.' Isabel's voice had an edge to it. 'If we can't find one, what are we doing here? All we need is some luck like yesterday when we got the coordinates of that wreckage.'

'It wasn't luck,' Ryder said. 'You can bet your life the boy was told to show it to us. Diaz arranged to have you grabbed to make us find all of the canisters for him.' He moved to stand beside the heater. 'What's the big deal about you staying?'

'You know.'

'Because you don't want to be a disappointment to your uncle and aunt?'

'The reason doesn't matter. If you send me home I'll tell them that you and Alexei are planning to sell off the plutonium your-selves.'

'Do you think they'd believe you?'

133

'Do you want to take the risk?'

With some reluctance, but half-persuaded that the recovery programme might now be easier than he'd thought, Ryder made his decision. 'OK,' he said. 'You can stay on one condition; you let Alexei bandage your wrists and you call Colombia right now.'

'That's two conditions. Suppose my uncle's not there.'

'He will be. If he's got any sense he'll still be in bed. There's no time difference between here and Cali.'

She picked up the phone and began pushing buttons, holding the receiver to her ear and turning her face away before she started speaking quickly in Spanish.

Ryder didn't listen, waiting until she'd finished the call before he asked her what she'd told her uncle and how the news had been received.

'I just said we'd been attacked.' She placed the phone carefully on the wooden bench-top. 'I told him you'd captured one of the men and found out that Señor Diaz was behind the whole thing. Uncle Miguel thinks the men were trying to get hold of our plane and the infrared detectors and stuff.'

'What's he aiming to do about it?'

'I didn't ask. He apologizes to you for the inconvenience and says he'll phone us back as soon as he's attended to the problem.'

'Didn't he want to know if you're OK?'

'Of course he did. I said we're all fine.' She attempted to smile. 'There's something I'm supposed to tell you. Uncle Miguel says he has absolute confidence in your ability to discriminate between risk and gain and that he trusts you to do whatever's necessary if things get too dangerous.'

A warning, Ryder decided, a reminder that, compared with Isabel's safety, the plutonium was valueless to someone as wealthy as Corrales.

'You're not going to change your mind about me, are you?' she said slowly.

'No.' He zipped up his jacket. 'I'm going for a drive.'

'Why? What for?'

'To bury that canister we got from the Agudelo boy. We need to run a live test with a thermal-imager before we start flying around searching for the others, otherwise we won't know what kind of heat signature we're looking for, and we won't know what altitude we ought to fly at.'

'You don't have to do it right now,' she said. 'You haven't eaten since yesterday. None of us has. We're not in that much of a hurry, are we?'

'I'll only be half an hour.' Ryder wanted to be by himself for a while, not yet certain how wise his decision had been, wishing she was already on her way home but glad that she wasn't.

'I'll get some food from the Jeep,' she said. 'Alexei and I can fix breakfast while you're gone.'

She accompanied him outside, drawing in her breath sharply when the cold air hit her lungs and coughing on the sulphur fumes as she walked with him to the edge of the airstrip where the Cherokee was parked.

'It isn't true what Alexei said.' She opened the tailgate for him.

'About what?'

'About me being ungrateful.'

'Good.'

'Is that all you have to say.'

'Yep.' Ryder gave her the first-aid kit and started unloading food boxes on to the ground. 'Tell him we need to be in the air before the sun breaks through this mist or cloud or whatever it is. The colder the ground is, the better the canisters are going to show up in infrared.' Closing the tailgate, he pushed past her, got behind the wheel and started the engine. 'And don't let Alexei bandage your wrists too tightly.'

'I'll do it myself.'

Sure you will, Ryder thought. Never accept help from anyone and never say thank you in case it looks as though you've forgotten about all the shit that brought you here in the first place.

Despite being cautiously optimistic, Ryder hadn't expected the day to be so successful. Identifying the infrared signature of the sample canister had been easy enough. Detecting its image from an altitude of over a thousand feet above the desert floor had been equally easy. But, simple though the location technique had proved to be, he'd still been caught unawares when, thirty-five minutes after they'd left the airstrip, a second flickering, green smudge had drifted into the viewfinder of his thermal-imager.

They'd been flying almost without looking, heading north-north-east to the area where the boy had showed them the section of wreckage. And there, not more than a mile and a quarter away, either because their luck had changed or because of Isabel's intuition, Ryder had picked up the unmistakable heat halo from the second, crucial canister.

The discovery had done much to improve Isabel's spirits and she had soon taken over the job of full-time navigator, using the Porter's flight instruments to direct Alexei and to suggest slight changes of course when she'd thought the ground topography could have deflected wreckage and canisters away from the long red line she'd drawn across her map.

In two hours of flying, Ryder had used their Magellan GPS unit to record the precise locations of fourteen canisters, a hit rate that yesterday he would have thought too improbable to be worth considering.

So far, of the fourteen, only three lay outside the general crash path. These were rogues, he'd decided, those that had either ricocheted on impact or broken free from larger pieces of white-hot wreckage that had survived re-entry only to slam into the desert at such a God-awful speed that there was nothing left of them except the tiny, crash-protected capsules of plutonium.

Ten minutes ago when Ryder had called out the coordinates of the fourteenth canister, even Alexei had expressed his surprise at their good fortune. The Russian had spent much of the flight discussing their route with Isabel, arguing with her on occasions and failing in his attempt to explain the difference between the true compass-bearing she wanted and relative bearing he'd been forced to adopt because of the wind.

For the moment she was silent, sitting tight-lipped in the cockpit, endeavouring to recognize features on the ground.

'We're drifting again,' she said. 'We're still west of the railway line.'

Alexei grinned at her. 'Then I shall make a correction, but only if you say by how many degrees.'

'Don't bother.' Ryder had been watching the fuel gauge for some time. 'We've already got a crash corridor that's nearly eighty miles long. Unless there was some kind of massive air-borne explosion, the wreckage wouldn't have spread any further than this.'

Isabel shook her head. 'There were eighteen canisters in the probe,' she said. 'What about the four we haven't found?'

'Three.' Ryder corrected her. 'You've forgotten the one I buried.'

'What's the difference? Why go back now?'

'Because we've got no idea how many survived re-entry. Anyhow, some of them could be in places where we wouldn't find them if we were out here for a week.' Ryder had stopped scanning, worried about the possibility of observers on the ground who could have already seen how straight and how predictable the PC-6's flight route had been.

After giving Alexei the turn-for-home sign he handed the imager to Isabel. 'We're heading back to the strip,' he said. 'You can double-check the coordinates of the canisters as we fly back over them. The more accurate our GPS readings are, the more time we're going to save when we come out in the Jeep to start digging.'

'Why not land the plane on the desert – like you did last night?'

Ryder had no intention of trying. 'If you'd seen our landing you wouldn't ask,' he said. 'It's too risky. If we tip over or end up in the bottom of another dust-bowl we'd be stuck out here without any way of getting anywhere.'

'The Jeep can get stuck just as easily.'

'We won't be taking off and landing it in fourteen or seventeen different places, will we?'

'I still don't see why we should stop searching now.' She was insistent, apparently expecting him to agree with her.

'Don't push your luck,' Ryder said. 'I'll let you know when you're in charge. Until we hear back from your uncle, we're not going to spend half a day in the air showing people what we're doing.'

'If anyone's watching.' She busied herself with the imager, adjusting the sensitivity control before she settled down with her face pressed against the cockpit window.

'I shall fly faster now?' Alexei enquired.

'Yeah.' Ryder was happier now he'd made the decision. 'It might be an idea to put on a bit of altitude too, in case we can save some gas.'

'We have sufficient for tomorrow but no more. After that, if you wish to continue it will be necessary for us to obtain more fuel from Tarija.' Alexei banked the PC-6, holding the turn until the nose was centred on some distant, unseen point. 'You believe now that this plane I bring is good?'

Ryder nodded, wishing he'd kept his mouth shut earlier in the flight when he'd made the mistake of suggesting that a Cessna might have been a cheaper and more fuel-efficient alternative.

'You have seen how a Turbo-Porter will land where other aircraft cannot.' Alexei said. 'When you invite me to join you in Bolivia, you say over the phone that the conditions will be very bad, so I think from a ten thousand foot-high airstrip in the cold and dust we do not want a toy plane like the one you mention.'

'Right.' Ryder had got the message. The Porter had proved its worth already, and after their success of today, fuel efficiency was not the issue it had been before.

He still found it hard to believe they had done so well. When he'd first discussed the project in Cali, Corrales himself had suggested that the recovery programme could take as long as three or four weeks. But at this rate, if their luck continued to hold, the tough part of the mission could be over in a matter of days. A bonus, Ryder thought, and Corrales would be happy with fifteen canisters, even if his niece was not.

Picking up the clipboard she'd been using, he inspected her map, remembering the summer day in Cali when she'd told him what she'd learned about the trajectory of the ill-fated probe.

Except for guessing the starting point of the corridor incorrectly, the original line of her map was no more than two or three degrees west of the line she'd drawn today.

The new one was shorter, crossing the Chilean border north of the canyon where she'd been held prisoner before it skimmed past the desert township of Cascada, heading almost exactly for the centre of the Salar de Uyuni, the huge dried-up salt lake to the north. But Ryder was certain that the wreckage could not extend that far. The last canister they'd located was a good fifty miles short of the lake's southern boundary, and it was unlikely that any wreckage could have travelled the extra distance.

He tried to visualize six tonnes of superheated metal plunging into the atmosphere at a speed of 7,000 metres a second, imagining how enormous the fireball must have been before it broke into a thousand pieces high above the Altiplano.

The picture was not an altogether reassuring one. How many of the canisters had survived intact, Ryder wondered? Were some of the heat images from them so bright and so clear because, over the years, their contents had leaked out into the surrounding ground?

For the remainder of the flight he continued to think about the possibility, keeping his concerns to himself and only abandoning his search for answers after they'd landed because by then both Alexei and Isabel had started questioning him about his plans for tomorrow.

Unlike day one, day two of their reconnaissance had been a frustrating failure. After spending over three hours in the PC-6, they had come back to the airstrip with nothing new to show for their efforts.

They had experimented with a variety of search patterns, they had surveyed the high plains from difficult altitudes, and they had surveyed it at different airspeeds, and twice Alexei had almost stalled the Porter after Ryder had insisted on checking out images that, on a slower fly-past, had proved to be either unreliable or non-existent.

In spite of the setback, Ryder had not been disheartened.

Instead he'd been busy. Since their return, over the course of the afternoon he had constructed a pair of wooden tongs with which to handle the canisters, and before the sun had begun to disappear he'd spent the best part of an hour mapping out his route for the ground search – if and when a ground search was to take place.

For some of the time, Isabel had helped him decide on the best route, checking every map she had for roads and tracks that passed closest to the hidden canisters that now had to be excavated from the ground. How deep they might lie was another of the unknowns – a less hazardous one than the level of radioactivity, but still potentially problematic.

By nightfall, Ryder had stopped anticipating complications. He'd also stopped trying to predict Isabel's reactions to things he recommended or things he did.

For reasons of her own, she had single-handedly prepared their evening meal, calling on Alexei's expertise with the drip-heater only to maintain the temperature of the hotplate on which she had done the cooking.

As a result of her labours they had dined well, enjoying the hot beans and the thick, kerosene-flavoured slices of bread and fried spam that Isabel had kept piling on their plates.

She'd eaten almost as much as Ryder, hungry after her day out in the cold and recovering from the events of two nights ago more quickly than he'd expected her to.

Now their meal was over, she was resting on the bottom bunk, hands behind her head, amused by Alexei's attempts to make himself comfortable on the wooden workbench.

'Looks like I'm on watch,' Ryder said.

The Russian lit a cigarette before he answered. 'I will do it,' he said. 'But I think it is OK if first I have a smoke in the warm.'

'I'll take the second shift.' Unwilling to use the upper bunk because of the sulphur fumes which accumulated beneath the ceiling, Ryder fashioned himself a cushion out of a sleeping bag and sat down on the floor.

'Maybe we don't need to keep watch.' Isabel glanced at him. 'If that truck was around we'd have seen it from the air.'

'Unless your friend with the scar has taken his men back into the hills. We won't know the coast's clear for sure until we hear from your uncle.'

She checked the light on the satellite phone. 'We'll have to start the generator in the morning,' she said. 'If we don't recharge these batteries we won't be hearing from anyone.' She paused. 'Perhaps Uncle Miguel will call tonight.'

'If he does we'll use the Jeep tomorrow,' Ryder said. 'We'll be getting cabin fever if we have to hang around here much longer.'

'Why not take the Jeep out tomorrow anyway – or do another search from the air? We don't have to go all the way in one day.'

'How are we going to use the plane when we've hardly got enough fuel left to make it to Tarija? And unless you want to get jumped on again we're sure as hell not driving the Jeep anywhere until we know it's safe.'

'They were just ideas. You don't have to snap at me.'

'Please.' Alexei eased himself off the bench. 'You squabble like children. If you cannot discuss things without banging your heads together, I shall go to sit alone in the Cherokee where I do not have to listen.' He collected the binoculars and the thermal-imager. 'I think it is better if you both get some rest.'

Ryder was inclined to agree. He waited for Alexei to leave the hut, then took the sleeping bag and dragged it with him up the ladder to the upper bunk.

'Set the beeper on your watch for me,' he said. 'Eleven thirty'll do. If I don't take over from Alexei he's liable to spend all night out there.' He waited for a reply that was not forthcoming. 'Did you hear me?' he asked.

'Yes, I heard you.'

Deciding not to say goodnight, he found a position that didn't hurt his stomach, then, trying not to cough from the fumes and after making certain he could feel the shape of the Winchester beside him, Ryder closed his eyes.

He'd been asleep for what seemed like only a few minutes when he was awakened by a rattle from somewhere inside the hut. The noise was too familiar to be alarming – the sound of someone turning off the drip-heater's supply valve.

141

It was Isabel. Enough moonlight was filtering through the lou-vres for him to see the white of the bandages around her wrists. And he could see how cautious she was being.

She waited for the flame to die before re-opening the valve, but made no attempt to relight the burner.

Good luck, Ryder thought. Now the damn thing was flooded she could have the job of getting it going again, and if she'd been too hot in bed, she'd be bloody freezing by the time she'd nursed it back to life.

Assuming she'd return to her bunk, he closed his eyes again only to be disturbed by her whispering something to him.

'What?'

'The heater's gone out. I can't get it to work.'

To save time, Ryder clambered down and went to experiment with a match, hoping there was sufficient heat left to evaporate the pool of fuel. His effort was rewarded with smoke, a puff of flame and more smoke. But at least it had started burning. All he had to do now was figure out why she'd been fiddling with it.

He had a foot on the bottom rung of the ladder when the sit-uation became clearer.

'That man,' she said, 'you know – the one who was going to rape me.'

'What about him?'

'Alexei said you were aiming for his shoulder.'

'Does it matter?'

'Yes. No. I don't know.' She slumped down on her bunk. 'Would you talk to me for a while?'

'Not if that's what you want to talk about.'

'It isn't. I don't care what. Anything. Tell me why you went to Canada.'

Because the air was cooler and cleaner at floor level, Ryder could smell the freshness of her skin – the faint smell of cut cedar and of something pleasant from his childhood that he couldn't quite identify. 'I told you why I went to Canada,' he said.

'To get away from the PAF?'

'Québec was as good a place as any.'

'Until I came along.' She looked up at him. 'I don't understand how the PAF ever got their hooks into someone like you.'

'Probably because they timed it right. It wasn't long after Grace's funeral. And their arguments sounded pretty good, I suppose.' He sat down beside her. 'Have you ever wondered what would've happened if Hitler had been assassinated before he could start World War Two?'

'Is that one of their arguments?'

'They've got dozens of them. When the PAF was first founded, the directors might even have believed they were doing the right thing. But it's the old story about power and corruption. Once they discovered they could make private fortunes through their own companies, the whole organization went rotten from the inside out.'

'It's good you met me then, isn't it?' She smiled slightly. 'Otherwise you wouldn't have a way of undermining it.'

'To hell with undermining it. Ballantine, Latimer and Poitou are causing more misery in the world than you could ever dream of. They need their hearts cut out.'

'My uncle can do that. He told me he could.'

'As long as the canisters aren't buried twenty feet down.'

'They won't be.' She drew her fingertips across the back of his hand. 'Tell me about those other jobs you did for the PAF.'

Although Ryder hadn't quite given up the idea of going back to bed, the more he considered it, the more conscious he was of the pressure from her fingers. She was still touching him, pushing down lightly on his hand as if to prevent him from leaving.

'Serbia,' she prompted. 'Bosnia and Somalia.'

Against his better judgement, almost certain he was making a mistake, he began to speak slowly, allowing pieces of the past to resurface so they could be reassembled into some kind of coherent order.

He started with Somalia, describing the little Mogadishu church and explaining how, because of his failure to safeguard the children, he'd never been able to forget their screams after the bomb had gone off.

To forestall her questions he carried on, providing an account of his subsequent overland escape to Baidoa where for days he'd hidden from the band of half-crazed soldiers that Farrah Adid had sent to kill him, and telling her about the nine-year-old girl who, in the end, had led him out to safety.

He was more circumspect with the descriptions of his other assignments, skipping over some of the details and only attempting to justify what he'd done in Sarajevo when she interrupted. Her questions brought him to a halt, and although he could detect no obvious antipathy in her voice, Ryder could not continue.

'I didn't realize,' she said quietly, 'how bad it was, I mean. I thought you'd make it sound exciting, but it wasn't, was it?'

'Parts of it were OK – until Alexei phoned me one day from Moscow. He'd just got back from Panama and wanted me to know that he'd found out what we were really doing.'

'Targeting the wrong people?'

'No.' Ryder shook his head. 'I've never shot anyone who didn't deserve a bullet, but Alexei and I had been given assignments for the wrong reasons. What we didn't know was that we'd been helping the PAF directors sell small-arms, rocket launchers and tanks to whoever the PAF had decided should have them. Find a country that's in the middle of a civil war or in a mess because of religious fundamentalism or political upheaval and you'll find the PAF supplying equipment to one side or the other.' Ryder endeavoured to gauge her reaction. 'The system works pretty well.'

'Because men like you and Alexei are hired to make sure the right sides win.'

'Yep.'

'The Peace Aid Foundation doesn't just deal in aid and military equipment, though, does it? You didn't say anything about their cocaine business.'

'Surprise.'

'I wasn't trying to score points.' She removed her hand. 'You don't know what I meant.'

He was still interpreting her remark when to his surprise she leaned across and kissed him gently on the forehead.

'You'll have to try harder,' she said. 'Then perhaps you'll be able to understand what that means.'

Chapter 10

MARKOVIC finished drying himself in the shower, wrapped the towel round his waist and padded out into the other room.

To his disgust he saw that the girl had gone back to sleep. She was lying on the bed, still smelling of sex and cheap perfume, half-covered in a sheet, with the money he'd given her clasped loosely in one hand.

Last night when he'd picked her up in the bar, the smell of her had been attractive enough, but this morning he found it as distasteful as her nakedness. In daylight her features too were unappealing – those of a peasant with coarse lips and a nose that was too large for her face.

She'd been a disappointment all round, Markovic thought, providing pleasure of the kind he wanted only after he'd hurt her and threatened to withhold the money.

To wake her, he picked up one of her shoes and brought it down hard across her buttocks.

She gave a little scream and sat bolt upright, clutching the sheet to her breasts.

'I told you to get out.' Markovic threw her clothes at her. 'Take those with you.'

Frightened now, the girl slipped off the bed and backed away from him while she gathered up the clothes and collected the shoes he kicked over to her.

'Get dressed in the corridor,' Markovic said. 'Shut the door behind you.'

As soon as she'd gone he stripped the bed, bundling the pillows, sheets and blankets into a cupboard so her smell would not remind him of an evening that had been less than satisfying in almost every respect.

It had been late afternoon when he'd arrived at the Potosí air terminal, and he'd been too weary after the long journey from Colombia to conduct his customary survey of hotels. As a consequence he had chosen unwisely, selecting the Residencial Villamontes partly on the advice of the taxi driver, but principally because it was the first one he found that advertised central heating. That the advertising was not borne out in practice had quickly become apparent, driving Markovic out of his room in search for warmer surroundings when he would have preferred to stay where he was.

His exploration of Potosí had led him first to a noisy restaurant near the bus terminal in the Plaza del Estudiante. From there he had moved on, sampling a succession of cafés and bars in his hunt for a young woman who could be used to while away an otherwise unproductive night in a city he'd already decided he disliked.

There was little left of the extravagance that the all-conquering Spanish had once lavished on Potosí. Now that the rich, underground veins of silver were all but worked out, Markovic had been able to find few traces of the city's former glory, and then only in narrow, unlit backstreets where he'd been more interested in the local girls than in local architecture.

This morning, viewed from his hotel window in watery sunlight, the whole place seemed to be rooted in another time, he thought, kept alive by what remained of the silver mines and by uninformed tourists who flocked here to suck up its colonial history and because, at an altitude of over 4,000 metres, Potosí was the highest city in the world.

He dressed slowly, choosing a business suit, a white shirt and the expensive, hand-lasted shoes he'd bought in London. Whether or not a suit would influence the outcome of his meeting was difficult to predict, but it was always better to look the part, he decided, and even if his journey here had been a wasted one, it would be safer to leave again with his identity intact or at least without it being questioned.

Sealing his Beretta automatic in a plastic bag, he dropped it into the toilet cistern then took the stairs to the ground-floor restaurant where, after helping himself to toast and coffee, he sat down at a table to prepare for his morning's work.

Not that there was much to prepare, Markovic thought. Having learned very little from his phone call of yesterday, there were only three possibilities: that he'd embarked on a wild goose chase; that the meeting would blow up in his face – or that the judicious application of money would pay immediate dividends because, here in South America, money greased the wheels of everything.

Unlike Canada where airline passenger lists had been unobtainable at any price, in Colombia the situation had been quite different. During his two-week stay there, for a modest outlay of US$100 a day, Markovic had been supplied with computer print-outs listing the destinations of every passenger on every flight that had departed from the Cali terminal.

Every morning, at precisely 9.00 a.m., a small boy on a bicycle had delivered the print-outs to his hotel, and on each of those mornings over breakfast, Markovic had patiently read through them until the names of the right passengers had finally appeared.

He still had no idea why the Englishman and the Colombian girl had travelled to Bolivia, nor did he yet have any means of confirming their rendezvous with the Russian. Nevertheless, that the three of them were in the country somewhere seemed to be a more than reasonable assumption. What they were doing, and where they were doing it were the unanswered questions that had brought him to Potosí – to the only place in Bolivia where the Corrales family had business interests and where perhaps, if things were to go well this morning, he would obtain the lead he wanted.

Over coffee he rehearsed the lines he would use, reciting them again silently to himself in the taxi and for one last time outside the grimy CMC building before he pushed through the swing doors and entered the Bolivian head office of the Corrales Mining Corporation.

The young woman at the desk had the similar high cheek-bones of the girl he'd enjoyed last night. Her mouth was slightly more inviting, but her teeth were not as straight and her waist was too thick.

He gave her his card. 'I have an appointment with Señor Castaña Diaz at nine twenty. He's expecting me.'

She smiled and pushed a button on her intercom, speaking in Spanish but having to stop to ask him how his name should be pronounced.

'Itch.' He returned her smile. 'I know it's difficult.'

'I am sorry for my English. If you will wait, Señor Diaz will meet you now.'

Markovich didn't have to wait. A short, stocky man had already emerged from a door behind the desk.

In his early fifties, wearing an ill-fitting, dark-grey suit, he had the face and belly of someone who lived too well, but the quick eyes of a man who missed very little.

He offered his hand. 'I'm Diaz. Please, you will come to my office so we may talk.'

Markovic followed him into a room that had at one time been decorated with some care but that, over the years, had been allowed to deteriorate. It was run-down to the point of being seedy, with a threadbare carpet, a scruffy desk, some old wooden chairs and a glass-topped table which had a large crack across one corner. Adding to the impression of seediness were several unopened cartons of Johnny Walker Scotch stacked in the door-way of a small adjoining bathroom.

Diaz sat at the table and looked pointedly at his watch. 'I regret I must leave before ten,' he said. 'However, if you would care to specify the ingot quality and quantity of tin your company wishes to purchase, I am sure we can agree on a satisfactory price.'

Markovic remained standing. He said nothing.

'Please.' Diaz waved a hand at one of the chairs. 'What grade or purity do you require?'

Before Markovic sat down he positioned his briefcase carefully on the table. 'I'm not here to discuss tin,' he said.

'I see. Or rather I do not see. Yesterday when you telephoned, you introduced yourself as a buyer for a consortium of European metal traders. Is that not so?'

'I was lying.' Markovic decided on a direct approach, judging that the Bolivian would be best unsettled by treating him as an underling.

'Then what is your purpose in coming to my office?'

Opening his case, Markovic took out two photographs and slid them across the table. 'Do you recognize these men?' he asked.

'I do not. And if I did, why should I tell you?'

'Because I'm offering two thousand American dollars to anyone who can put me in touch with them.'

Diaz stood up. 'I am sorry,' he said. 'I cannot be of help to you. Now please forgive me, I have another meeting to attend.'

Markovic stayed where he was, removing the colour print from the envelope that had been couriered to him the day before he left Colombia. 'Perhaps this'll change your mind.' He laid the photograph on the table. 'I'm sure you know who she is.'

Diaz sat down again.

'She's travelling with the two men,' Markovic said. 'I need to know where they are.'

The Bolivian placed both hands on the tabletop. 'So Mr Markovic, you are a buyer after all, but not of metals.'

The remark was ambiguous. Did Diaz regard him simply as a buyer of information, Markovic wondered? Or was he missing something?

'Señor Corrales is not a man who is easily deceived.' Diaz smiled. 'He should not have trusted you. But you are very wrong to believe I can be deceived in a similar manner. After you have learned Corrales will soon have a large quantity of plutonium for sale in Colombia, you decide to bypass him. Is that not the case?'

Not a muscle moved in Markovic's face. His eyes revealed nothing, his body position remained unaltered and his hands were completely still.

'Allow me to inform you now that you will not bypass me.' Diaz inspected his fingernails. 'You may have been clever enough to follow Señorita Corrales and her friends here to Bolivia, but you will not be permitted to buy or steal the plutonium from them. If you wish to do business, you will do it with me and only with me. Do you understand?'

All Markovic understood was that he'd stumbled on something of great significance, but without any real knowledge of what it was. He decided to broaden the conversation. 'Whether you and I can do business depends on the quantity and the price,' he said.

'How many grammes do you wish to purchase?'

Markovic shrugged. 'It depends. Corrales just said he'd have a lot of it and that the grade would be extremely high.'

'It will be weapons-grade plutonium-238 – perhaps as much as two hundred grammes. Is that suitable for your purposes?'

'If the price is right. What are we talking about for a full two-hundred-gramme consignment?'

Diaz smiled again. 'For whom do you work?'

Markovic pretended to contemplate the question. 'My principals prefer to remain anonymous,' he said. 'You know how these things work.'

'I would still like their names.'

'So you can rack up the price depending on my answer?'

'No. So I may check out your credentials.'

'You don't want me to tell you to get fucked, do you?' Markovic said pleasantly. 'You'll get names when I'm ready to give them to you. I don't work for some rat-arsed terrorist organization, Señor Diaz; I represent the interests of the Libyan Government. If that's not good enough for you, all you have to do is say so.'

'It was not my intention to be rude.'

'Good.' Aware that he was improvising dangerously, Markovic struggled to think. 'Are you going to quote me a price, or not?' he said.

'It will be less than five million US dollars. At the moment I cannot be more precise.'

'I see.' Staggered by the figure, Markovic slowly collected the photographs and returned them to his briefcase. Determined now to learn more, but worried that he'd be unable to maintain his pretence if the conversation was to take an unexpected turn, he risked another question. 'How do I know you can guarantee delivery?' he said. 'The girl and the two men aren't working for you, are they? They're working for Señor Corrales.'

'Mr Markovic, I assure you that in one week I shall have free title to the material. Until then I suggest you avoid meddling in matters which do not concern you, and over which you can have no influence.'

'In that case I'll need a minimum of one gramme for analysis.' For a second, Markovic thought he'd gone too far. But he'd misread the change in the Bolivian's expression.

Diaz consulted his watch again. 'A sample may be difficult,' he said. 'The material is in sealed capsules. I think it will be better if we discuss the details elsewhere.'

'I haven't come all the way from North Africa to be given the brush off.'

'That is not what I meant. I am more than willing to explore how we may best come to an arrangement, but, as I have explained, I cannot do it now.' Diaz left the table and disappeared into the bathroom. 'Where are you staying?'

'At the Villamontes.' For the second time this morning Markovic found himself disgusted. Through the open bathroom door he could see the Bolivian standing in front of the mirror. The man had flopped out his prick and was pissing into the washbasin while he adjusted his tie and combed his hair.

Diaz continued the conversation without turning round. 'If you will come to my home this evening I will have a more accurate price for you. Doubtless by then you will have made phone calls to finalize your own position. Please tell your principals that if they require assistance to ship the plutonium out of South America, I can make the necessary connections for them.'

'For a fee?'

'Of course.' Having completed his toilet, Diaz returned to escort his visitor politely from the room. 'My secretary will give you my home address,' he said. 'She can also call a taxi for you if you require one.'

Because there had been no sound of running water from the bathroom taps, with some reluctance Markovic shook hands to say goodbye. 'What time this evening?' he said.

'Shall we say seven?'

'I'll be there.' Once Diaz had left the building Markovic turned his attention to the girl at the desk, finding rather to his surprise that, because of her crooked teeth, his interest in her had been replaced by thoughts of what promised to be a more attractive and an altogether more rewarding proposition.

In their enthusiasm to promote Potosí as the world's highest city, the publishers of the local guidebook had neglected to mention that Potosí also had the lowest daytime temperatures and by far the most primitive and inefficient telephone system of anywhere Markovic had ever been.

For a good part of the last six hours he'd been endeavouring to refine his information base, first by telephoning the public library and the offices of local organizations, and only extending his search for data after becoming so discouraged that he was left with no alternative but to spend money on expensive international phone calls.

How well spent the money had been was open to speculation. From a variety of sources he had learned a little about the world market for illicit plutonium, and he had discovered that there were no nuclear reactors in Bolivia where the material could have ever been produced. By lunch-time, from a contact in Belgrade, he had found out that at least five kilogrammes of enriched plutonium are needed to construct a nuclear weapon and been told that a purity level of greater than ninety per cent is usually required.

The same contact was reluctant to disclose the names of current buyers although, rather as Markovic had expected, the big money was being offered either by rogue countries that were eager to establish a nuclear capability, or by well-organized terrorist groups who had the financial means to fulfil their private agendas.

The existence of a fertile market was beyond question. Nor did Markovic have any reason to disbelieve what Diaz had so foolishly told him. But the involvement of the Englishman, the Russian and the girl remained a mystery.

Only recently in the latter part of the afternoon, and with the help of some more surprisingly good coffee in the hotel restaurant, had Markovic been able to make sense of his thoughts on the matter.

Whichever way he looked at it now, the answer seemed to be the same. As a result of the girl's abortive effort to kill the Englishman in Canada, some peculiar kind of alliance had been established between Ryder and the girl's uncle. And because of that, Ryder, Volodya and the girl were here in Bolivia to procure a quantity of plutonium that was large enough to whet the appetite of anyone who knew about it.

Diaz in particular had already staked his claim, anxious to find a buyer and more than willing to double-cross Corrales in order to get his hands on what he called the capsules before they could be smuggled out to Colombia.

Which left the PAF, Markovic thought, the internationally respected aid foundation who, by putting him on the trail of the two men and the girl, had unwittingly introduced him to a potential pay-off that could be thirty times greater than the one he'd been anticipating. Or even more, he realized. If the estimates were right, eliminating Diaz would alone yield anything up to five million. But that was without the $150,000 the PAF had agreed to pay him for the contracts.

Except that no project was ever as straightforward as it seemed – a rule it would be unwise to overlook. For his plan to succeed there was still much to do: the requirement to cultivate his association with Diaz until the whereabouts of the plutonium became clearer, and the need to keep the PAF entirely in the dark while he broadened the scope of his assignment.

He left the restaurant shortly before five o'clock, returning to his room to consider the approach he should take at his meeting this evening and to make his weekly report to the PAF.

It took him less than five minutes to rehearse his statement for the phone call to Bonn and another two minutes to get a connection. By then, Markovic was ready to dictate his message, confident that the three directors would be unable to see through his lies.

Speaking clearly and deliberately, he began his report in the usual way:

'This is Markovic. Message dated Thursday, 12 July. The following information is confidential, intended only for the offices of Sir Richard Ballantine, Senator George Latimer and Monsieur Gerard Poitou. Gentlemen, I'm speaking to you again from my hotel in Cali. However, unlike my report of last week, I'm pleased to inform you that all the items have now arrived in Colombia. Consequently, I expect our contract to be concluded inside a period of one week. I shall, of course, be in touch with you again then. Message ends.'

He replaced the receiver, conscious of a slight tingling in his fingertips that had been absent for some weeks. Even last night when the girl had eventually done what she'd been paid to do, there had been no trace of the sensation. So what had brought it on now? The prospect of a $5 million windfall? Or because, thanks to Diaz, the Corrales girl would soon be within easier reach?

Wondering which explanation was correct, he laid her photograph on the table in front of him.

Judging by the light and the depth of field, the photo had been taken at evening time through a powerful telephoto lens, although the definition of the print was still excellent. The girl was wearing a thin beige-coloured jacket and carrying a shoulder bag, standing near a small jetty, her figure outlined against a backdrop of trees and what Markovic thought was a lake rather than the sea.

Where and how the picture had been taken was immaterial. What mattered was her extraordinary prettiness. She was so pretty that it was a waste if the Englishman was fucking her, and a shame the photo showed her fully clothed.

He indulged himself by imagining what she would look like naked, tied to a bed while he took his own pictures of her.

The PAF's terms were imprecise, Markovic decided, requiring him to submit evidence of the contract's completion, but not specifying the point at which the evidence should be obtained – in which case, to satisfy his obligations, it would be prudent to photograph her before and after she was dead.

Provocative though the idea was, by six o'clock the tingling had not returned, allowing him to leave the hotel with a clear mind, reminding himself now of the other rule by which he led his life – that the greatest rewards came not to the deserving, but to the strong and to those who made the least number of mistakes.

The Diaz residence was situated in a side street not far from the cathedral. Like other houses in the neighbourhood, it was reasonably modest, somewhat out of place in a part of town that was more commercial than suburban, but well cared for and with a tiny garden that was illuminated by a single outside light.

Markovic paid the taxi driver, opened the gate and walked up a short path to the front door. He had his hand on the knocker when he realized the door was ajar – by no more than a few millimetres, but definitely unlocked.

Remaining where he was he pushed on it lightly, waiting to hear the chink from a tightening safety chain.

There was no chink, nor were any other sounds coming from the house.

His decision to leave the Beretta behind had been a mistake. In a city like Potosí, where an unlocked door wasn't an invitation but a warning, Markovic knew he was at a disadvantage, out in the open with no idea where the danger lay.

A parked car in the street? From a window of an adjacent home? Or from inside? The open door meant nothing – except perhaps that the invitation was too obvious.

He considered his options, knowing it would be foolish to walk away when there was so much at stake, but taking his time to weigh up all the risks. His visit here was entirely innocent, he concluded. He'd been in Potosí for less than two days and, except for Diaz, few people knew he was in Bolivia let alone Potosí – facts that hardly added up to the possibility of a trap.

Keeping his eyes on the street, he stepped to one side then acted out the role he'd come to play by banging hard on the knocker. 'Señor Diaz,' he called. 'Good evening to you. Are you there?'

Although the door swung open, Markovic waited for a moment before he entered the house. He moved with extreme caution, holding his briefcase in front of him and closing the door behind him with his foot.

The lighting in the hallway was barely adequate, leaving deep shadows at the far end where a large wooden dresser stood against the wall. Closer to him a number of open doors led into rooms which were all unlit and all equally silent.

His nerves were on edge, suddenly made worse by a disturbing smell.

Markovic knew what it was before he located the right doorway and switched on the light.

The room was a study, furnished with prints of impressionist paintings, a cocktail cabinet, an expensive desk and a comfortable leather chair.

The chair had been pulled out from the desk. And slumped on it was the body of Castaño Diaz.

He had died unpleasantly, voiding the contents of his bladder before his life had been taken from him.

So distasteful was the smell of urine that Markovic held his breath while he approached the chair. After establishing that the body was cold, he was in the process of examining a curious weal around Diaz's throat when he heard the creak of a floorboard.

He froze, cursing himself for not searching the house more thoroughly, then, very slowly he straightened his back, holding out his hands so they could be seen.

The intruder was behind him. Markovic could sense his presence and even detect where he was. But who he was he could not be sure.

'I know you're there,' he said. 'If you think I did this, you're wrong.' Still moving slowly he turned, waiting for a muzzle-flash, prepared to act if he had to because a bullet would be a better option than a steel wire around his neck.

A stranger was standing in the doorway. He was travel-stained, wearing heavy boots, army fatigues and a filthy sheepskin-lined jacket. From the look of him he'd been living rough for some time. Stubble covered his face, exaggerating a white scar on his left cheek and he smelt powerfully of stale sweat, diesel fuel and woodsmoke. A large automatic in his hand was pointing at Markovic's stomach.

The man was relaxed, showing no signs of being jumpy. 'What is your name?' he asked.

'Markovic.'

'You can prove this to me?'

'In there – on the desk.' Markovic pointed to his briefcase.

The man went to it, using his free hand to shuffle through the contents. After inspecting Markovic's passport he withdrew the three photographs. 'You know these people?' he asked.

'Not exactly.' Markovic was regaining confidence, beginning to believe he'd overestimated the threat. 'Are you going to tell me who you are?' he said.

'I am called Vargas.'

'And you had a little disagreement with Diaz?'

The man spat on the floor. 'You do not understand. We share the same family. Señor Diaz is my cousin.'

'Not any more he isn't. Are you holding that gun on me because you think I killed him?'

'He is dead before you arrive in your taxi.' Vargas lowered his gun. 'I have been away in the Cordillera mountains, but I today return here to see my cousin. This morning while we drink coffee together he has told me of someone who comes to Bolivia to buy plutonium for a foreign government.'

'And you and me and Diaz were all supposed to have a nice talk about it together?'

'My cousin asks me to visit with him this evening at his house where he says a Señor Markovic will also be present. But Diaz has

159

not yet obtained the plutonium so, even if you are here earlier, I think there is no reason for you to do this.'

'If you or I didn't kill him, who did?'

'I do not know.' Vargas put the automatic in his pocket. 'But I have many friends. With their help I shall find out who has shot him.'

'He wasn't shot,' Markovic said. 'Someone wrapped a steel wire round his throat. The poor bastard was choked to death.'

'That is not correct. I have checked. After the wire, he has been shot in the head.' Vargas walked over to the body. 'I will show you. Look.'

Stepping carefully over the puddle, Markovic went to see, discovering that there was indeed a powder burn and a wound in the skull. The entry point was behind Diaz's right ear, a tiny almost bloodless hole, much smaller than that made by a round from a .38 or a .32, but slightly larger than a hole from a .22.

'The bullet stays inside his head,' Vargas said. 'It has not come out.'

Markovic took his word for it. He gathered up his photos from the desk. 'You know where these people are, don't you?' he said.

'Perhaps.'

'Yes or no?'

'When it is dangerous for anyone from the CNPZ to travel so far alone, why else would I be in Potosí?'

'If that's yes, I think you and I can do business.' Despite never having heard of the CNPZ, Markovic was pleased, congratulating himself on an evening that had turned out to be well spent after all.

Slipping the photos back into his case, he smiled agreeably at his newfound friend. 'How about us finding a nice warm bar?' he said. 'We've got some things to discuss.'

On his way from the room, for the sake of orderliness, he switched off the light and closed the door. It was a pity about Diaz, he thought, but in the circumstances a fitting enough end for a man who knew no better than to piss in his own washbasin.

Chapter 11

AS usual, this canister wasn't in the right place either. Except for the second one they'd dug up yesterday, none of them had been where they were supposed to be.

Instead of searching for it Ryder switched off the Geiger counter and began walking, using his compass and counting his steps until he reached a small, protruding ridge of rock.

'Not far enough,' Isabel called. 'You haven't counted properly.' She was some distance away, sitting on the bonnet of the Cherokee to keep warm and pointing ahead of him.

Ryder ignored her, reactivating the Geiger counter and sweeping the head backwards and forwards over the little ridge. Already the clicks were coming faster, indicating that the canister was almost exactly where he'd thought it might be. Like some of the others, it had either bounced or burrowed on impact, only coming to rest because of harder ground or because it had smacked up against the line of underground rock.

He spent another minute or two listening to the signal, then began to use his spade, digging carefully in case the canister turned out to be cracked.

So far none of them had been. Of the eight they'd recovered yesterday, and of the three today, all had appeared to be in good condition apart from some deep scratches and slight traces of corrosion.

This one too seemed to be intact. Ryder could see the end of it, another tiny, grey-coloured cylinder that had thawed out the frost from the surrounding soil.

Easing it out of the ground, he inspected it more closely, gently rolling it along with the tip of his spade until he was certain there were no obvious signs of damage. By now, his safety precautions were second nature. Once they'd discovered that their GPS readings were in error by a more or less constant twenty-two feet in a south-easterly direction, finding the canisters had proved fairly simple, although without a Geiger counter the task would have been impossible.

Determining the danger was more difficult, a crude technique that also relied on the Geiger counter. Ryder had originated the procedure after checking out the first two canisters from a safe distance, persuading himself that others should register similar or identical levels of radioactivity unless they were damaged in some way.

Because he had no real idea of how hazardous the procedure was, he opened the lead-lined container, then used his wooden tongs to quickly transfer the canister, dropping it into a vacant compartment before he slammed the lid.

'Have you got it?' Isabel called.

'Thirteen down. One to go. Drive the Jeep over.'

She jumped off the bonnet, but instead of doing what he'd asked her to do, she walked over carrying his rifle. 'I saw a pair of vizcachas.' She handed him the Winchester. 'If you can shoot one, we can have it for dinner.'

'Sledge hammer to crack a nut.' Ryder smiled at her. 'There wouldn't be anything left.'

'Try anyway.' Leaving him standing beside the container, she returned to the Jeep.

Suspicious though he was, it wasn't until he saw her pointing the video camera at him that he realized he'd been set up.

Early yesterday morning, after her uncle had phoned with the news they'd been waiting for, she'd unpacked their camera gear, delaying their departure while she shot some video tape and two rolls of 35-millimetre film. She'd photographed the hut, the sheds, the airstrip, the morning mist and irritated Alexei by

insisting that he pose alongside the plane while she photographed him from a variety of angles. Today, it was evidently
Ryder's turn.

He was pleased for her sake, glad she'd been able to overcome
her embarrassment and that she'd recovered so well from the
incident of four days ago. On the other hand, he wasn't keen on
being filmed, and with a canister yet to find before the evening
mist came down and the cold began to bite, this was not the time
to be messing about on the Altiplano.

'Bring the damn Jeep,' he said. 'I'm not carting all this stuff
over to you.'

'Wait a second. Wave your gun at me.' She tried to hold the
camera still, then suddenly burst out laughing.

He went to see what was so funny, but could get no sense out of
her. She was still giggling, leaning against a mudguard, refusing
to look him in the face.

'What?' he said. 'Tell me.'

'You.' She managed to stop for a moment. 'It's you.'

He'd never seen her quite like this before. Her smiles had
come more often lately, but few had lasted very long. This was different. For the first time since he'd met her she seemed to be not
just amused but positively cheerful.

She wiped away some tears. 'Alexei calls your Winchester a cowboy gun,' she said.

'So?'

'Our cover story. We're supposed to be an American TV crew –
remember?'

Ryder hadn't forgotten, but it didn't help.

'It's Alexei's fault,' she said. 'I photographed him again this
morning before we left. He was covered in dust where he'd been
working on the plane, and he looked so wonderfully grizzled.
Don't you see? He's a great Butch Cassidy.'

Now Ryder understood, not entirely comfortable in his incar-
nation as the Sundance Kid, but unable to do much about it.

'You're perfect,' she said. 'You haven't shaved for days, you're
wearing that awful man's jacket, and you're dirtier than Alexei
was. All you need is the right hat.'

'Shoot the tape,' he said. 'It might come in handy if we have trouble getting the canisters through customs.'

'It wouldn't work. The Sundance Kid was more handsome than you are.'

'Thanks.' Ryder got into the Cherokee, drove it over to the pile of equipment and started loading up. Like her, he was in better spirits than he had been for weeks. It was a refreshing feeling to be back in control, and since they'd received the all-clear from Corrales and managed to recover so many of the canisters, there had been a step-change in his mood. How much of it was the result of an improvement in Isabel's demeanour, he didn't know. Over the last two days she'd been a good deal more helpful, and unless he'd been imagining it, she'd gone out of her way to spend as much time as she could with him.

Whether her kiss meant anything was still hard to tell, although he was inclined to believe it had been nothing more than a belated thank you – disguised perhaps, but not necessarily out of character.

He shut the tailgate and peered into the distance, searching half-heartedly for signs of a road or a track that might lead them to the coordinates of the last canister.

With the one from the boy and with thirteen others safely in the box, why not leave the damn thing where it was, Ryder thought? Or come back for it another day in the PC-6 and risk the take-off and the landing? If they did that, maybe there'd be more time for him to discover how long lasting her new attitude was going to be, or at least find out if she was playing games with him.

'What are you looking for?' she asked.

'Nothing. I don't know where the hell we are.'

'I'll show you.' She unfolded the map. 'Look, if we carry on going south, we can use the road for a few kilometres before we have to turn back into the desert. It shouldn't take us more than half an hour.'

'OK. You drive.' Ryder took the map from her. 'I'll use the Magellan so I can yell at you when you go off course.'

'No you won't. You'll go to sleep like you did yesterday.'

'Alexei was driving yesterday. He's better at it than you are.'

164

'Really.' She slipped into the driver's seat and started the engine. 'If he's Butch Cassidy and you're Sundance, maybe you'd both be happier on horses.'

Ryder didn't answer, settling back for the next leg of their journey, welcoming the warmth from the heater as the Jeep gathered speed, travelling towards a part of the Altiplano where the temperature was likely to be even lower, and into an area more desolate than the one they'd left behind.

Isabel had underestimated. It took them over an hour – sixty-eight minutes of lurching and scraping their way around rocks and holes, through patches of deep gravel, thick dust and along old creek-beds that were as cracked and arid as the pot-holed section of the road.

Throughout it all the Cherokee was uncomplaining, spinning all four wheels on occasions, but always managing to keep going, even when Isabel made the mistake of slowing halfway across a soft patch.

She too had been uncomplaining, but now they'd stopped, Ryder could see blood seeping through the bandages around her wrists.

Before he could say anything, she got out and went round to open the tailgate.

'You should've let me drive for a while,' he said.

'Your stomach's no better than my wrists. I've seen the painkillers Alexei's been giving you.' She consulted the GPS unit. 'We're too far east. I don't think this thing works properly while we're moving.'

Ryder could feel the cold. It was already cutting through his gloves, and even with his hood up, the tips of his ears had begun to hurt. By now he was wishing Alexei had come with them. In country like this, the Russian would have been good insurance – particularly if there was the danger of them getting stuck somewhere on their way home.

Isabel had read his thoughts. 'We're not lost,' she said. 'Even if we were, Alexei wouldn't be any help.'

'He's a handy guy to have along.'

'Why did you say he could stay behind then?'

'I didn't. All I said was that you and I could handle things without him. He did more than his fair share yesterday as well as all the driving. Anyway, he had to fix that fuel leak on the plane.'

'I don't believe you. Is there something you want to say to me – something you don't want him to hear?'

'No.' Taking the Magellan from her, he set off by himself, reading the numbers on the display while he walked in a large circle until he was certain of the correct position and ready to step out the twenty-two foot offset. He used the Geiger counter now, listening to the click frequency as he swept the sensing head across the ground.

Isabel had already decided where he should be looking. 'Right in front of you,' she said.

Not really believing she was right, he went to fetch the spade and the tongs, but by the time he returned she'd kicked a shallow hole in the dust to expose the cylinder.

This one had hardly burrowed at all. It was lying on its side, no more than an inch or two beneath the surface.

Once he'd checked it for fractures and corrosion, he picked it up at arm's length with the tongs and carried it back to the Jeep where Isabel had the container open ready.

She was over-anxious, dropping the lid and trapping the tongs before he could withdraw them.

'I'll let you dig up the next one,' Ryder said.

'There isn't a next one.' Her eyes were sparkling. 'We've got them all.' Stepping aside she executed an impromptu pirouette.

In spite of her bulky clothing it had been surprisingly well done, but so incongruous that Ryder couldn't keep a straight face.

'You didn't know I'd been to ballet school, did you?' She started laughing again. 'I'm usually better than that, but my leg's stiff because of the cold.'

He'd seen her limping now and again, but hadn't thought to ask about her injury. 'We'd better get moving,' he said. 'You stick your feet up – I'll drive. Go to sleep if you want.'

'You'll never find the road without me navigating.'

'Watch me.' Ryder packed away the things, took a last look around and made a silent promise. Never again, he told himself.

If more canisters lay buried out there somewhere, they could stay buried. And if anyone ever suggested a return trip he knew what he'd tell them.

They were on the main road south, twenty-five minutes into their journey home, when a shredded front tyre gave Ryder cause to repeat his promise – this time out loud to Isabel.

But she said nothing, either because the place where he stopped to change the wheel was disconcertingly close to the mine, or perhaps because she was absorbed in her own thoughts.

The sun was low when they skirted the barren shoreline of the Laguna Colorada, and the first faint traces of sulphur began to contaminate the air.

The smell was familiar and no longer quite so unpleasant. For the last four days it had marked their safe return to the little hut where, no matter how primitive it was, there was always warmth, hot food and shelter from the wind.

On this, their final evening, although the wind was dropping, the hut was an especially welcome sight.

Nearby on the runway the PC-6 was parked ready for Alexei's departure in the morning, and smoke pouring from the hut's chimney was a sign that the Russian was already cooking dinner.

He met them at the door, waiting expectantly for good news or bad news.

'Got the bloody lot,' Ryder said. 'All fourteen of the bastards.'

'It is what I have hoped to hear.' Alexei was clearly pleased. 'So tonight I shall see if you and the little *señorita* are glowing in the dark from radioactivity.'

Isabel climbed out of the Jeep. 'There's something you ought to know,' she said. 'The next time you call me the little *señorita*, I'm going to throw all your cigarettes into that revolting toilet.'

'I apologize.' Alexei smiled at her. 'Perhaps I will be forgiven when you see what I have done.'

'I can already see. You've got on a clean sweater, you've scrubbed the oil off your hands and you've shaved. What a pity.'

'I have done wrong?'

'Isabel figured you made a pretty good Butch Cassidy,' Ryder said. 'But you've blown it.'

167

'Ah, then it is fortunate I have other skills. Please.' Alexei held open the hut door and bowed. 'The best table in the house awaits you.'

The best table in the house was the wooden bench. It was laid with three place settings, each with a knife and fork, an enamelled plate and a coloured plastic cup. At each end of the bench, candles were adding to the light from the drip-heater, creating an ambience spoilt only by the cobwebs and the odour of unburnt kerosene.

Isabel was impressed. 'Where did the candles come from" she asked.

'They are hidden on a shelf in one of the huts. But I have something better.' From behind his back Alexei produced an unopened bottle of Posolskry vodka. 'I have been saving this for such an occasion.'

It was a nice touch, Ryder thought, a reward and a great way for them to celebrate their last night together.

'Please help yourself,' Alexei said. 'For entrée there are sardines fresh from the can, and for the main course the finest beef, although you may find the flavour and texture similar to the corned beef we enjoyed for breakfast.'

Ryder was so hungry that he wouldn't have cared what he was eating. Standing beside Isabel at the bench, he munched on thick toasted sandwiches, washing down each mouthful first with bottled water and then with vodka, feeling the warmth from the alcohol spread out through his stomach to create a sense of genuine well-being.

That a failed Russian space mission had brought him from Canada to Colombia and to Bolivia was extraordinary in itself. That the Mars-96 probe could be the means to sink the PAF was even more unlikely – a proposition that until now he hadn't really believed would work. But Ryder believed it now. After a disastrous beginning that could have cost Isabel her life, the visit to the Altiplano had yielded precisely what Corrales had predicted it would yield, opening up a future that was neither unrealistic nor unattainable.

Isabel interrupted his thoughts. 'Shall we phone Uncle

Miguel?' she asked. 'We ought to tell him, don't you think?'

'Do it in the morning.' Ryder sat down on the lower bunk. 'There's a whole bunch of things we need to talk to him about.'

'No, there's not. He's already said what he wants us to do with the canisters. Once we've got them to La Paz and someone's collected them from us, our job's over. We don't have to smuggle them out of the country. Uncle Miguel's arranging all that. He's going to organize everything from now on – you know – about getting the PAF interested and the tapes and stuff.' She looked at Ryder. 'You don't trust him, do you?'

'If I didn't trust him, I wouldn't be here. You wouldn't be either.'

'Tonight you will not argue.' Alexei topped up their drinks. 'We should be thanking Señor Corrales for his foresight.'

'Yes, we should.' Isabel raised her cup. 'To my uncle.'

'And to you my little *señorita*.' Alexei smiled. '*C angelame ti morzesh zit vechno.*'

She frowned. 'Are you making fun of me?'

'It's a toast,' Ryder said. 'May you live forever in the presence of angels.'

'How do you know?'

'Alexei told me what it means. You're lucky. He only says it to people he really likes.'

'Oh.' Her frown disappeared. 'Nobody's ever made a toast to me before. It's lovely. Thank you.'

Alexei held up a packet of cigarettes. 'So you will not throw these away?'

'Not this time.' She sat down beside Ryder with her drink. 'Won't it be nice when our lives don't have to revolve around a drip-heater?'

'You might be too warm when you get home. It'll be coming up to mid-summer.'

'Mm.' She turned to Alexei. 'It'll even be warm in Moscow. Or aren't you going there?'

Alexei shook his head. 'First I must find a buyer for the PC-6 so I may pay back some of the money for it to your uncle. Then I shall return to Angola where I have unfinished business.'

'Have you got someone lined up to buy the plane?' Ryder asked.

'I believe the people I acquired it from in Buenos Aires will repurchase it if the price is right. They have two other Turbo-Porters for smuggling cocaine and heroin across the borders into Paraguay and Brazil. As I have already showed you, no other plane can operate from such short airstrips in the mountains.'

'Sell it somewhere here in Bolivia,' Isabel said. 'My uncle won't care how much you get for it. Then you can come back with us to Cali for a few days.'

Her statement came as a surprise to Ryder. This was the first time he'd heard anything about him returning to Colombia with her. Once the canisters were off his hands there was no reason for him to stay in South America, nor would she be his responsibility for much longer. Now that Santos or some other Corrales family minder had warned off Diaz, somewhere in Potosí she had a ready-made escort who could take her home. So why was she expecting him to accompany her?

She wasn't, he decided. It had been a throwaway remark – a polite way of inviting Alexei to Cali in case he was expecting her uncle to thank him personally for his help.

She was sufficiently close for Ryder to smell her skin again – the same fresh smell he remembered from their first meeting at the lake. Like her mannerisms, her body language and the shape of her mouth, the fragrance was as much a part of her as the way her eyes flashed when she was angry – details that even in such dismal surroundings were as compelling and diverting as they'd ever been.

His awareness of her was being exaggerated by their living conditions, he told himself, the closeness forced on them by circumstances. But it was more than that – an attraction that had been there from the beginning – even before the day he'd gone to visit her in hospital.

'What's the matter?' she asked.

'Nothing.'

'That's what you always say. You're thinking about tomorrow, aren't you?'

'Only about how early we need to start.'

'If we're starting early I'd better get the video camera from the Jeep.' She stood up and went to the door. I want Uncle Miguel to see what we had to put up with here.'

While she was gone Ryder took the opportunity to raise the matter of money with Alexei. 'I'll send you half of what I get from Corrales,' he said. 'It'll probably take a few months.'

The Russian shrugged. 'It is not necessary. I shall make a big profit in Angola. I ask only that you let me know when I can stop looking over my shoulder for the PAF.'

'I'll leave a message on the Luxembourg number – unless you want to try calling me in London. I'll be at Grace's flat.'

'Chris, that is a bad idea. It is easy for Ballantine and the others to trace you there.'

'I didn't mean right away. I'll find somewhere else to go first.'

'Like Colombia?' Alexei lit a cigarette.

'I don't think so. Isabel's still got those photos of my assignment in Medellín.'

'But she understands why you had to do what you did?'

'Ask her.' Ryder had no wish to discuss it. He reached for the vodka, intending to pour himself another drink, but was interrupted by Isabel's return.

She was straight-faced, and instead of bringing the camera, she was holding an infrared detector. 'Someone's out there,' she said. 'I'm sure there is.'

Ryder felt his hand tighten on the bottle. 'Did you see them?'

'No. Just a light at the end of the airstrip. It was only there for a second.'

'What kind of light?'

'I couldn't tell. It's creepy in the dark.' She gave him the detector. 'If I'm right we'll be able to pick up a heat signature, won't we?'

Alexei was swearing in Russian, loading a magazine into his M-16 while Ryder blew out the candles and turned off the drip-heater.

'What are you going to do?' She was apprehensive.

'Find out who the hell it is.' Ryder struggled into his jacket and

171

grabbed the Winchester and a handful of ammunition. 'You stay here.'

He opened the door cautiously, breathing in the cold air to clear away the effects of the vodka.

Outside, the wind had died completely, allowing a thick mist to envelop the runway. Light from the moon was being scattered by the moisture, creating a white curtain through which he could see very little until his eyes grew accustomed to the night. Even then, the Jeep and the PC-6 were no more than shadows on an airstrip that stretched away into a blur of emptiness.

For over a minute Ryder listened, hoping to hear a muffled cough or the sound of breathing.

There was nothing. The strip was as silent as the desert, and unless Isabel's imagination had got the better of her, whoever was out there was being careful to remain hidden.

Ryder loaded the Winchester with a single round, then used the imager, clamping the body of it against his rifle with one hand to keep his trigger-finger free.

The still-warm engine of the Jeep was easy to detect, and he could pick up residual heat coming from the PC-6 where Alexei had started the turbine at some point in the day.

But it wasn't images from the Jeep or the PC-6 that made his stomach churn. Floating in the centre of his screen was another much brighter halo – one that had the unmistakeable characteristics of a truck.

It was four or five hundred yards away, stationary, parked in a direct line with the airstrip.

As well as being able to recognize the heat spots from its engine and its radiator, Ryder could see a faint glow coming from the tyres and from a bonnet that had been strengthened to carry a machine-gun.

What he saw next was even more alarming. Wherever he pointed the imager there were other halos – the distinctive green smudges of other vehicles. Like an invisible pack of wolves they were grouped in a semi-circle around the runway, all concealed in the milkiness of the mist, all waiting for the signal to converge on the hut.

Ryder didn't stay to count them, nor did he waste time trying to understand how in God's name he could have ever let this happen. Still holding the imager to his eyes, he pushed open the hut door with his back and called to Isabel.

'Can you see anyone?' She came to stand beside him.

'Get your gloves and parka on. We've got people all around us. You'll have to watch. Let me know the minute any of them start moving.'

Nervously she took the imager from him.

'Don't make a sound.' Ryder said. 'And don't get rattled. They can't see you, and they don't know we're on to them.'

Inside the hut, Alexei was assembling flashlights, hand-grenades and ammunition on the bench top. 'We must deal with more than one?' he asked.

'The bastards are everywhere. Our friends from the CNPZ have got themselves some reinforcements.'

'Then Corrales cannot have attended to Diaz as he has told us. He has lied.'

'Maybe he phoned too early. Either that or there's been a monumental fuck-up.' Ryder was assessing their position. Besides being outnumbered, they were trapped, surrounded by anything up to half-a-dozen cars or trucks, one of which was armed with a machine-gun – a predicament that didn't bear thinking about.

'We shall use the plane,' Alexei said.

'Forget it. We'd never get off the ground.'

'They have guessed we have the plutonium, I think.'

'That's why the plane's no good. It's no big deal to them if they shoot it down. They'll just get the canisters out of the wreck.' Ryder pushed more cartridges into the Winchester. 'There's only one way we're getting out of this: can you rig the PC-6 to taxi by itself?'

'For a diversion?'

'It'll buy us a head start in the Jeep.'

Alexei frowned. 'But a waste of a good aircraft. Señor Corrales will not be happy.'

'Happier than he'll be with no plutonium and a niece with her head blown off. Have you got a better idea?'

173

Alexei took his time to answer. 'I shall require three or four minutes to jam the controls,' he said. 'And without a pilot I cannot guarantee how far it may travel.'

'Never mind how far. It's going to be full of holes before it reaches the end of the runway.' Ryder was thinking ahead, uncertain of the road conditions further south where he'd never been before, but beginning to believe they had an even chance of outrunning the opposition. 'Well?' he said.

The Russian smiled. 'This will be more exciting than digging up the little canisters, but there will be more danger.'

An understatement if there had ever been one, Ryder thought. 'Let's get to it then,' he said. 'Isabel can drive. You and I will have to see if we can slow the bastards down.'

'Instead of the .44 it is better you use the Kalashnikov I bring from the mine.' Alexei pointed to the hand-grenades on the bench. 'They also may be of some help to us.'

'Leave all that to me. I'll sort things out here while you set up the plane. We'll be waiting for you in the Cherokee.'

'I shall be as quick as I can. Please tell Señorita Corrales that, once we start, she must drive very fast.'

Isabel had overheard. 'To where?' She spoke without lowering the imager, still scanning the Altiplano but with hands that were shaking slightly.

'Anywhere,' Ryder said. 'Just keep on the road and head south.'

'Then what?'

'I'll figure out something.' He watched Alexei trudge off into the mist.

'Where's he going?' she asked.

'To start the PC-6. It's all we've got to buy ourselves some time.'

'Oh.' She gave him the imager. 'I can't hold it any more. My arms are hurting.'

'Did you see anything moving?'

She shook her head. 'It's the same men, isn't it?'

'Same truck.'

'Why not use the satellite phone?' She looked awkward. 'I suppose that won't help.'

'We'll be fine in the Jeep. It's fast enough to give us an edge. You go and get in. Take the Winchester with you – I'll bring the rest of our stuff.'

To minimize weight, apart from the AK-47, the ammunition and the grenades, Ryder left everything else in the hut. For the same reason he emptied the back of the Jeep, jettisoning their water containers, spare bedding, clothes and every scrap of their remaining food supplies.

'Hey.' He spoke to Isabel through her open window. 'You can do this.'

'I'm too scared to do anything.'

'Have you got the transfer case in four-wheel-drive?'

She nodded.

'OK. Now listen. Don't start the engine until I say, and don't switch on your headlights too early.'

'Do you want to put the plutonium in the front with me?' She tried to smile. 'We'd look silly if it fell out, wouldn't we?'

He relocated the container, stacking photographic equipment around it to wedge it in place while Isabel scanned the airstrip with the imager again.

With nothing left to do but wait, Ryder was getting jumpy. 'Where the hell's Alexei?' he said.

'Outside the plane. He's standing on one of the wheels. No he's not.'

No further explanation was necessary. Without warning, the silence was broken by the whine of the Porter's turbine.

The noise was startling in its intensity, building rapidly to a whistling roar that seemed to be coming from all around them.

The moment Ryder saw Alexei running towards him, he smashed out the Jeep's tail lights with his rifle, climbed in the back and instructed Isabel to start the engine.

The Russian was out of breath, glancing over his shoulder as he arrived.

'Forget the bloody plane,' Ryder shouted. 'Get in.'

Isabel had been holding the Cherokee on its brakes. She waited for Alexei to throw himself alongside Ryder then put her foot to the floor. At the same time the Porter began to taxi, the back draught from its propeller dispersing the mist and stirring up a whirlwind of surface dust.

Gathering speed, but already travelling off course, it had nearly vanished from sight when headlights from the truck came on. A second later the whole airstrip was bathed in light as other vehicles followed suit.

By now the plane was nearing what Ryder guessed was its normal take-off speed, still on the strip but veering on to the corrugations along the edge. He watched the wings start to judder, saw the muzzle flashes spit out at it and heard the chatter of a machine-gun.

Believing the Jeep was under fire, Isabel wrenched on the wheel.

'It's OK,' Ryder yelled. 'They're not shooting at us.'

'Not yet.' Bracing himself against a wheel-arch, Alexei pulled back the bolt on his rifle. 'But they have seen where we are.'

Accelerating down the strip, one of the vehicles was in pursuit. It turned on to the road 200 yards behind them to take up the chase, its lights on high beam, temporarily blinding Ryder.

'What's happening?' Isabel shouted.

His reply was drowned out by the hammering of at least a dozen automatic weapons. They were being fired at the stricken Porter, raking it from nose to tail, perforating its rudder and fuselage until half of the undercarriage started to collapse.

Ryder expected the plane to topple, but somehow it had gained sufficient speed to carry on, travelling in a long, sickening curve. The end came when a wing tip ploughed into soft ground on the eastern edge of the runway.

Still the guns kept firing, pouring round after round into the smouldering wreckage until, at last, the smoke gave way to sparks and sparks gave way to billowing orange flames.

Ryder's view of the fire was being obscured by the Cherokee's tailgate. With each bump in the road it was swinging up and down, making it impossible for him to see either the flames or the following vehicle.

He solved the problem by lying on his back and kicking out

the gas struts. There was a squealing noise of hinges tearing away, and a glimpse of the tailgate breaking free.

Without it more dust was being drawn back into the Jeep, but his sight picture was unobstructed now, allowing him to steady the AK-47 against a rear pillar.

'Wait,' Alexei grunted. 'We are gaining ground.'

The vehicle behind had swerved to avoid the tailgate, losing speed in the process. But its place had been taken by other head-lights – many more of them, some casting their beams out across the desert instead of along the road.

'They try to cut us off,' Alexei said. 'I think we must show them our teeth.'

'You take the ones on the left.' Ryder was worried about Isabel, knowing that from inside the Jeep the noise of the gunfire would scare her silly if she wasn't expecting it.

He turned to warn her, but Alexei had seen something Ryder had missed – the shape of a pick-up that had appeared from nowhere. Travelling without lights, it was fifty yards off the road, racing to intercept them.

Alexei's first burst was low. His second was not.

Death for the driver was mercifully swift. What happened to the two gunmen in the back, Ryder never knew. The pick-up flipped and rolled twice before it was swallowed up in the mist.

'Keep going,' Ryder yelled at Isabel. 'You're doing fine.'

She was working hard, switching on her lights only when she was forced to and successfully skirting the worst of the potholes she could see.

Despite her efforts, so rough was the ride that Ryder had given up trying to hold his rifle steady.

Alexei was experiencing the same difficulty. 'Chris,' he said. 'Although we are faster, they know twists and turns in the road that we do not. There will be many places where they can take short cuts.'

'Try these.' Ryder gave him a hand grenade.

'First we must slow down so they believe they are catching us.'

Of the four sets of headlights behind them, two were an imme-diate threat. Ryder concentrated his attention on them, guessing they were the lights of four-wheel-drive vehicles that could match the Jeep's performance on or off the road.

The drivers were keeping their distance, trailing by about a 120 yards, either unwilling or unable to narrow the gap.

Telling Isabel to back off the throttle, he lay down on the floor, adjusting his grip on the Kalashnikov while he experimented with the sights.

The improvement was marginal. For a fraction of a second he could hold a bead, but the mist was adding to the problem. Where it was thick, his targets were lost in a blanket of white haze, and in the few patches where visibility was better, the headlights quickly became too bright for him to look at them.

Alexei was ready with the grenades: one in each hand, and another two gripped between his thighs. 'It is good I steal these from the men at the mine,' he said. 'I shall enjoy returning them.'

Minute by minute, the chase vehicles were drawing nearer. The drivers were taking their cue from Isabel, swerving all over the road to avoid the holes she'd already bypassed or crashed over.

'What's the fuse time on the grenades?' Ryder shouted.

'We shall see.' Using his teeth, Alexei pulled the pin from one and dropped it out on to the road.

Ryder's attempt to count off the seconds was cut short by flashes of light stabbing out at him, and the dreadful noise of bullets ripping through the roof.

Praying that Isabel was still alive, he returned the fire, holding back his trigger until the grenade exploded. It went off in the centre of the road, but was too early to be effective.

Unharmed but in trouble, Isabel was sawing on the wheel, endeavouring to punch out the crazed glass of the windshield. Three bullet holes in it showed how narrowly she'd escaped, one so close to her head that Ryder couldn't imagine how it had missed her.

He used the butt of his gun to smash out the glass. 'Do what you can,' he said. 'Drive like hell.' His stomach was in knots now and he knew that if his plan had ever been any good, the last few minutes had showed how wrong he'd been. They were running out of options, running out of time and, unless he could find a way to exploit their speed advantage, in a matter of minutes they'd be running out of luck as well.

Alexei was disposing of the grenades, tossing them carelessly overboard as though they were tennis balls. Like Ryder, he'd realized they were useless unless the chasing vehicles were allowed to get dangerously close.

'We must stop them with long range shooting.' The Russian's face was expressionless. 'We cannot continue in this manner for much longer.'

Another vehicle had joined the pursuit. Ryder thought it was the truck. Its lights were smaller, riding higher, visible only now and again through the fountains of gravel being thrown up by the exploding grenades.

He sighted on it, taking a wild guess at the range, welcoming the kick of the Kalashnikov, but knowing he was fooling himself. Irrespective of how reassuring it was to squeeze off burst after burst, without results he might as well not have bothered.

The truck was still coming. And because Alexei had been equally unsuccessful, the other lights were still there too.

Ryder tried again, aiming at the flickering flashes of the machine-gun until he'd exhausted his magazine.

The machine-gunner was frighteningly accurate. The ground was erupting all around them, some of the bullets ricocheting off rocks to scream past both sides of the Jeep.

Holding his breath, Ryder waited for one to hit their fuel tank or destroy a tyre.

Alexei was less fatalistic, continuing to return the fire until he suddenly lowered his rifle. 'They are slowing,' he said. 'Their courage has deserted them.'

He was mistaken. Isabel had begun reducing speed as well.

The reason lay ahead – a quarter of a mile ahead where, through the mist, the road and the desert were being flooded by a brilliant beam of light. It was an icy blue colour, approaching at tremendous speed.

Ryder had seen enough halogen lights to know what it was and what it meant. Despairingly he loaded another clip, no longer believing there was the slimmest chance of them ever getting out of this.

'Chris, no.' Alexei pushed away the barrel of Ryder's gun. 'They have radioed for air support. We cannot fight a helicopter gunship.'

With no cards left to play, Ryder did the only thing he could do. He told Isabel to stop, hoping against hope that by handing over the plutonium he might just be able to save her life.

It was a bad decision.

So swiftly was the helicopter closing that, before the Jeep could shudder to a halt, salvos of rockets came streaking out towards them.

Chapter 12

TERRIFIED and blinded, Isabel flung open her door and was halfway out when Ryder managed to grab hold of her belt.

'Wait,' he yelled. He'd seen what she hadn't. The rockets were flashing overhead, their warheads detonating over a hundred yards to the rear of the Jeep. And the helicopter had gone. Instead of hovering in front of them, it had passed them by.

The pilot was banking, not to return, but to correct his flight-path. Ryder watched as a four-wheel-drive roadster was caught in the light, its driver trying desperately to escape. The roadster was being put into a series of slides, throwing up enough dust to conceal its position, but no match for the gunship.

Two rockets hit it simultaneously, leaving only fragments of broken metal and burning debris to show where it had once been.

By now, every vehicle was in retreat, the muzzle flashes from the guns no longer directed at the Jeep. They were pointing skywards, firing at a gunship that was hunting them down as though they were ants in a sandpit.

The pilot was relentless, using his guns to destroy two other vehicles before he broke off the chase and swung back towards the Cherokee.

For several seconds he hovered nearby, probing with the light, scouring away the dust and mist with his rotor and creating so much noise that conditions inside the Jeep became intolerable.

Ryder got out and waved, keeping his back to the gale, holding on to the door to maintain his balance.

He felt sick. The rescue – if that's what it was – had very nearly come too late. Another hundred yards, another burst from the machine-gun two or three inches closer, and there would've been no one left alive to rescue.

Alexei knew it too. He crawled out on his hands and knees and said something Ryder couldn't hear.

'What?'

The Russian spat out a mouthful of grit and tried again. 'Cavalry,' he shouted.

'Maybe.' After what had happened, Ryder was wary, not yet prepared to believe their fortunes could have improved so quickly.

He went to check on Isabel who was still in the driver's seat. She was biting her lip and had both her hands locked on the wheel.

'Switch off the ignition,' he yelled. 'We're not going anywhere.'

She stared at him but remained silent.

The gunship was moving away, its investigation completed, the beating of its rotor changing note as it landed sixty or seventy yards along the road where the surface was flatter and comparatively free of holes.

Now it was being illuminated by the Jeep's headlights, Ryder had his first good look at it. Painted in desert camouflage and equipped with rocket-launching pods, it was an Aerospatiale or a Western Gazelle – formidable enough against unarmoured, civilian trucks and pick-ups, but not against much else.

What mattered were the two markings on its fuselage. Ryder could see them clearly – the unmistakable insignias of the Bolivian Air Force.

He helped Isabel out, reassuring her because of her reluctance to accept that the danger was over.

'Suppose it isn't the air force,' she said.

'Pretty damn good imitation if it isn't.' Ryder was forcing himself to remain calm, mystified by the arrival of the helicopter, but beginning to believe he might have been wrong about their luck running out.

'The gods have been kind,' Alexei said. To offer thanks to

whatever gods he had in mind, he wrapped his arms around Isabel and lifted her high in the air. '*Moya marlenkaya dickaya-coshkar,*' he said. 'Behind the wheel you are truly a little wild-cat. '*Ti chudo, vek budu pomnet.*'

'Put her down,' Ryder said. 'We've got company.'

A man had emerged from the helicopter. He was walking unhurriedly towards them, apparently unarmed, wearing full military battledress and carrying a powerful flashlight.

Approaching Alexei first he bowed slightly. '*El Comandante de Escuadrón Ramírez,*' he said. 'Squadron Leader Ramírez. Am I addressing Mr Christopher Ryder?'

'Over here.' Ryder shook hands with him. 'Thanks for your help. We'd be in a hell of a mess if you hadn't showed up.' He introduced Isabel and Alexei, volunteering their names because it seemed pointless to do otherwise.

The squadron leader turned to Isabel, speaking formally in a pronounced American accent. 'I trust none of you are hurt.'

'I don't think we are.' Although she'd stopped biting her lip, she was still struggling to pull herself together.

'We're fine,' Ryder said. 'A bit ragged round the edges, that's all.'

'And no doubt angry at the loss of your aircraft. I'm sorry we couldn't provide the protection we should have done. My government and your producer are not going to be at all happy about this.'

Isabel was quicker than either Ryder or Alexei. 'TV producers are never happy about anything,' she said. 'How did you know about our plane?'

'I'm pleased to say that even this far west, terrorist rabble like the CNPZ don't always have things their own way. Thanks to your Mr Santos we've had the region under surveillance for the last two days.'

Ryder became uneasy. 'Have you been watching us?' he asked.

'Not at all. I've had a man stationed south of the red lake and another near the geothermal hot springs.' Ramírez switched off his light. 'My orders were to make certain no one interfered with your filming and to see if there was a chance for us to kill or capture Jorge Vargas.'

183

'Who's he?' Ryder said.

'A breakaway CNPZ guerrilla leader. According to intelligence Mr Santos has obtained, it was Vargas who attacked you during your first day on the Altiplano. I'm afraid Bolivia's acquiring a bad reputation for holding foreigners hostage. We have terrorists operating in nearly every corner of the country.'

The picture was getting clearer, but Ryder decided to tread carefully. 'Was it your men who saw what happened at the airstrip?' he said. 'Did they radio for backup?'

'They requested airborne firepower. They'd already reported an unusual number of night-time vehicle movements and been instructed to move in closer to the meteorological station. Then, of course, after I heard about the gunfire and the destruction of your aircraft, I realized we'd underestimated things.'

'So you sent a helicopter.' Isabel put on her best smile. 'Alexei thought you were the cavalry.'

Returning her smile, Ramírez reached into his pocket and produced a pair of tiny silver wings. 'Air cavalry,' he said. 'These were presented to me on my graduation from the academy in West Virginia where I received my combat training. It's also where I learned my English.' He turned to Ryder. I apologize for arriving late. We had little warning.'

'Vargas didn't have any,' Ryder said. 'With any luck you might've nailed him with one of your rockets.'

'If not, there will be other opportunities.' The squadron leader spoke into a hand-held radio before using his flashlight to inspect the interior of the Jeep. 'Is your vehicle still roadworthy?'

Isabel answered the question. 'Except for some bullet holes and no windshield,' she said.

'Good. In that case, once you and your things have been transferred to my helicopter, one of my officers will drive it back to the airbase for you.' Ramírez shone his light on the plutonium container. 'Is this your photographic equipment?'

'Just thirty-five millimetre film.' Isabel lifted the lid to reveal the rows of canisters. 'On overseas assignments like this, we have to use these special boxes to stop the negatives from getting fogged by airport metal-detectors. I'm afraid it's awfully heavy.'

'My men will treat it carefully.' Ramírez started gathering up the rifles.

'Leave the damn things where they are,' Ryder said. 'We won't be wanting them again.'

Ramírez looked awkward. 'I have orders to provide you with whatever security you require,' he said. 'My government is most anxious for an American television programme to be made here. The spin-off would benefit our tourist industry and help us earn valuable foreign currency. I can guarantee an incident of this kind will not occur again. You have my word.'

'It's OK,' Ryder said. 'We've got a fair idea of the locations we can use. We just need to get our photographic stuff home. The equipment we left at the hut isn't important.'

'It's important to me. I'll arrange for it to be collected and sent on to you.' Ramírez used his radio again, speaking in Spanish to relay a message that sounded more involved than Ryder thought it should.

Isabel was listening but she appeared to be unconcerned, placing a finger on her lips when he glanced across at her.

'My orders have been changed.' The squadron leader was pleased. 'Instead of taking you to my airbase at the sulphur springs where the accommodation is unsuitable, we'll be flying directly to Tupiza. Hotel reservations are being made there for you. Will that be satisfactory?'

'Fine,' Ryder said. 'What's special about Tupiza?'

'Mr Santos suggests it's the most convenient place for him to meet you. He's already left Potosí, but I'm not certain if he's travelling overnight by train, or whether someone's been assigned to drive him.'

Ryder had begun to think that Santos was making too many waves. The Bolivians were already uncomfortable about tonight's incident, and blowing it out of proportion could do more harm than good.

'There are flasks of hot coffee in the cockpit,' Ramírez said. 'If you'll accompany me, we'll find somewhere warm for Miss Corrales to sit down.'

Ryder hadn't appreciated how badly she was shivering. She was suffering from let-down, trying unsuccessfully to stop her teeth from chattering.

'Come on.' He put his arm round her. 'You'll be soaking in a hot bath before you know it.'

'I'm all right. I just feel a bit funny.' She let him help her, walking along unsteadily beside him. 'I shouldn't have drunk all that vodka. Is Alexei bringing the container?'

'It is not necessary.' The Russian had caught up with them. 'If you look, you will see men are already coming. They will collect our cameras and the box.' He bent down to speak more confidentially. 'It was clever to show the canisters to the squadron leader.'

She shook her head. 'It's Santos who's been clever. I never thought we'd need a cover story, but it's worked out really well for us, hasn't it?'

'About time something did.' Ryder smiled at her. 'Sorry I screwed up.'

'You didn't. How were you supposed to know the CNPZ would attack us again?'

'Someone knew. If Diaz didn't organize it, who did?'

'It doesn't matter now. Ask Santos; he might have some idea.' Disengaging herself from his arm, she walked on alone to the helicopter's hatch.

'She does not understand how lucky we have been.' Alexei stopped to peer back over his shoulder. 'You and I know that in this business there can never be certainty. But, unlike us, she is learning to rely on the influence of her family and expects to live forever. It is a dangerous lesson for a young woman.'

Alexei had got it wrong, Ryder thought. Isabel wasn't here to learn. She'd been sent to unlearn, and, in this particular instance, if her uncle hadn't despatched Santos to Bolivia, by now there was every chance they'd all be dead.

He took a last look around what little he could see of the Altiplano, the moonlit, mist-shrouded high desert where, for much of the time, he'd felt no lonelier than he'd felt anywhere else – a part of the world best left to itself – unfriendly to the point of being hostile; windswept, cold, desolate and unchanging, but utterly unforgettable.

So where to now, he wondered. Did it matter? If this place was so unforgettable, but apparently no more lonely than any other place, why the hell bother about where he was going next?

Ryder was in no hurry to get up. The bed was warm, comfortable and, after the squalid conditions at the hut, extravagantly luxurious. The whole room was luxurious. Better still, as he'd discovered late last night, Tupiza itself lay in what was regarded as the heart of Cassidy and Sundance territory.

Because of the town's location, and because word of the American TV crew had evidently reached the hotel before their arrival, they'd been greeted effusively by the manager, shown to the best rooms the Residencial Palmira had to offer and provided with electric razors, hot towels, and fresh clothes – although finding things to fit Alexei had caused some temporary consternation amongst the staff.

This morning, Ryder was less concerned about the exploitation of their cover story. If the Bolivian government wanted to make amends for an unprovoked terrorist attack on innocent Americans, then so they damn well should do. And if the efficient squadron leader had managed to slow down the CNPZ for a while, that was as helpful to the local authorities as it was a useful means of safeguarding the plutonium.

He remained in his bed for a few minutes longer, going over the events of last night in his mind before deciding that he should find out if Isabel was willing to travel home with Santos as her escort.

If she wasn't, hard bloody luck, Ryder thought. Alexei had better things to do with his time, and so did he – even if he wasn't yet sure what they were.

He'd finished dressing and was about to go down for breakfast when someone knocked gently on the door.

It was Isabel, dressed in black, bootcut jeans, a red belt and a tight-fitting, cream-coloured sweater. She was also wearing make-up, giving Ryder the impression that this was more than a casual wake-up call.

'Hi.' She remained standing in the passageway. 'Are you going to ask me in?'

'Depends who you are.'

Wrinkling her nose at him, she pushed past and held out her arms to display her clothes. 'What do you think?'

'Do I get my parka back now?'

'I've thrown it away. Have you just woken up?'

'I'd forgotten what it's like to sleep in a decent bed.' Ryder closed the door. 'Have you had breakfast yet?'

'I had it with Santos. He arrived about an hour ago. That's why I'm here. I have to ask you something before you see him.'

'About what?'

She sat on the edge of the bed. 'Alexei's hoping you'll go with him back to Angola, isn't he?'

'I've already turned him down.'

'Because you're going somewhere else?'

'Yep.'

'Like where?'

'I haven't decided. Greek islands, the Caribbean – some place I haven't been before. Somewhere warm.'

'It's warm in Cali. You're the one who reminded me.'

'I've already been there.' Although Ryder knew what was coming, he wasn't going to make it any easier for her to say what she wanted to say. 'You don't need me to hold your hand anymore,' he said. 'If you're not straightened out by now, you're never going to be.'

'That's not what I meant.' She studied the carpet. 'If you don't come with me to Colombia, how will you get your ten per cent from my uncle?'

'I don't expect to get paid until he's sold the plutonium. And that's going to take a while, seeing as how the PAF don't even know about the stuff yet.'

'Don't you remember I'm supposed to take you on a guided tour of Popayán? We were too busy before. There are other places to go as well.'

Ryder was tiring of her game. 'Look,' he said, 'you and I have started getting on pretty well, but you're not ever going to get past the fact that I killed your father, are you?'

'It's a stupid question. That's like me asking if you'll ever be able to forget what happened to your sister.'

'I didn't say forget. I said get past. There's a difference. Why would you and I want to spend more time together?'

'If that's how you think, I can't answer your question.'

Ryder wished he hadn't asked it to begin with. She'd become defensive again, and it was fairly obvious that her reason for inviting him back to Cali wasn't the right one. 'I'd better find Santos to say hello,' he said.

'So you can hand me over?'

'So I can hand over the canisters. They're worth more than you are.'

'How would you know how much I'm worth? Those men who kidnapped me had more idea than you do.'

Ryder ignored the remark. 'Is he downstairs?'

'He's with Alexei. Alexei won't leave his room because the plutonium's there. He's playing guard dog.'

'I'll go and let him off his chain. Do you want to stay here?'

'No.' She left the bed and went to the open door. 'If I stay here how are you going to get rid of me?'

Ryder propelled her out into the passageway. 'Don't mention anything about me not going to Africa,' he said. 'It's nothing to do with you.'

There was no need to hand over the plutonium. Santos had already taken charge of it. He was seated at a table in Alexei's room, busy wrapping layers of adhesive tape around the container.

'Ah, Mr Ryder.' He nodded his greeting, but continued working. 'I am pleased we meet again. Señor Corrales has asked me to give you his best regards.'

Ryder had forgotten how small Santos was. The Colombian was half Alexei's height, and almost as slightly built as Isabel.

'Why the tape?' Ryder enquired.

'On Bolivian trains there are sometimes young children who are trained as pickpockets. After all your trouble, we must not lose any of the canisters.'

'Do you figure it's too risky to go by plane?' At one point Ryder had been considering it.

'In these circumstances Señor Corrales thinks air travel would be inadvisable. There is good security at Bolivian airports. There are x-ray machines even for internal commercial flights. By train we avoid these difficulties.'

'What happens when you get to La Paz?'

Santos smiled. 'Arrangements have been made for a private jet which will fly us directly to Colombia. In my own country, air-ports and customs are not a problem.' He withdrew an envelope from his pocket. 'Squadron Leader Ramírez was kind enough to make flight reservations for us, but I have explained how we pre-fer the train in case there is good scenery for you to film on the way.'

'So he's bought us train tickets instead?' Isabel said.

'Yes. To repay his generosity I have said the military are wel-come to keep the Jeep with its bullet holes. He is most grateful.' Santos removed four tickets from the envelope. 'These are for first class travel on either the *Tren bala* or the *Tren especial* from Tupiza to La Paz.'

'You can give two of those back,' Ryder said. 'Alexei and I aren't going with you. We'll be picking up flights out of Tarija.'

'I see.' Santos glanced at Isabel across the table. 'It is not what Señorita Corrales has told me. She assured me you would both be coming with us.'

'When did she do that?'

'This morning – after she has seen the fax from her uncle and I explained to her how there may still be some small chance of danger.'

'Danger from Diaz?'

'No, no. It is not possible. But perhaps from a man called Vargas if he is still alive.'

'Let's go back a step,' Ryder said. 'What do you know about Vargas?'

'He is the cousin of Diaz. In the Cordillera mountains he acts for the Nestor Paz Zamora Commission. It is an anti-government rebel group.'

'Who told you?'

'Diaz.'

'He just happened to mention it, did he?'

Santos spread his hands. 'Unless I had extracted this information from him, I could not have enlisted the assistance of the Bolivian authorities.'

So far, apart from learning that the reason for Isabel's early morning visit had been more complicated than he'd thought, Ryder had heard nothing he hadn't expected to hear. 'What else did you get out of Diaz?' he asked.

'He explains how his cousin keeps watch on you in the desert and speaks of a buyer he has found for the plutonium – a man named Markovic who deals with the government in Libya. I have already discussed this with Alexei.'

The Russian took the opportunity to join the conversation. 'Chris,' he said, 'perhaps it is this Markovic who pays the CNPZ to attack us last night.'

'Why him? Vargas and his friends could've decided to have another go themselves. Either that or Diaz gave them some extra money.'

'No.' Alexei shook his head. 'The CNPZ would not act alone. Without the right business connections, no terrorist group can hope to sell plutonium on the world market. And it was not Diaz. I promise you he could not have been involved in any way.'

Alexei's subtlety had failed. Before he'd finished explaining, Isabel had turned furiously on Santos.

'You're worse than an animal,' she said. 'Diaz worked for my uncle for nearly seven years.'

'For which he was paid more than he deserved.' Santos was unmoved. 'Had he not betrayed the trust of your family he would still be alive today.'

'Were you told to kill him?'

'You know very well that Señor Corrales would never issue an instruction of that kind. I was simply doing what was necessary to protect Señor Ryder, Señor Volodya and yourself. If I have somehow caused offence, you must accept my apologies.'

'Don't you dare tell me what to accept. You're a murderer.'

191

She spat in his face, swung round and left the room, using all her strength to slam the door behind her.

Santos wiped his cheek with a handkerchief. 'She does not like me,' he said. 'This has happened before.'

Ryder wasn't surprised. She'd done much the same thing to him in Canada, and although she was being more than usually unreasonable, it was a nice change to see someone else on the receiving end of her temper.

'What's in the fax from Corrales,' he asked.

'I have it here. He sends it to you, but I think it does not matter that the *señorita* made me show it to her first.' Santos slipped a sheet of paper out of the envelope. 'It comes because of my telephone conversation with him. Perhaps it will change your mind.'

The fax was handwritten, short and to the point:

Dear Mr Ryder
Although I am, of course, delighted with your success, I cannot help but feel responsible for the problems you have encountered.

To avoid further difficulties during phase two of our project, I believe it is essential for us to discuss The Foundation in rather more detail than we have done to date.

Accordingly, so that we may together develop a strategy, I hope you and Mr Volodya will accept this invitation to be guests at my home.

It goes without saying that I will also feel more comfortable knowing that Isabel is in your care during her return journey to Cali.
Sincerely yours
Miguel Corrales

Ryder handed the fax to Alexei. 'This is the second invitation I've had in half an hour,' he said. 'How do you feel about lying in the sun for a couple of days?'

'There is sun in Africa.'

'But no Las Caleñas – the most beautiful women in Colombia. The streets are full of them. Ask Isabel.'

'At present it is too dangerous to ask her anything.' Alexei grinned. 'I think there is little information we can give her uncle, but if you must extend your fishing trip for a short while, I shall go with you. If I do not, who else will prevent you from acting unwisely?'

The whole damn exercise had been a fishing trip, Ryder thought. He'd known that from the beginning. So who cared if there was nothing at the end of it, and why stop acting unwisely now?

Chapter 13

MARKOVIC saw the waitress coming. She was hurrying across the restaurant, pointing towards the lobby and repeating the word telephone.

'OK. Thanks.' He stopped pouring milk on his cereal. 'I understand.'

Because he'd been expecting to receive the call last night, he had a feeling that perhaps things were not going to plan. On the other hand, late news was better than no news, and there was no reason to assume anything had gone wrong.

Leaving the table, he made his way to reception where a woman at the desk smiled her good morning to him and handed over the phone.

He spoke guardedly into the receiver, making sure it was Vargas before giving his own name and asking for a progress report.

'There has been a big problem,' Vargas said. 'We are attacked in the dark by guns and rockets from a helicopter. Nine of my men are killed, and my truck and many cars have been destroyed.'

Markovic was more annoyed than surprised. 'How did Ryder get hold of a helicopter?' he asked.

'Not Ryder. I think he radios for help from the military airbase at the sulphur springs.'

'I didn't pay you two thousand dollars for a fuck up,' Markovic said.

'What I have not spent to pay my men I shall return to you.'

The offer was so improbable that Markovic didn't bother to pursue it. 'What's happened to the material?' he asked.

'I do not know. But I have other information. There is a boy with the name of Agudelo who works for me. Did Diaz speak of him?'

'No.'

'It is he who finds the first capsule in the desert. When the Englishman and the girl come here, they pay the boy to show them where they should go.'

Markovic had no idea where this was heading. 'What about it?' he said.

'The boy learns that if anyone asks what the man and the girl are doing, he is to explain they are from an American company who wishes to make television programmes in Bolivia. Do you understand?'

'No.' Markovic controlled his impatience. 'Are you saying the boy knows where these people are now?'

'He has no further knowledge. But if you read page four of the Potosí newspaper this morning, you will, I think, be able to narrow your search for them.'

'Really?' Doubting that information in a local paper could be of any value, Markovic decided it was time to cut his losses. 'Is that all you can tell me?' he said. 'Is that the best you can do?'

'I am sorry it is not more. I had hoped we would together make much money from the sale of the capsules, but the costs are too great. You must remember how my cousin has already died because of them.'

Markovic had lost interest. He told Vargas to send the refund to the hotel and hung up, still annoyed, realizing he'd been stupid to rely on some idiot terrorist who, in his haste to get his hands on the plutonium, had probably tortured and killed his own cousin. It was a lesson, Markovic thought, another example of why it was always advisable to work alone.

He collected a copy of the morning paper from the front desk and went back to the restaurant to finish his breakfast, ordering a fresh bowl of cornflakes before he began looking for the article on page four.

As a result of his stay in Colombia and of his more recent visit to Bolivia, Markovic's Spanish had improved considerably. In both Cali and Potosí, once he'd been able to find his way around and discovered that a mixture of Spanish and English was a useful combination, he'd rarely been caught out in everyday conversation. Reading, though, was less straightforward, and this morning he was anxious to avoid any misinterpretation.

Attracting the attention of one of the younger waitresses, he handed her the folded paper together with a one-hundred-boliviano notc. 'Could you translate something for me?' he asked. 'You speak English, don't you?'

'I have learned it.' She quickly concealed the note. 'What part should I read?'

'There.' He showed her the column near the top of the page. 'Do you mind?'

'It is my pleasure.'

'Sit down.' Markovic pulled out a chair for her.

'It is not permitted.' She smiled awkwardly. 'The restaurant manager will be angry with me.'

But for her exceptionally good English, Markovic would have selected a more attractive waitress. This one was either too young for her body to have developed properly, or she was never going to have breasts at all. Except for her hair, she was not unlike a girl he'd found one night in Rotterdam about a year ago – an underage, flat-chested little bitch with long, slender legs who'd fucked as though every time was going to be her last. He'd spent two days playing with her before ending it, exploring every pore of her body, teasing and stroking hour after hour until he'd been no more able to control her than she'd been able to control herself.

'You have need for the headline?' the waitress asked.

'I'm sorry.' Markovic made the effort to concentrate. 'Please. Read the whole thing.'

She cleared her throat, speaking slowly to begin with. 'It says Air Force clashes with CNPZ near Salar de Chalviri.' She looked at him. 'I am not certain of the word clash. It is like fight.'

197

'Just carry on,' Markovic said.

'I read the smaller print to you now.' She seemed more confident.

'Members of a United States television company were last night confronted by armed terrorists at a meteorological station south of the Laguna Colorada. It is believed a Swiss-built, Pilatus PC-6 Turbo-Porter aircraft was destroyed, and reports have been received of damage to a four-wheel-drive vehicle in which the two men and a woman made their escape unharmed.

It is rumoured that the attack was led by Jorge Vargas, nephew of Señor Castaño Diaz whose body was found at his home in Potosí two days ago. A connection between the two events has yet to be established.

Thanks to swift action by the crew of an Air Force helicopter, several CNPZ vehicles were disabled, and a number of bodies have been recovered from the high desert where the attack took place. It is not known if Vargas is among the dead.'

The waitress gave the paper back to Markovic. 'These Americans are your friends?' she asked.

'No. I'm a journalist. I work mostly out of Chicago, but I've got business interests down here. I just thought there might be a follow up story in this somewhere.'

'I am sorry I cannot be of more help.' She smiled again. 'If my manager asks, you will please say my English is good.'

'I'll do that.' Markovic wasn't listening.

'My grandfather teaches me. He comes here from Australia many years ago to work in the silver mines.'

The last thing Markovic wanted to hear about was her wretched grandfather. He wanted her to go away – now, before she became more of a nuisance than she was already.

When she opened her mouth again, he stood up from the table, brushing her aside and only half-hearing what she was saying as he left the room.

In the lobby, the same woman was behind the desk, surreptitiously drinking a cup of coffee.

Markovic showed her the newspaper article. 'I'd like to speak to someone who knows about this.' He gave her the last of his one-hundred-boliviano notes. 'If you can get hold of the right person I'd be grateful if you'd transfer the call to my room.'

'I will try.' She opened her phone directory. 'Is it permissible to give them your name?'

'I'll do that. You just say it's important.' Markovic had reservations about how successful this was going to be. He had similar reservations about placing phone calls which could be traced back to him at the hotel, although with any luck he'd be checking out before this evening. Luck was going to play a minor part, he decided. Success would depend more on whether or not the air force was eager for positive media exposure.

The answer was not long in coming. He'd been back in his room for less than ten minutes when the phone rang.

Markovic waited for a moment before he picked up the receiver. 'This is Chuck Jackson,' he said. 'Who am I talking to?'

'I'm Squadron-Leader Ramírez. I believe you have some questions.'

'Good morning to you.' Markovic adjusted his voice, employing a not altogether convincing American accent. 'Look, I'm real sorry to disturb you. I work for one of the big Press agencies in the United States. I've just read a piece about American nationals being attacked by a bunch of shit-heads somewhere down south, so I figured a couple of West Coast US dailies might run an inside story if I can get one.'

'Where are you calling from, Mr Jackson?' Ramírez sounded guarded.

'I'm in Potosí, but I can meet you anyplace. I'd kinda like pictures of the plane wreck and maybe of the guys who were flying your chopper. I can pump up their side of things a bit – you know – unless you rather I didn't.'

'It's a long way for you to come,' Ramírez said. 'I'm speaking to you from Tupiza. And, as far as I know, there's little left of the plane to photograph.'

'But you're the guy I need to contact, right?'

'I commanded the operation.'

199

'No shit? Hey, that's great.' Markovic kept his voice level. 'Listen, I've got a rental car. If I leave right away, I can be in Tupiza late this afternoon. I've been hoping to get hold of these TV people, but if I can't find them it doesn't matter now. Your story's going to make better copy.'

'They're here in Tupiza,' Ramírez said. 'Unfortunately that's not going to help you much. They'll be leaving for La Paz at three o'clock.'

'Tell you what – see if they'll catch a later flight. Say I'll be there by four.'

'I'm afraid they're going by train. There's no air service to or from Tupiza. I'm sorry.'

'Jesus. Wouldn't you know it? I trip over something like this and half of it goes down the goddamn toilet.' Sensing that Ramírez had lost some of his suspicion, Markovic waited.

'Perhaps not all is lost,' Ramírez said. 'I believe the train stops for a short while in Uyuni. Why not travel there and see if you can interview them at the station?'

'Hey, you're a genius. Do you know that?'

'You'll have to ask someone what time it gets in, but it should be around six, I think.'

Having learned far more than he'd hoped to learn, Markovic resisted the temptation to end the conversation early. 'OK,' he said. 'Here's the deal. I'll say my hello to these people tonight, then drive down to see you first thing tomorrow morning. I'll take you out to lunch. How do I find you?'

He paid no attention to the address Ramírez gave him, waiting for an appropriate moment to assure the squadron leader that he was looking forward to their meeting before he said goodbye and hung up.

Things had turned out remarkably well after all, Markovic thought. In the end, the failure of Vargas and his men had actually proved to be advantageous, not only eliminating the need to involve a group of incompetent revolutionists, but creating a new and very much better opportunity.

Encouraged by events, he used the phone again, asking for a railway timetable to be delivered to his room before he set about making his plans for the day.

By lunchtime they were all but complete. He had memorized the route which the train would take from Uyuni, made arrangements to ship a cargo of valuable items across the border into Peru and considered several different means of satisfying his contract with the PAF directors.

Only two small matters continued to nag at his mind – how had the plutonium arrived in Bolivia to begin with, and if Vargas hadn't killed Diaz, then who had?

Because there seemed to be no simple answer to either question, he shelved them temporarily, concentrating instead on his preparations for this afternoon and for tonight.

As a first step, after retrieving his Beretta from the bathroom cistern, he stripped and cleaned the gun, lubricating each component, not with oil which could become sticky at low temperatures, but with teflon spray, reassembling the parts with great care and working an entire clip of cartridges through the action to remove any residue.

He was equally fastidious with his knife, checking to make certain the spring and the blade release button were free of dirt or grit.

The camera, though, required no such attention. He'd bought it new before leaving Cali, a cheap Polaroid that for too long had remained unused in its box – a reminder of how many weeks it had taken to reach this point in his project.

Still, Markovic thought, with so much more at stake, setbacks and complications were bound to arise. At least things were coming together nicely now. In a few short hours, the plutonium would be delivered to him, and an hour after that, either on the train, or in the comfort of a hotel bedroom somewhere, he'd be enjoying the pretty Colombian girl in ways she could never have imagined – a change of fortune for him and for her, and proof of how quickly bad news could become good news.

In the London headquarters of the PAF, only part of the news was good. The best of it had come in a hand-delivered letter that had arrived in Ballantine's office an hour ago – a brief note from the

201

Principality of Monaco to say that, from mid-August to mid-September of this year, the luxury, twelve-berth motor-yacht *Valencia* had been reserved for the exclusive use of the PAF directors, their families and their friends. As usual, the letter confirmed that, in recognition of the Peace Aid Foundation's important international work, the Principality would be pleased to provide both yacht and crew at no cost.

More good news was contained in the larger of the two reports on Ballantine's desk. Embossed with the letters PAF at the top, and with the initials of James Latimer at the bottom, it gave the names of those dignitaries from the UN and from UNICEF who had already agreed to speak at the PAF's autumn fund-raising dinner in Geneva.

There were the names of other people, too; influential US politicians, a few Hollywood celebrities who, in the scramble for self-promotion, had suddenly become concerned at the plight of third world countries, and a list of US business leaders who hoped commitments would allow them to attend.

The last page of Latimer's report gave an estimate of how much money the PAF might raise from individual US sources.

Even Ballantine should have been impressed by the figure. Instead, because of the second report, he'd hardly given it a thought.

This one was from Poitou. Although little more than a collection of photocopied documents, so disturbing was the information in it that Ballantine had spent the entire morning trying to decide how best to distance himself from the implications.

Because the matter required immediate attention, he elected to forego lunch, asking his secretary to hold all calls before he started reading through the documents again.

They were universally damning, providing a snapshot of someone far removed from the detached professional that Markovic had claimed to be.

The first sheet was the most shocking of them all, dated only a month ago and printed under the imposing seal of the International War Crimes Tribunal in The Hague:

CONFIRMATION OF INDICTMENT

Form.. WCT.3/48Z

First Name: Haxhi   **Last Name:** Markovic

Place and Date of Birth: Raska, Serbia. 1981   **Sex:** M

Other Names: Murat Noic. James Jefferson. Djuro Tafili.

Weight: 75–80kgs (probable)   **Blood Type:** O

Height: 180cms (witness estimate)   **Colour of Eyes:** Grey(?)

Colour of Hair: Varies   **Dentition:** No records

Distinguishing Features: Partially descended left testicle/monorchid (unconfirmed).

Summary of Charges: Genocide.

Breaches of the 1949 Geneva Convention.

Violation of the laws and customs of war.

Ethnic cleansing.

Crimes against humanity.

Formal Evidence Submitted By:

- UN Commission on Yugoslav War Crimes – File 393.1 (c)
- Chief Prosecutor for the International Criminal Tribunal for the former Yugoslavia – Microfiche 211/3
- Office of the European Union (Ms Mihrije Imeraj, Paris)
- NATO (Commander R.F. Court, Brussels)

Written Eyewitness Affidavits: All names withheld. Four adults, one child aged five.

Additional Information: Markovic is wanted by civilian and military authorities in the following countries: Kosovo, Holland, Albania, Spain and Turkey.

Criminal charges include: sexual violation, torture, mutilation and murder, The subject is believed to be responsible for political assassinations in both France and Algeria where arrest warrants are in force. Photographs and photocomposites can be transmitted electronically on request together with DNA test results obtained from skin, hair, saliva and semen samples.

Markovic is a deviant sexual predator who is known to be active in a number of countries. The subject's present whereabouts is unclear. Information leading to his apprehension should be forwarded immediately to this office for the attention of Ms Louise Dykstra.

Other documents in the report provided similar if less comprehensive descriptions of a man whom Ballantine was wishing fervently he'd never heard of, let alone met.

That Markovic had been here in the London office was worrying enough; for him to be currently working in Colombia as an employee of the PAF was nothing short of alarming.

To contain an already dangerous situation, after considering his options, Ballantine made the decision to act unilaterally. For the next hour he remained at his desk, placing discreet phone calls to unlisted numbers, issuing instructions to his secretary, shredding documents and sending faxes to both Poitou and Latimer, informing them of what had been done and why it had been necessary to do it.

By three o'clock he was feeling less threatened. The telephone number in Bonn no longer existed and had, in fact, never existed. All records of it were gone. The taped messages were also gone, as was evidence of Markovic's bank account in Zurich.

The exercise had been time-consuming and exhausting. But it had been extraordinarily thorough – a cleansing operation of which, had he known about it, Markovic himself could have been quite proud.

Chapter 14

RYDER should have known the train trip would be an anti-climax. At the start, because of the extraordinary scenery around Tupiza, the journey had been interesting enough, taking them through countryside that was unlike anything he'd seen before – a southern hemisphere version of the old American West that no camera could hope to capture.

Set in a valley formed by the rugged Cordillera de Chichas, Tupiza was surrounded by an amazing landscape of cactus forests, mountains, hillsides, rainbow-coloured mesas and canyons. There were pinnacles, deep gorges, rock spires and dry washes, all predominantly red, but flecked with cream, green, blue and even violet.

The contrast with the flatness and drained-out colour of the Altiplano could hardly have been more striking, but spectacular though it was, Ryder's appreciation of what he saw had been dulled by the prospect of the long haul to La Paz. In the age of air travel, he'd forgotten how slowly miles could drift by, and how easy it was to wish them away instead of enjoying the unfolding landscape for its own sake.

The sense of slowness was being exaggerated partly by the ongoing tension between Isabel and Santos, but also because the train had provided him with the opportunity to once again question the wisdom of what he was doing.

The train itself was more comfortable than he'd expected it to be, consisting of two air-conditioned but almost empty first-class Pullman-type carriages, a dining-car and seven second-class carriages that were so crammed with adults, children, chickens, sheep and goats that passengers were forced to get out at each stop to stretch their legs before resuming their journey.

At both Oru Ingenio and at Atocha, Alexei had disembarked as well, returning empty-handed after fruitless searches for American cigarettes and for something more palatable than the suspect vodka he'd obtained from a helpful attendant in the dining-car.

Only Santos seemed unconcerned by their rate of progress. Insensitive to the changing scenery, he'd spent the journey in contemplation, his feet resting on the plutonium container and with his eyes half-closed. For the last hour, since making the mistake of arguing with Isabel, he'd said nothing at all, sitting facing her in the compartment, but refusing to be drawn into conversation, apparently content to keep his peace.

From past experience, Ryder knew it was the best strategy, although he doubted that even Santos could maintain his silence for the whole way to La Paz.

To ease the disagreeable atmosphere he left his seat and went out into the corridor, guessing that Isabel would follow him.

She did, shutting the door behind her and coming to stand beside him at the window. 'Let-down,' she said. 'Or are you bored?'

'Neither. I figured you and I ought to have a talk about Santos.'

'Oh.' She stuck her hands in the pockets of her jeans. 'I don't want to talk about him.'

'You're being unreasonable,' Ryder said. 'Stop waiting for him to say something so you can shoot him down.'

'He came to Bolivia to murder Diaz. He wanted to do it.'

'That's crap. Who do you think sent those men who tried to rape you?'

'Diaz wouldn't have told them to do that. It was their idea.'

'Sure. Just like it was their idea to visit us at the airstrip. If Santos hadn't been around, you wouldn't be going home now. You'd be dead. He was just doing his job.'

'So it's all right if someone has a job that involves killing people?' She looked at him. 'I suppose you'd know all about that.'

'Canada,' Ryder said. 'Lake Lesage. I don't remember you being too hung up about what you were doing there.'

'That's not fair. I didn't know what I was doing. How could I when my uncle and aunt hadn't told me the truth?'

'You don't judge people by what they know or what they don't know. You judge them by what they do at the time.'

'So because I tried to shoot you I'm no better than Santos. Is that what you're saying?'

'I'm saying you don't have to keep on at him. We've got a long way to go.'

'And we all have to sit together in a tiny train compartment. What a shame.' She turned to go. 'I'm sorry I'm annoying you.'

Ryder spun her round. 'Listen,' he said, 'it's Santos you're trying to annoy. Leave him alone. I'm on this train because your uncle's asked me back to Cali, not to be some kind of referee.'

'I asked you back to Cali too. But you turned me down. I wonder what that means.'

'No one's counting points,' Ryder said. 'You're playing by yourself.'

'If this is a game to you, why would you care what I say to Santos?' She paused. 'I thought you and I were supposed to be getting on well together.'

'We are.' He grinned. 'It's just that you're hard work sometimes.'

'It's not me; it's you. You're so busy building fences round yourself that you've forgotten what they're for.'

If she was right, for her and only for her, Ryder would have torn them down. But she'd never complained before, and unless he'd misunderstood, she was only complaining now to justify the stand she was taking.

'You haven't the faintest idea what I'm talking about, have you?' she said. 'Nothing's changed. You don't believe I'm any more straightened out than I ever was. You think I'm the same poor little rich girl you met in Québec, don't you?'

'No. If I had to go back out on to the Altiplano on a dark night, I'd rather have you with me than anyone else.'

'Except Alexei.'

'He wouldn't go again – not without a real good reason.'

'What about the three canisters that are still lying around there somewhere? Wouldn't they be a good reason?'

'Not for Alexei. If Vargas can find them he can have them. They'll buy the CNPZ a fleet of new trucks and some nice shoulder-held anti-aircraft missiles. All they have to do is phone their order through to the PAF. I should've given Vargas the number.'

'He's probably dead,' she said.

'What if he is? South America isn't short of people like him. You know that. There are more of them in Colombia than there are here.'

'I don't see why we're talking about this.' She took his arm. 'Do you want to go to the restaurant car with me?'

'Not without Alexei. He'll start feeling neglected. You go on.'

'Oh.' Her expression changed. 'All right then.' She walked off, only just managing to keep her balance as the train swayed and rattled over another level crossing.

Alexei was showing few signs of neglect. He was engaged in an earnest conversation, thumping the seat with his hand to support the argument he was having with the Colombian.

'Ah, Mr Ryder.' Santos removed his feet from the container. 'I have recently learned of a wonderful village in Russia where all the women are virgins, but I do not believe it.'

Ryder grinned. 'Don't believe anything he tells you. There aren't any virgins anywhere in Russia. Look, are you happy staying here with our cargo for a while? Do you mind if Alexei and I go for some coffee?'

'I shall stay. It will be good for my friend to fill himself with caffeine.'

Alexei stood up and stretched. 'I will bring back a drink for you.' Following Ryder from the compartment he paused outside in the corridor to light a cigarette. 'Where is the *señorita?*' he asked.

'In the restaurant. She gets scratchy if she spends too long with Santos.'

'I have much in common with him. He has worked in many of the places I have been.'

'He's pretty tough for a little guy,' Ryder said.

'I think it is Señor Corrales who is the hard man. He pays Santos, does he not?'

'You haven't met Corrales yet. He's OK.'

'Chris' – Alexei drew deeply on his cigarette – 'there is something I must say to you. I have said it before, and I know you do not wish to hear it, but you must listen to me.'

'Don't bother,' Ryder said. 'I haven't forgotten.'

'Yes, you have. I am certain there is not a man who could walk away from Señorita Isabel without wondering what she would be like in bed. I have sensed this in myself, I sense it in others, and every day I see it in your eyes, but there will always be too much between you. If you must make love to her, then do it soon. If you do not, I fear these weeks you have spent in her company will occupy your mind forever.'

'Is that it?' Ryder said. 'Have you finished?'

'I am sorry for the lecture.' Alexei smiled. 'I am also sorry for making you angry. If she was not so pretty, things would have been easier for you.'

Ryder couldn't remember the last time anything had been easy. 'Come on,' he said. 'She'll be wondering where we are. You can try your theory out on her.'

Isabel had chosen a table at the far end of the dining-car where the windows were free of condensation and the smell of cooking from the galley was less intrusive. In front of her, three cups of coffee stood beside a pile of magazines and a bowl of *chuño*, freeze-dried potatoes.

She waited for Ryder to sit down before repositioning the coffee cups and handing round the bowl. 'It's not long before we stop again,' she said. 'I asked someone.'

'We're still not going to get in to Oruro before midnight.' He looked out of the window. 'So much for the *Tren especial*. At this rate it's going to take us all bloody night to reach La Paz.'

'You shouldn't be in such a rush to get everywhere.' Isabel was amused. 'This is a really fast train. There's another one called the *Tren rápido* that stops at every single station. It's worse than being on a tram.'

He didn't answer, gazing out at a depressingly familiar vista of darkening desert. Without him realizing it, they had all but reached the centre of the Altiplano – the bleak, otherworldly town of Uyuni where they'd spent the night at the Hotel Avienda before picking up the Agudelo boy on the following morning.

After everything that had happened, it was hard to believe they'd come full circle, but not so hard to recall Isabel's confession at the little restaurant in the Plaza Arce where, for the first time, she'd acknowledged her father's guilt and admitted that she felt she was being punished for it – precisely what Alexei had been trying to say, Ryder thought, how everyone's future was shaped by their past, and why the trip had so far solved none of' the problems he'd hoped it might solve.

Already the train had begun to slow, the clack of the wheels neither as rhythmic nor quite so sleep-inducing as it had been, and the dining-car no longer swaying from side to side when they passed over bridges and the increasingly frequent number of intersecting tracks.

Outside, it was completely dark now, and all Ryder could see through the window were the occasional lights of cars or distant houses. It was just as well, he decided. For the moment he didn't want any more reminders of this cold, unfriendly place, and it was better to look forwards to the warmer days in Cali where the ends of another circle would finally be brought together.

He finished his coffee, wondering whether a refill would help counteract his tiredness. Alexei was equally weary, only half-heartedly attempting to keep awake, leaning back in his seat, his eyelids drooping, the same unlit cigarette in his hand that had been there for the last five minutes.

Isabel disturbed him by removing it from his fingers.

'I apologize.' He sat up straighter. 'We are there?'

'Pretty soon,' Ryder said.

'Then, before I see if there is a shop at the station that sells something better than horse dung to smoke, I shall take refreshments to Señor Santos. It is bad manners to sit here sleeping while he has only himself to talk to.'

'He's used to it,' Isabel said. 'No one at home talks to him apart from Uncle Miguel and one of the housekeepers.'

'He will have to wait, I think.' Alexei pointed to a neon sign and a cluster of flashing lights. 'We are arriving.'

Unlike the modest, wooden buildings at Oru Ingenio and Atocha, the station at Uyuni was on a grander scale altogether. Running parallel with the tourist office on the eastern flank of the plaza, it was well lit, over a hundred yards long and surprisingly busy.

People on the platform had assembled in groups, most standing at the southern end where the second-class carriages and the *bodega* boxcar were expected to stop. Some of the groups were families, the children so bundled up against the cold that they were indistinguishable from the sacks of grain and vegetables that stood waiting to be loaded, while, here and there, a number of down-at-heel Indian *quirquinchos* were standing in the shadows or turning away their faces as the leading carriages passed by.

No sooner had the train squealed to a halt than first-class passengers began emerging from what looked like a restaurant or bar at the northern end of the platform. Apart from a young woman carrying a baby in her arms, all were businessmen – half a dozen of them, all hurrying to claim an unoccupied compartment for their journey to Oruro or La Paz.

Having boarded at the front of the train, the woman with the baby was the first of the passengers to come through the diningcar. Nodding pleasantly at Isabel, she continued on her leisurely way, unflustered by the impatience of the people behind her.

Isabel received a smile from one of the businessmen – a tall, smartly dressed young European who seemed less preoccupied than his briefcase-carrying companions.

Instead of returning his smile, she made a point of ignoring him, keeping her eyes fixed firmly on Ryder until they were by themselves again.

Why she had done it was unclear, but the suggestion of possessiveness had been so slight that he chose to disregard it.

'We might as well have a meal while we're here,' she said. 'If we go back to the compartment, you two are going to fall asleep and miss out on dinner.'

211

Alexei slid out of his seat. 'Señorita Corrales, you will order for me please,' he said. 'South American food is a mystery to me, so I shall rely on your good taste. Perhaps I can bring you back something from the shops?'

'Hershey's chocolate,' she said. 'But there won't be any.'

'I shall try for you. I will return shortly.'

Isabel had been maintaining a straight face, but now Alexei had gone she was giggling. 'He's always so serious,' she said. 'Doesn't he ever laugh?'

'Sure he does. He's still unhappy about the plane. He'll be fine when we get to Cali.'

'I'll get Aunt Christíana to adopt him,' she said.

'Alexei's a bit on the big side for adoption, don't you think? The Spetsnaz used to call him the *bolshoi medved.*'

'What does that mean?'

'Big grizzly.'

She toyed with the corner of the tablecloth. 'I'm not sure whether he'll like my uncle and aunt. Do you think he will?'

'He likes you, so he'll like them.'

'Oh.' She was pleased with his answer. 'You and Alexei are the same. Did you know that? It's funny, at one time I decided you'd be like Santos. But you're not. Alexei isn't either.'

Great compliment, Ryder thought. With Santos the least favoured flavour of the month, she might as well have said nothing. To change the subject he handed her the menu. 'You can order for me too, if you want.'

'All right.' She called over a waiter and began speaking to him in English, but quickly switched to Spanish when he asked her to slow down.

Instead of listening, Ryder was watching a woman outside on the platform who was struggling to tow along a young male goat. The animal was bracing its legs, fighting against the rope until it suddenly gave in and scampered off taking the woman with it.

There was little else to see. By now the majority of passengers were on board, although a few stragglers were still arriving, all but one heading for the rear carriages or the boxcar.

The exception was the tall young man who had smiled at

Isabel. Either because he'd been forced to go back for something, or perhaps because he'd wanted to check that his luggage had been safely stowed, he was boarding for the second time.

To Ryder, neither explanation seemed satisfactory. The man was being careful not to hurry, walking casually towards the back of the train instead of to the front.

Excusing himself, Ryder left his seat.

'Where are you going?' Isabel put down the menu.

'To see if Alexei's had any luck getting your chocolate. I'll only be a second.' Before she could protest, he squeezed past the waiter, made his way from the dining-car and disembarked.

Outside, the temperature was already below freezing, made colder by a breeze that was stirring up eddies of grit from the deserted platform.

The restaurant too was nearly empty. At the counter, a woman was sitting alongside a half-drunk Indian who had fallen asleep, while at the entrance to the kitchen the barman and a waiter stood smoking cigarettes.

Ryder didn't bother to ask if they'd seen Alexei. There was nowhere else he would have gone, and only one possible reason for him not to be here.

The men's toilet was at the north end of the building, clean and well appointed with hand basins and urinals along one wall facing a row of cubicles.

Ryder should have been relieved to find one of the cubicles occupied. Instead, all he experienced was dread.

He was unable to move, transfixed by the sight of something on the tiles at his feet – an empty box of Polaroid film.

There was no need to kick the door down. It was unlocked, already open wide enough to warn of the horror inside.

Blood was everywhere, smeared over the cistern, spattered up the partitions and still accumulating in pools all over the floor.

Alexei's lifeless body was wedged between the toilet-pan and the left wall. His eyes and mouth were open, his head tipped back to display the gaping, blood-filled gash across his throat.

Chapter 15

AN awful calm had come over Ryder. He welcomed it, recognizing it for what it was – not a fence but a temporary barrier to insulate him from reality so he could go on to do what had to be done now. There was no revulsion, no stomach-churning sickness, no trace of rage, no sense of loss. The calm was everything, so all-enveloping that he could feel nothing at all.

In the time it had taken to distance himself from the atrocity, all he had fought for three years to overcome and to forget had suddenly been brought back into focus. And with it had come what he knew would come – the clarity of mind that would allow him to rely entirely on instinct, experience and training.

He was already running, trying to pick out the right window of the dining-car, wrenching open the door of the nearest carriage and swinging himself on board a second before the train began to move.

In another second he had Isabel out of her seat, scattering coffee cups and magazines in his haste to get her on her feet.

'What are you doing?' She was startled. 'What's the matter? Where's Alexei?'

'Alexei's dead.'

'Oh God.' She gripped the edge of the table, then put her hands over her face. 'No. He can't be. He isn't. You don't know what you're saying.'

There was no time for nicety. 'We've got to find Santos fast.' He pulled away her hands. 'You go first. If you see that guy who

215

smiled at you, hit the floor and yell. It might just keep us alive. I'll be right behind you. Do you understand?'

She nodded.

'Go on. Do it.'

Holding her hand to prevent her from getting too far ahead, Ryder waited until they'd cleared the dining car before he started walking backwards, watching for a flicker of light from behind a curtain and listening for the telltale click of an opening door. He was calmer than ever, controlled and ready, prepared for the worst when Isabel stopped outside their compartment.

The curtains hadn't been drawn when Ryder left; now they were.

Making her stand aside, he crouched, sliding open the door with his foot.

Nothing happened.

Certain he was going to find Santos dead inside, he launched himself resolutely through the doorway.

The Colombian was very much alive, standing on the seat with a silenced automatic levelled at Ryder's head.

'Jesus.' Ryder slithered to a halt.

'I am sorry.' Santos lowered the gun. 'I did not know it was you. Something is wrong?'

'Yeah.' Ryder pulled Isabel inside and shut the door.

'Alexei is not with you?'

'Someone cut his throat in the station. He's dead.'

Santos was shaken, grim-faced and visibly distressed. 'Then we have been followed,' he said slowly. 'The man Vargas is with us on the train.'

'No he isn't. What was the name of that guy who wanted to buy the plutonium from Diaz?'

'Markovic.' Santos got down from the seat. 'You believe it is him? You think he comes to steal the canisters from us?'

'He's got something else in mind as well.' Ryder was planning his next move. 'He'll be working for the PAF.'

The news was another shock for Isabel. 'You can't know that,' she said.

'Trust me.' He wasn't going to tell her about the empty box of film. 'You bought lipstick and stuff in Tupiza, didn't you?'

She nodded.

'What about a mirror?'

She went to her bag and took out a cheap powder-compact. 'What do you want it for?'

This guy knows we're in first class: he knows Alexci's dead, and he probably knows we're sitting on five million dollars' worth of plutonium. We can't afford to be surprised.'

After crushing the compact under his heel, Ryder picked up the two largest pieces of broken mirror, giving one of them to Santos. 'You take the left side of the door,' he said. 'I'll take the right. You're looking for a tall guy wearing a dark suit, a white shirt, a tie and good shoes.'

'It is better if I go to find him.' Santos slipped the automatic into the pocket of his jacket. 'I am not someone he has seen before.'

'Bad idea,' Ryder said. 'Unless you've got another gun.'

'I have only this one.'

'Then you're staying here. We don't know where the bastard is. You could be searching the front end of the train while he comes at us from the back.' Ryder glanced at Isabel. 'Switch off all the lights. Smash the bulbs if you have to.'

Santos was already using his piece of mirror, resting his hand against the doorframe and positioning himself to obtain a clear view of the corridor.

'Let me have the gun,' Ryder said. 'This is my job, not yours.'

The Colombian unscrewed the silencer before handing over the little automatic. 'This will make it simpler to use,' he said. 'The noise, I think, is not important now.'

With its silencer removed, the gun was lost in Ryder's hand. It was the same .25 calibre Iver Johnson that Santos had used in Montréal, a gun so tiny that it would be ineffective at anything except point-blank range.

On the positive side, now Isabel had extinguished the compartment lights, it was easier to keep the corridor under observation, although Ryder knew the technique for doing so was

217

unsustainable. Steadying the mirror was difficult enough: holding it in place for God knows how long would be nearly impossible.

He was reconsidering his options when Isabel came to stand behind him. She stood close, wrapping her arms around his waist and holding on to him.

'I don't know what to say,' she whispered. 'If I'd never gone to Canada, Alexei wouldn't be dead.'

'It's not your fault.'

'If you see that man, you're going to kill him, aren't you?'

He didn't answer.

'You don't know the PAF sent him. How can you be sure?'

He prised her arms away. 'If Alexei was alive, he'd tell you how. If you don't like what's going to happen, don't think about it.'

'You still haven't said what you're going to do.'

'OK. How about I shoot the motherfucker four times in the stomach, then throw him off the train so he dies out there alone in the cold? Is that all right with you?'

'You're wrong about me.' She stepped away from him. 'I don't care what you do. I'm only trying to explain something.'

He never found out what it was. At the end of the corridor two children had appeared. They'd come from the carriages at the rear – a boy and a girl, both dirty and poorly dressed, hesitating now they'd entered forbidden territory. Behind them, half-hidden in shadow, was the figure of someone wearing a dark suit.

Ryder adjusted his grip on the automatic, angling his mirror in an attempt to see the man's face.

'He comes?' Santos enquired.

'Maybe.'

'When he is close, you must aim here.' The Colombian put a finger to his head. 'The gun is not good at longer ranges.'

Ryder wasn't listening. He was watching, waiting for the man to walk out into the light.

Suddenly, both children started running, laughing and shouting as they scampered past towards the dining-car. The man, though, was in no such hurry. Nor was he anyone Ryder had seen before. He was a stranger – not the man called Markovic, if that was his name, and not the threat Ryder had thought he was.

Santos was still tense, continuing to scan his end of the corridor, but having to relax one hand and hold the piece of mirror in his other. 'Mr Ryder,' he said, 'with so many hours ahead of us, I believe we will grow tired.'

'Have you got any ideas?'

'The train stops only at Colchani and at Rio Mulatos. Until then, there is nowhere for this man to hide. If the three of us go together, surely we will trap him.'

'We're not dealing with some hired gun off the street,' Ryder said. 'The PAF don't employ amateurs. If he's not looking for us, he'll be expecting us to look for him.'

'We can't all go,' Isabel said. 'Not unless we take the canisters with us.'

'Please be silent.' Santos had become more alert. 'There are people coming.'

It was another false alarm. An attendant from the dining car was escorting the children back to where they belonged, pretending to chase after them when they stopped to make rude signs at him.

By now, judging by the dwindling number of lights outside, the train was leaving the outskirts of the city, still travelling slowly and not yet clear of the points that marked the intersection of the north-bound tracks with the south-eastern lines to Chiguana and the Chilean border.

For Ryder, the speed of the train was unimportant, of no more consequence than its destination. He was aware only of the calm – the unforgiving, dispassionate resolve that, despite his three-year effort to bury it, had tonight resurfaced as though it had never gone away.

The third false alarm was not an alarm at all – the return of the dining-car attendant who spoke briefly to Santos on his way past, apologizing for any noise or inconvenience.

For the next five minutes the corridor remained unoccupied, but the respite was not to last. Shortly after the train had been overtaken by a faster-moving express, a reflection in Ryder's mirror told him that all his instincts had been right.

'Here we go.' His pulse quickened. 'Guess who.' For a moment he delayed, then, holding the automatic in both hands, he stepped out into the corridor.

The man was less than thirty feet away, inspecting a vacant compartment.

'Hey, Markovic,' Ryder called.

So rapid was the response that Ryder only caught a glimpse of the gun. He saw it swing upwards towards him, and just for an instant saw fear in the eyes of the man he was about to kill.

Ryder never squeezed the trigger. Blocking his view was the woman with the baby. She was leaving her compartment, closing the door behind her, ignorant of what was going on.

Unwilling to take the chance of hitting her, Ryder held his fire. Markovic had no such reservations.

The first shot shattered a pane of glass beside Ryder's head: the second splintered woodwork by his hip. At the same time the woman started screaming, clutching her baby, trying frantically to reopen her door as Ryder dropped his gun and sprinted past her, narrowly escaping a third bullet by throwing himself at Markovic.

The man was strong, but not strong enough.

Ryder slammed him back against a bulkhead, seizing his gun hand and swinging him round to break his elbow or dislocate his shoulder.

Had there been more room, he might have been successful. But Markovic was using his feet, levering himself away from the bulkhead, fighting for his life, sinking his teeth into Ryder's shoulder and just managing to break free.

Before Ryder could grab him again he was gone, pocketing his gun and disappearing into the dining-car.

Instead of pursuing him, Ryder retrieved the automatic and returned to the compartment where Santos was waiting with a length of thin steel wire in his hands.

'You won't be needing that.' Ryder pushed it away. 'I know where he is.' He paused. 'If I screw up, he can only come at you from one direction. All you have to do is watch the north end of the corridor.' He gave Santos the gun. 'Don't mess around. He's pretty fast. If you see him, you kill him.'

The Colombian nodded. 'You go to find him now?'

'Yeah.' Ryder glanced at Isabel. 'Promise you'll stay right here.'

Santos interrupted before she could reply. 'I shall accompany you,' he said.

'Like hell you will. You're not going anywhere. If I don't show up again, you don't leave this compartment until the train reaches La Paz. If either of you wants to go to the toilet, you go on the floor. You don't go to sleep and you never ever stop watching.'

'Then it is better you take the gun,' Santos said.

'I won't need it. You might. I'm relying on you. If anything happens to Señorita Corrales I'll be looking for you first. Do you understand me?'

Isabel had blocked the exit to the compartment. 'No,' she said. 'Ryder, this isn't going to bring back Alexei.'

'I know.'

'There's another reason, isn't there?' Slowly she lowered her arms. 'If you don't do this, you think he'll find you somewhere else, don't you?'

'You saw how it works up in Québec. He won't give up; the PAF won't let him. Look, everything's OK. I'll be back before you know it.' Ryder left her standing in the doorway, trying not to remember the way she'd been looking at him and wondering vaguely how so much blood could be leaking from his shoulder when he could feel little or no pain from the bite.

Markovic was seated at a table in the dining-car, clearly ill-at-ease, his eyes flicking from side to side, his face displaying signs of obvious anxiety. In front of him, an open magazine concealed the gun he was holding.

Ryder kept his own hand in his pocket, gripping an imaginary automatic while he continued to advance.

Here and there, people were sitting at other tables, the woman with the baby thankfully not among them. They were talking or eating, oblivious to the danger they were in, several of them in the direct line of fire if Markovic was to risk another shot.

Ready for one, on his toes, Ryder had his whole attention

focused on the magazine, knowing he'd have less than a second in which to duck for cover.

He was ten feet away when the tall man made his move.

But there was no shot.

Intimidated by Ryder's determination, instead of making a stand, Markovic retreated from the dining-car, backing away either as part of a predetermined strategy, or because he was afraid.

Ryder rushed him, almost getting a hand on the gun before Markovic kicked open a door on the left side of the carriage and leaped into the darkness.

For the briefest of moments Ryder hesitated, then he too made the commitment, swinging outwards wildly on the door before dropping into space.

Travelling at nearly fifteen miles an hour, he made the mistake of landing on his feet, jarring his knees and ending up in a heap, slithering face-down over an embankment of rocks that split open his chin and lacerated both his hands.

Once he'd stopped sliding, he stayed where he was, waiting for his eyes to become accustomed to the dark before he stood up to take stock of his position.

The moon was rising, still low, partly obscured by some streaks of cloud that were being dispersed by the wind, but providing sufficient light for him to get his bearings.

To his astonishment he knew where he was.

He'd never been here, but he'd seen this place before. Isabel had pointed it out from the road on their drive south into Uyuni a week ago. He was in the railyard – or what had once been a railyard.

All around him were the hulks of disembowelled steam loco-motives – dozens of them rusting away in the salt-laden air of the desert or lying in truck-sized pieces that were casting shadows everywhere.

Ryder could not have wished for more ideal surroundings. With all the cover he needed on a partially moonlit night, conditions would favour the hunter not the prey, and if he'd been able to choose his ground, he could not have chosen anywhere better.

He listened now, knowing that success depended on the detection of sound rather than movement, attempting to filter out the background noise. There was none. Except for the almost inaudible moaning of the wind, the railyard was eerily quiet – another plus, another edge – this one based on his experience over the last week out on the cold and equally silent Altiplano.

Tonight Ryder was insensitive to the cold. He couldn't feel anything, detached so completely from himself that he was aware only of his reliance on the intuition that had kept him alive in similar situations.

At night in the African jungle, the hum of insects had been unceasing. In the ruins of Sarajevo, the sounds had been of muffled gunfire, distant traffic and of people shouting. But here, the only sounds were that of his own breathing and the slight crunch of gravel whenever he took a step.

The railyard was covered in the gravel – acres of it, crisscrossed with tangled tracks and littered with the remains of the locomotives that, like Markovic, had been delivered here to die.

It was the gravel that made it easy for Ryder. He was wearing the boots he'd had on for weeks. They were broken-in, soft-soled and made relatively little noise on any surface. But the man he was hunting was less lucky. Markovic was wearing expensive city shoes. Ryder remembered seeing them on the train, just as he remembered seeing the fear in the eyes of the man who wore them.

He set off along the base of the embankment, walking cautiously but quickly, counting off a hundred paces before stopping to recalculate. If the train had indeed been travelling at fifteen miles an hour, and if he'd jumped from it twenty seconds after Markovic, then their initial separation would have been around 150 yards.

But what was the distance between them now? Had Markovic made use of his headstart? Or elected to lie in wait? Was he fifty yards away somewhere in the shadows? And if he was closer than that, how good a shot was he in the dark?

To find out, Ryder made the decision to continue, skirting the western edge of the embankment, walking steadily, aware that each step could be taking him deeper into danger.

How much danger depended on two things, he thought: on the accuracy of his calculation, and on who would reveal themselves first.

It had been ten minutes since the tail-light of the boxcar had disappeared into the night – long enough for the tall man to have made his way to safety unless he'd suffered injury in the fall. But if he was still here – where the hell was he? Did he know he'd been followed off the train? Had it been too dark for him to see?

The answer to Ryder's questions was nearly fatal. The bullet caught him under the right armpit, ripping him open and smashing one of his ribs.

This time there was pain. It was as though a nail had been driven through him, burning and twisting inside him as he ran, making him sweat and slowing him down before he could reach the cover of a derelict locomotive tender.

The wound was severe, already bleeding badly, and he could feel the broken ends of the rib that had deflected the bullet. But he'd seen the muzzle-flash – the only analgesic he needed – the give-away that told him exactly where he should begin his hunt.

For the next thirty minutes he became part of the night, unconscious of the blood trail that marked his passage across the gravel from one shadow to another, inching forwards, listening to each footstep, watching each shaft of moonlight and, above all, waiting – only moving when Markovic moved, gaining ground on each occasion to relentlessly reduce the gap between himself and the man he was tracking.

Not until he was in striking distance did he stop, standing motionless behind a pile of rotting railway sleepers, drawing on the pain to sharpen his senses, once again adopting the strategy that favoured the hunter – the ability to remain unseen for hour upon hour if necessary, increasing the pressure on a quarry who had no idea where the danger lay.

Markovic was the first to break. His nerve gone, unable to stand the strain any longer, he appeared from nowhere, gun at the ready but facing in the wrong direction. He was walking backwards, keeping in the shadow of the sleepers, looking nervously over his shoulder, but not often enough.

Before he knew what was happening, Ryder had him.

There was no struggle. So unequal was the contest that a man of twice Markovic's strength would have had lost the fight before it had begun.

In one smooth movement, Ryder had locked a forearm hard around his neck, choking off his windpipe and all but lifting him from the ground.

'Drop the gun,' Ryder commanded.

Markovic released it from his fingers.

'If you're working for the PAF, raise your right arm.' Ryder tightened his grip.

A gagging sound was accompanied by a delayed and almost imperceptible shaking of the man's arm.

'Do they know about the plutonium?' The nail in Ryder's side had been replaced by a white-hot iron. He was able to see that Markovic's arm remained stationary, but that was all he could see. His vision was blurring, he was dizzy and he could feel himself becoming weaker from loss of blood.

'One chance,' he said, 'the only one you're going to get. Swear you'll testify against the PAF and you might just live for another day.'

Choking on his own vomit, trembling and desperate to save himself, Markovic raised his arm.

'You lying piece of shit.' Ryder steeled himself. 'This is for Alexei. *Fgore v ardu.*' Using what strength he had left, he jerked Markovic's head sideways with his other hand, hearing the snap of the two vertebrae before the body twitched and suddenly went limp.

The execution had been as swift as it had been brutal, but now it was done – now it was over – Ryder couldn't bring himself to release his grip, wanting more than retribution, demanding it, searching for some sense of closure or satisfaction that he knew would never come.

In doing what Alexei would have expected him to do, he had achieved nothing. Worse still, by his own actions he had awakened a part of himself that should have been locked away forever.

He let the body slip from his grasp, but stayed in the shadow of the sleepers for several minutes, only stepping out into the moonlight when he realized that the calm and his sense of purpose had evaporated.

He was freezing, so cold that his hands and feet were numb. And he was shivering, finding it impossible to think coherently until he lay down on a slab of rust-streaked iron that he feared might well turn out to be the resting place where he would stay.

His hands and his shoulder were bleeding, blood was dripping from his chin, and for over half an hour, the flow of blood from his ribs had been continuous and unstemmed, saturating his clothes and running out sticky over his belt. How much he'd lost he didn't know. Not that it mattered. Not even the lost years and wasted opportunities mattered anymore. What regrets he had were not of the past, but of an unfulfilled future he'd once thought Isabel had held for him.

The moon was his reminder of her – of their first night in Canada, of their evenings in Cali and of the time they'd spent together out on the empty, windswept reaches of the Altiplano.

Tonight the moon was as white as he'd ever seen it, still rising over the railyard, but high enough for him to curse it for bringing back his recollections of her.

He shouted at it, raging against the PAF for making him into someone he could hardly recognize, denouncing everything that had brought him here to another killing field where, by avenging Alexei's death, he had succeeded only in creating a final, dreadful memory for himself.

His last thoughts were more muddled, and the images more confused. He was looking in a mirror at a reflection of the old man he would never be – grey-haired and frail, lips blue from the cold, his face a wrinkled mask with skin as thin and colourless as the moonlight.

Chapter 16

THE nightmare had been the same as the others. As usual he'd woken with a jolt, bathed in sweat, his heart pounding, knowing it had been a dream, but for a second or two unable to clear it from his mind.

This morning he could remember only fragments – the old man who'd summoned help after finding him dying in the railyard, the awful blank expression on Alexei's face, Pablo Corrales, the cabin burning at the lake, the Mogadishu church and the PC-6 slewing off the runway – overlapping pictures that, since his discharge from the hospital in Uyuni, had returned night after night in unpredictable and varying detail.

The antidote was sunshine – the more the better, because the more there was, the quicker the dreams could be dispelled, and the easier it was to pretend they would not recur.

In Cali at this time of year, sunshine was not in short supply. Every morning for the last four mornings it had come streaming through his bedroom window in great gushes.

Today was no exception. The whole room was filled with light. And the air was warm, bearing the scent of flowers from outside where there was the sound of bees already going about their business in the garden.

As was her custom, it was Aunt Christíana who brought him toast and coffee. She entered without knocking, smiling a good morning when she saw he was awake.

'You don't have to do this, you know,' Ryder said. 'You're making me feel like an invalid.'

'You should not be such a stubborn young man.' She placed the tray on the table beside the bed. 'You wish to show that your injuries are nothing, and that you are already as good as new.'

'Not quite.' Sunlight or not, Ryder was painfully aware of his rib, his shoulder, his chin and of the cuts in his hands. 'Is Señor Corrales back yet?'

'He has returned home last night. He says he is looking forward to seeing you again.' She helped Ryder sit up. 'It is not often my husband will admit to being wrong, but this time he believes he has made a very large mistake indeed. He understands how negligent he has been and blames himself for the death of your friend.'

'It's more my fault than his.' Ryder leaned back against his pillow. 'Maybe Alexei's too. He was pretty drunk. We both underestimated the PAF. If we hadn't done that, everything would've been fine.'

'You are too cynical. I cannot accept such a thing so easily. Until I made Isabel explain the marks around her wrists, I had no knowledge of the danger you had all been in because of my husband's foolishness. For a few hundred grammes of plutonium he has placed people other than himself at grave risk – something he has assured me he will not repeat.'

'He's on a fairly safe bet.' Ryder smiled at her. 'Unless the Russians try to launch another probe to Mars.'

'You do not know him as I do. He will soon find another project. He is the same as you.' She turned to go. 'Isabel says you also are searching for something.'

She left the room before Ryder could ask her what it was. When he wasn't sure himself, it was interesting to hear that Isabel had already decided – a sign that he either had some catching up to do, or that she'd reached yet another wrong conclusion about what he wanted, or where he was planning to go.

The time he'd spent in the Uyuni hospital had done little to help refine his ideas about the future, and even after the entirely unexpected arrival of Corrales at his bedside on the afternoon of his third day there, he'd been unable to clarify his thoughts about anything worthwhile.

In the short term, Corrales had solved the problem by arranging for Ryder to be driven to the airport at Sucre where, after being put on a pre-booked commercial flight to La Paz, he'd been whisked out of the country on the private jet that had brought him here to Cali.

Because it happened so rapidly, and because Corrales had remained behind – ostensibly to hire a new manager for his Potosí tin mines, unofficially to buy the silence of the old tramp who had saved Ryder's life in the railyard – it was only yesterday that the question of tomorrow or next week had assumed any real importance. But in preference to thinking about it, Ryder had chosen not to think about it, using the pain in his ribs as an excuse, taking each day as it came, trying without much success to forget what had happened at the station and in the locomotive graveyard while he regained his strength and pretended not to notice the attention he was receiving from a new and very different Isabel.

The change in her was all the more remarkable for being genuine – or what he imagined was genuine. To begin with he'd been wary. He'd seen her like this before – polite, self-assured and confident on her home ground now she believed she had nothing more to prove. But on this occasion, from his very first day back at the Corrales hacienda, as well as being perfectly natural, she'd seemed protective and unusually anxious about him – not necessarily as a result of family pressure, Ryder had decided, but because the uneasy truce between them had developed into something more long-lasting, or at least something to make her realize how closely they'd been drawn together by events.

Each evening without fail she'd changed the dressing on his shoulder, checked the stitches beneath the bandage where his bullet wound had been sewn up and inspected his hands to satisfy herself that the cuts were healing properly.

He'd become used to her breath on his face, to the touch of her hands, to the fragrance of her skin and the fresh smell of her hair. But he was under no illusions. Alexei had been right all along. In spite of any attraction she felt for him or how attracted he was to her, the gulf between them would always be there – an unwanted legacy that was unlikely to go away.

He dressed slowly, then went to find her, knowing where she'd be because at this time of the morning she was always swimming in the pool.

Today she wasn't. There was no sign of her. Instead, Miguel Corrales was standing alone at the poolside.

'Mr Ryder, good morning,' he said. 'I am pleased to see you are better. If you are looking for Isabel, I'm afraid she's not here. She has gone to collect one of the cars.'

'Where's she off to?'

'I understand she proposes taking you to Popayán. It is a long drive, but I believe you will enjoy your visit there.'

'Did you get things cleared away in Uyuni?'

'Of course. I am sorry it took me so long, but I thought it prudent to stay in Bolivia until the possibility of complications has passed. I consulted twice with the old man, and agreed to send him more money in four weeks' time. He is happy to co-operate.'

'What about Markovic?' Ryder asked.

'I made no enquiries, but in a place like Uyuni I can guarantee there will be no repercussions from the discovery of his body. Do not concern yourself.'

Ryder wasn't concerned. He was thinking, staring at the mosaic of the giant puma that decorated the bottom of the pool. When he'd seen it last, he'd considered it tasteless. Now he didn't. In the four days he'd been here he'd become accustomed to the way the Corrales family lived their lives, and this morning the display of affluence seemed if anything to be discreetly understated.

The collection of pre-Hispanic pottery was no more ostentatious than the cabinetfull of Calima gold or the Negret sculpture standing at the entrance to the patio, and just as his first impressions of Isabel had been wrong, so had his opinion of her family been distorted by the actions of her late father and by the undisguised wealth of her uncle.

'Mr Ryder.' Corrales cleared his throat. 'We have some things to discuss. If you would care to come to my study, perhaps we could go over them. I'm certain Isabel will not mind waiting for you.'

'Sure.' He was less than enthusiastic. Alexei's death had undermined his will to take on the PAF irrespective of how much help Corrales was willing to provide. Ryder didn't want help; he wanted peace – something unachievable unless he could start afresh by forgetting about Alexei, the PAF, the plutonium, Markovic and maybe even Isabel.

He followed Corrales to the study, watching while the Colombian opened a drawer in his desk and took out a scale model of a missile mounted on a launch pad.

'Mars-96,' Ryder said.

'Indeed. I had intended presenting it to you to commemorate the recovery of the canisters. However, I believe now that you may not wish to keep such a thing as a memento.'

Together with its probe, the missile stood nearly twelve inches high, a detailed replica of the Russian Proton rocket that had failed so spectacularly over the Bolivian high desert.

Although Ryder knew that turning down the gift would be ill-mannered, he was reluctant to accept it. 'Where are the canisters?' he asked.

'They are being utilized in the manner in which we agreed. You have completed your side of our bargain; I promise I shall complete mine. The sale of the plutonium is my responsibility.' Corrales looked awkward. 'I do not mean to be rude,' he said. 'only to assure you that I will fulfil my obligations.'

Ryder didn't doubt it. But he didn't much care. 'Do you still want information on the PAF?' he asked.

'Since Isabel has returned she has learned a great deal more from the Internet and from other sources – enough, I think, for our purposes.'

'Enough for you to have sent Santos to Europe? Isabel says you won't tell her what he's doing there.'

'It is better neither of you know. After the mistakes I have made, perhaps I do not deserve your trust. Nevertheless, from here on I would be grateful if you would leave things to me.' Corrales slid an envelope across the desktop. 'Mr Ryder,' he said, 'at the hospital in Uyuni I endeavoured to express my regret over what has occurred, but I believe I have not conveyed my true feelings. Because of my stupid ideas I have not only caused the death of your friend, but exposed both you and my niece to great danger. Had I suspected Diaz would betray my confidence, I would never have asked you to go to the white desert in Bolivia. I can only hope you will forgive my poor judgement.'

'It's OK. It's done.'

'But I remain in your debt.' Corrales hesitated. 'Without your courage, my niece would have perished in Canada. I have also learned that last week you again risked your life on her behalf. So, because I do not know how to thank you for what you have done, I would like you to accept an advance payment against the sale of the plutonium. Inside the envelope is a cheque for five hundred thousand American dollars.'

'Keep your cheque.' It was Ryder who was feeling awkward now. 'Shaft the PAF, then send me what you owe me.'

'If you will not accept my money, will you consider taking a position in the Corrales Corporation?'

'Couldn't you get anyone to run your mines in Potosí?' Ryder intended the remark to be a joke, but it had fallen flat.

Corrales was embarrassed. 'I have explained myself badly,' he said. 'Nothing could be further from my mind.'

Ryder pushed away the envelope. 'Look, you've already had to write off the cost of a PC-6 and a Jeep Cherokee, and you've been paying to fly people all around South America. Let's wait and see how things turn out, shall we?'

'Mr Ryder, my project has cost your friend his life. Compared with that, my personal expenses are of no consequence. There must be something I can offer you.'

'I don't want anything. Just keep in touch so I know what's going on.'

'I am sad to hear you intend leaving us soon, but understand you have not yet decided where you are going. To keep in touch, I will need an address.'

Ryder retrieved the envelope and scribbled on the back of it. 'Phone number in Luxembourg,' he said. 'It's the one Alexei and I used. You can leave a message on it any time.'

'I see this other number is for a post office box in London.'

'Right. In case you want to mail me something.'

'Have you thought that England may not be your best choice?'

'I'll be OK there for a while.' Ryder had given it no thought at all. 'The PAF have to hire themselves another gun before they can try again.'

'But you have somewhere to stay in England?'

'Grace's flat. You know – my sister's old place.'

'Of course. Forgive me for asking.'

Ryder wished he'd kept his mouth shut. 'It's sort of handy as a base,' he said. 'I haven't got any real plans.'

'I am in a similar position. My wife says she will not permit me to consider another project for a period of one year.' Corrales went to place the model on his bookcase. 'May I ask you something personal?'

'Sure. Go ahead.'

'I would like to know if you find my niece attractive.'

As much a loaded question as a personal one, Ryder thought. He was curious, wondering what had prompted it, but was prevented from finding out by Isabel's untimely return.

She came across the patio, limping slightly, swinging a video camera by its strap and waving a set of car keys at her uncle. 'I've brought the Mercedes,' she said. 'Is that all right?'

'Provided you drive with care.' Corrales frowned. 'Our guest, I'm sure, will appreciate a gentle ride.'

'Oh – yes.' She turned to Ryder. 'I thought we could go to Popayán, but I should've asked about your rib, shouldn't I? We don't have to go. We can have lunch in Cali if you'd rather. I know a place that makes the most amazing *lechona*. They play live salsa too.'

'Popayán's fine.' Ryder didn't mind where they went. As long as she was happy, one place was much like another, and unless she was going to surprise him, today was likely to be as uneventful as yesterday or tomorrow.

*

Popayán had not been the disappointment he'd imagined it might be. Instead it had proved to be one of the most beautiful cities he'd ever seen – a tranquil place of open streets, white-washed, colonial mansions and fifteenth century churches with magnificent high altars and breathtaking frescos.

Equally breathtaking was the young woman in whose company he'd spent the day. She'd changed into a strapless evening dress and was standing at a window in the lounge, staring out over the dark V of the valley towards the lights of Cali – the same young woman who had once tried hard to kill him, but who, over the course of the last few weeks, had transformed herself into someone else altogether.

Since their return to the hacienda, apart from insisting on using up the tape in her camera, she'd been quiet and uncharacteristically reserved, content to let Ryder get on with his drinking and only breaking her silence to ask if he was all right when she noticed how restless he was.

Ryder didn't feel restless. Now the Scotch had dulled the ache in his ribs and clouded his mind, he was able to watch her without considering whether leaving would be worse than staying, and over the last quarter of an hour, he'd even managed to stop wondering why she was so addictive and why it should be that fate had dealt them both such lousy hands.

'I ought to change your dressing for you,' she said. 'It's getting late.'

'Tomorrow'll do. You don't have to stay up because of me.'

She came to sit beside him on the sofa. 'Is that what you think?'

'What?'

'That I spend every day with you because you saved my life and stopped me from getting raped – because of everything that's happened to us.'

'No.'

'No what?'

'No, I don't think that.' All Ryder knew was that she was sitting too damn close. He could feel the warmth of her thigh against him, smell her perfume and imagine how wonderfully smooth and silky her skin would be to touch.

As though sensing his awareness of her, she leaned across and kissed him softly on the lips. 'Do you want to take me to bed?' she whispered.

So desirable and so irresistible was she that the temptation was overwhelming. For weeks he'd been anticipating what it would be like to kiss her open-mouthed, to undress her and to make love to her.

But something was wrong with the invitation – not an invitation, but an enquiry. Not, 'please take me to bed'. Not, 'I want you to', but a peculiarly hollow question.

A thank you? He wondered. Or worse still, in place of him accepting a job with her uncle or an advance of half a million dollars, was this his promised reward for services rendered to the Corrales empire?

He rejected the idea, determined not to have his fantasy about her spoiled. But fantasy or not, and no matter how impersonal the invitation had been, he knew he was incapable of turning down her offer – not simply because Alexei had foreseen the inevitability of this, but because, for a long time now, Ryder too had suspected that only by making love to her would he ever find the peace of mind to somehow and somewhere get on with what was left of his life.

He was too late making his decision. In the few seconds it had taken him to examine his motives, her confidence had gone, and he had lost her trust and wasted the opportunity.

She was crying, refusing to let him touch her, unable to face him, her expression confirming beyond doubt that the gulf had always been, and would always be, too wide for either one of them to bridge.

It had taken them two days to repair their relationship and to recover the ground they'd lost – two leisurely days spent either in the cool of the garden or out in the sunshine beside the pool, going over what had happened on the Altiplano, talking quietly about Alexei, about the Agudelo boy, Vargas, Diaz, Ramírez and about the man called Markovic.

Although their hours together had been spent well enough, not once had they touched on the poison that again had come between them on the evening after their visit to Popayán, and not once, as if by some unspoken understanding, had they discussed the future.

For both of them the prospect of a new future should have held some interest. But on the morning of the third day when she drove him to the airport, he found he could hardly bear to look at her. And because of the tears streaming down her cheeks when she kissed him goodbye, he could think of nothing at all to say.

Chapter 17

AT this time of the afternoon, the loch was invariably still and glassy, its surface unbroken except for streams of bubbles, or by ripples where fish were rising to snap at unwary flies.

Today, at the north end of the loch, the only disturbance was being caused by a manmade fly. For the last two hours Ryder had been casting it in the same place where the water was deeper and where he was sure the big fish was still lurking. He'd seen it twice in the last ten minutes, but because it had made no attempt to strike, he was beginning to think his afternoon would be no more successful than the others had been.

In the six weeks he'd been here he'd caught plenty of fish, but not the one he was after now. He'd first seen it about a month ago, an enormous brown trout that had made its home near the mouth of the river that connected Loch Calder to the sea. For Ryder the fish had become a challenge – sufficient justification for him to have rented the crofter's cottage and to have based himself in this part of Caithness where his only company had been the odd weekend fisherman or a passing hunter.

He was enjoying his time in Scotland, whiling away long, late-summer days with a fly rod in his hands, observing changes in the character of the loch in different weather, watching how the clouds gathered over the hills each evening and venturing into Halkirk only when he ran out of supplies or decided that he had to buy a new variety of fly.

The fly he'd bought yesterday wasn't working. It was indirectly responsible for his present mood. If he hadn't gone to town, he wouldn't have been near a telephone, and if he hadn't been near a phone, he wouldn't have made the mistake of ringing the Luxembourg number. He'd made the call on impulse, wishing almost at once that he hadn't because yesterday, for the first time in over two months, there had been a message on the tape.

It had been left by Miguel Corrales – a brief recorded statement from the Colombian saying he hoped all was well, and that a package had recently been airmailed to Ryder's post office box in London.

How long the message had been on the tape, Ryder didn't know. But its existence had been an intrusion, an unwelcome interruption when he'd been trying to persuade himself that the loch in Caithness was not dissimilar to the lake in Québec, and that his journey from one to the other had not necessarily been a complete mistake.

The fish had come to the surface again. Ryder could see it, but no sooner had he cast his line than, as if to demonstrate its indifference, the trout slapped its tail to drown a floating butterfly before disappearing in a swirl of water.

Tomorrow, Ryder decided, or maybe the next day if there were to be more cloud or perhaps a return of the misty rain which seemed to favour the angler rather than the fish.

He packed up his gear and walked back to the tiny stone cottage, endeavouring to decide which fly he should try next, but finding that his thoughts were elsewhere.

The message had done more than spoil his mood. By serving as a reminder of unfinished business, last night, for the first time in twelve nights, Isabel had played a part in the dreams, and today the bright water, the clouds and the heathland were no longer the catharsis they were supposed to be. They would always be here, but to be part of them – before he could properly find the peace they offered – Ryder knew there were two last steps he had to take – one that with any luck would enable him to stop treating every stranger with suspicion, and another that might allow him to remember Isabel only when he wanted to, and only on his own terms.

In the cottage, still lying on the table where he'd left it, was his most recent reminder of her – a pencil stub he'd found in a kitchen drawer – an old, wooden pencil that each time he sharpened it produced the fresh, clean smell of cedar.

Why it should have brought back his recollection of her so vividly, Ryder wasn't sure, although one evening two days ago when, for no particular reason, he'd identified the other fragrance that was a trigger for his memories, the same thing had happened. Then, it had been jasmine – some faint, long-remembered smell from childhood visits to his grandmother's garden. But since he'd started resharpening the pencil and been able to combine one fragrance with the other, Isabel had been occupying his mind more and more often.

To avoid thinking about her, after cleaning up and making himself some sandwiches, he divided his evening into two, spending the first half at the table while there was still daylight, retying half a dozen flies to make them more attractive in cloudy conditions, before he lit a candle and settled down to consider what the package from Corrales might contain.

By eleven o'clock, with the candle burning low, he'd grown tired of guessing and had stopped trying to decide whether or not he should bother to find out. But by the next morning, partly as a result of an unsettling dream in which Markovic had featured, and partly because the day had dawned fine and sunny without a hint of cloud, Ryder found that his plans had undergone something of a change.

Certain that the trout would remain where it was until he got back, he left the cottage early, throwing a few essential things into the back of his rental car before setting off towards the A882 for the twenty-mile drive to the little airport at Wick.

The woman who was supposed to be cleaning and looking after the flat was either doing a lousy job or not doing it at all. A layer of dust covered the furniture and the windowsills, and in spite of the summer weather, the lounge and bedrooms smelt musty and disused.

Ryder opened all the doors and all the windows before he checked to make sure everything was where it should be, going

239

through the ritual he went through whenever he came here because somehow it seemed to be important – a tenuous link with the family he didn't have and all that remained to remind him of his sister.

Her photo stood on the mantelpiece, a colour photograph that had been taken on her twenty-first birthday – a year after the car accident in Turin that had claimed the lives of both their parents, and eighteen months before she'd gone to Medellín to be a bridesmaid for her friend Dolores Moncado.

The longer Ryder studied the photograph the less inclined he was to open the parcel from Corrales. The parcel was another link to the past – not just the recent past, but to what had happened seven years ago in Colombia, a connection he himself had chosen to remake, and one that was now proving difficult to break.

An hour ago when he'd collected the parcel from the Cricklewood post office, he'd been looking forward to spending a couple of days in London – now he was less sure, wondering if he should have stayed up at the loch where the main unknowns were whether or not it was going to rain, and what kind of fly to select if it did.

He'd decided against opening the package in the taxi, realizing there was little point in doing so because, judging by its size and shape, it was almost certainly a video tape. But there it was, lying on the coffee table in front of him – half disturbing, half intriguing – another communication from South America to reinforce the link.

Rather as he'd thought, the parcel contained a VHS video tape. It also contained two envelopes in one of which was a cheque for US$525,000 drawn on a bank in Zurich.

The contents of the second envelope were more interesting – a receipt for a DM5,000 donation that had been made to the PAF by a Doctor Rudolph Schneider, and an embossed white card inviting the same Doctor Schneider to a major fund-raising dinner that the Peace Aid Foundation was holding in Geneva in two days' time.

In case the purpose of the invitation was unclear, Corrales had been thoughtful enough to include a slip of paper confirming a pre-paid, four-night reservation for a Mr Christopher Ryder at the Jet d'Eau hotel on the Geneva lakefront.

Ryder didn't know whether to be pleased or not. But for his chance call to the Luxembourg number he wouldn't have received the message from Corrales, and if he'd put off collecting the parcel until the weekend, the PAF function would have been over and done with before he'd known anything about it.

But he did know about it, and any idea of not bothering to view the tape seemed as stupid as pretending he could somehow sever his involvement with Corrales, with the Mars-96 project or with the PAF.

Wondering if he was about to discover whether the Colombian had completed his part of their agreement, Ryder switched on the television, loaded the tape into the VCR and sat back to watch.

The tape had been shot professionally in full colour with none of the shake or graininess he'd been expecting, and with high quality sound to match. The first frames set the scene – colourful images of Monaco on a sunny day showing tourists gathered outside the cathedral and the Royal Palace, and a number of views of the waterfront. Close-ups of street signs and hotels were interspersed with pictures of exclusive shops, and there was even a short clip of a bikini-clad girl falling off her jet-ski in the harbour near a cluster of expensive motor-yachts.

One of the yachts had been singled out especially. Except for being large and fairly modern it was unremarkable, but obviously important in some way. Several shots of the name *Valencia* on its bow were followed by a sequence during which the camera zoomed in to show the face of a man who, having alighted from a taxi at the harbourside, was about to board the boat.

The man was Santos, smartly dressed and instantly recognizable, not just by his ponytail and diminutive stature, but because of the heavy container he was carrying.

Ryder was fascinated, watching as the Colombian walked down the gangplank and waved to someone on the *Valencia* who was waiting to greet him.

Three people were on deck, all captured unknowingly by the camera almost as though they'd been posing to have their pictures taken. Ballantine and Latimer were wearing sunglasses, but at close range as unmistakable as Santos and the Frenchman, Poitou, who suddenly turned and disappeared down a companionway.

The next segment was more relevant – selected footage from two cameras hidden on the boat, one located in a wood-panelled lounge somewhere below decks, the other carried on board by Santos himself, either concealed in the plutonium container or perhaps in the lapel of his suit.

These pictures were less clear than the ones taken in bright sunlight from the shore, but what they showed was dynamite.

The coverage was of three separate meetings between Santos and the unfortunate and unsuspecting PAF directors. At the first meeting, Ballantine did most of the talking, asking questions and occasionally taking notes or pausing to speak privately to Latimer and Poitou.

Throughout the discussions, not once did Santos blink or falter, explaining how, at some considerable cost to himself, the canisters had been smuggled out of the Russian Krasnoyarsk-26 nuclear processing factory in Siberia, and that accordingly the plutonium was guaranteed to be weapons-grade material. His answers on why he'd approached the PAF were equally plausible – well-rehearsed statements portraying the Colombian as a procurer of some sophistication, but who nevertheless needed the marketing expertise of internationally respected traders in order to maximize the return on his investment.

Ryder had already seen enough of the tape to know he was not only watching a clinical exposure of the men who ran the Peace Aid Foundation, but witnessing the end of an organization that had been rotten from the day of its inception.

He'd underestimated Santos, he realized. In every scene the Colombian was utterly controlled, displaying just the right degree of confidence, always well mannered and polite, and always taking negotiations one step further whenever there was a sticking point or some disagreement over terms.

Despite heavy editing, the evidence the tape presented could not have been more condemning, showing the PAF directors in a light that the most jaded businessman would have flinched to see. Minute by minute, hour after hour, meeting after meeting, by using the spade Corrales had given them, Ballantine, Latimer and Poitou had dug themselves into a hole from which they would never be able to get out.

By now Ryder was fast-forwarding the tape, slowing it only to view those sections which seemed to be particularly incriminating. The best of them came near the end. It showed Ballantine puffing on a cigar while Latimer placed a number of overseas telephone calls via the *Valencia*'s land-line – calls that were the equivalent of the last nails in the PAF's coffin.

What viewers of the tape knew, but what Latimer didn't, was that the phone line had been tapped, allowing both sides of the conversation to be recorded.

Four calls were made; one to Syria, one to Pakistan, another to Iraq and one to a gruff-sounding gentleman in Israel who wisely refused to divulge his name.

The conversations were wide-ranging, dealing principally with such matters as the purity of the merchandise, the quantity of it, the method of delivery and, inevitably, the price – discussions with people in countries that were either fledgling nuclear powers or with leaders of well-known, international terrorist groups.

At a quarter of its length the tape would still have been the most comprehensive indictment that Ryder could have hoped for. He was amazed, wishing Alexei could have known, wishing things could have turned out differently in Uyuni, but believing for the first time ever that what he and Alexei had set out to do had finally and irrevocably been done.

He remained seated in front of the television for several minutes staring at the blank screen, relieved and pleased – but no more than that, searching again for a sense of satisfaction that was as absent now as it had been in the railyard after he'd taken the life of the man who had killed his friend.

But what the hell was he expecting? When the costs of the project had been so high, and success so long in coming, satisfaction would always be elusive, he decided, which was why, instead of dwelling on what might have been, it was better to concentrate on the positives.

Over the last few weeks, besides making a lot of money for himself, the ghost of Isabel's father had been laid to rest, and thanks to her uncle, to Santos and to Alexei, the PAF had committed a spectacularly public suicide. Or was that yet to come? Was that the reason for his mysterious invitation to the PAF's fund-raising dinner in Geneva?

An hour ago he'd had every intention of returning to Scotland tomorrow, but since viewing the tape, a quick trip to Switzerland no longer seemed such a bad idea – particularly when he was already halfway there. A good enough excuse, he thought. And even if it wasn't, he owed it to Alexei to see things through to the end, whatever kind of end that might turn out to be.

Ryder was enjoying Geneva. He was also in better spirits than he had been for some time. In London he'd felt threatened by the crowds, but here along the tree-lined quayside of Lake Geneva where everyone had room to move, and where there were plenty of open spaces, he was not uncomfortable at all.

This evening, the majority of people were in no hurry to go anywhere – either tourists enjoying the sight of the fountain or young lovers who were preoccupied with each other.

Ryder wasn't preoccupied with anything. Apart from an occasional thought about the trout and the odd twinge of loneliness, he was managing to keep his mind off the past, curious about the dinner he was about to attend, but pleasantly detached from the events that had brought him here on this warm, summer night.

To enjoy his newfound freedom, instead of taking a taxi from his hotel, he'd elected to walk the few blocks to the PAF's conference centre on the Rue de la Terrassière, mixing with other guests who had made the same choice. Ryder could pick them out – the truly wealthy, the industrialists, and politicians and dignitaries accompanied by their wives – all immaculately dressed and all on foot to show how unassuming and how very ordinary they were.

The famous and the new-rich had no such pretentions. They were arriving outside by the carload – overweight, middle-aged men attended by uniformly attractive young women displaying the latest creations from Galliano, Dior or Valentino, all long legs and smiles as they alighted from their limousines to wave at the paparazzi.

Ryder joined them at the entrance, showing his invitation to a doorman who, after checking a list of names, directed him to table number thirty-five.

In a room of more than a hundred tables, the noise level was already extremely high, all but drowning out the music from a string quartet that was doing its best to contribute atmosphere to another glittering occasion in the Geneva social calendar.

To Ryder, the occasion seemed more surreal than glittering. Along the lakefront the crowds were fine. This was different. After weeks out on the Altiplano and up at the loch, so foreign was the environment that he was on the verge of making a tactical withdrawal when the sight of two people at table thirty-five caused him to reconsider.

'Ah, Doctor Schneider.' Santos was smiling broadly as he stood up to greet him. 'I am glad you were able to come. May I introduce my wife, Carlotta? She has been looking forward to meeting you.'

Carlotta Santos was no taller than her husband, but rather plump and voluptuous with large brown eyes. She was adorned in gold bracelets to match her necklace and wearing a startlingly low-cut evening gown. 'Mr Ryder,' she said, 'this is a great pleasure for me. Señor Corrales was not certain you would receive his message, so he will be happy to learn you are here tonight. May I ask if you have travelled from Canada?'

'No. I've been up in Scotland for a while. You've come a lot further than I have.'

She smiled. 'My holiday is a present from Señor Corrales. He is grateful for the work my husband has done, so he pays for my airfare. This is very exciting for me. I have not before been to Europe.'

'You like the tape?' Santos enquired.

Ryder nodded. 'What have you done with it?'

'One month ago, copies were supplied to Interpol and to authorities in four different countries. I understand they have expressed great interest in what they have seen.'

Ryder could imagine. 'What about the plutonium?'

'The PAF have paid much money for it, so for the moment it is in their care. But last week I have had some frank discussions with a gentleman from the Russian Embassy. He is expecting to receive the Mars-96 canisters on behalf of his government some-time tomorrow morning.'

'After Interpol's got tonight out of the way.'

'I believe we will not have long to wait.' Santos checked his watch. 'Although we must first hear an address by Ballantine, I am told that before the meal is served we can expect a small sur-prise.'

'Why so public? Why not just lock up the bastards and throw away the key?'

'The Swiss police wish for the best coverage from the interna-tional Press. It is not often conspiracy on such a scale can be exposed, and since there are other people here who have been doing business illegally with the PAF, it is a good place for a net to be cast a little wider.'

If police and undercover agents were hanging around some-where, Ryder couldn't detect them. Except for two men checking out the public address system on the stage, there weren't even any likely candidates.

Carlotta Santos reached across to touch his arm. 'Mr Ryder,' she said, 'I was so very sorry to hear about your friend Alexei. After this evening, I hope you will feel better.'

Ryder didn't think it would alter things much. He was still detached, watching what was going on around him, but knowing he wasn't part of it, and wishing this was over.

On the rostrum now, where the members of the string quartet were putting away their instruments, spotlights had come on to illuminate a large green flag bearing the PAF's olive branch logo.

The directors emerged from the wings one at a time, Ballantine first, then Poitou and then Latimer, their attitude one of fawning gratitude, their smiles as false as the rising swell of applause from the audience.

After Ballantine had found a microphone he stepped forwards into the lights and waited for the room to become quieter. 'Ladies and gentlemen,' he said, 'honoured guests and friends of the PAF; on behalf of the orphans, the dispossessed and of all the victims of war, may I extend the warmest of welcomes to you.'

'First I have a confession to make. When my fellow directors proposed that we launch another international appeal for the refugees of Kosovo, I must tell you that I was reluctant to believe we could raise sufficient funds to carry on our work. With so much suffering in so many countries, and when the international community is continuously bombarded with requests for money, medicine and aid, there is a real danger of reaching a plateau of donor exhaustion. For this reason I feared we would be less than successful in our efforts.' Ballantine paused for effect. 'How very wrong I was. I am humbled not only by your attendance at this dinner and by the donations you have so generously made, but by your willingness to assist those people of the world who are less fortunate than us. They are everlastingly in your debt for your unselfishness, your kindness and more than anything because of the simple humanity which you all bring with you to this dinner.'

Ryder couldn't listen, sickened by the overblown rhetoric that for the last seven years had diverted a torrent of funds into PAF-owned companies whose dealings had taken a thousand lives for each one they'd ever saved.

If Santos shared Ryder's disgust, he showed no sign of it. Instead he was sitting on the edge of his seat, plainly anticipating a change in tempo. 'Mr Ryder,' he said, 'this is what we have come to see. I believe you will not wish to miss it.'

Ryder wasn't listening to Santos either. He was elsewhere – back in the canyon on the border of the Altiplano, his Winchester centred on the chest of the man who was going to rape Isabel. The need to squeeze a trigger now was no less than it had been then, but tonight he knew that somehow or other he would have to accept the serving of justice in a very different form.

Ballantine had started reading out a list of causes that were supposed to benefit from the dinner when the spotlights went out, and six men walked on to the stage. Unarmed and casually dressed, they acted in pairs, speaking briefly to Latimer, Poitou and Ballantine before each director was handcuffed and led down a short flight of steps at the front of the stage.

One of the men remained behind, tapping the microphone to make sure it was working. 'Ladies and gentlemen,' he said, 'please remain seated. There is nothing to be alarmed about. I'm sorry to inform you that what you have just witnessed is the arrest of the organizers of this dinner. I am not prepared to elaborate on the reasons; however, I can tell you that charges include threats to the security of several overseas governments, terrorism, treason, illegal supply of arms, extortion, the widespread violation of international treaties as well as a number of other wide-ranging charges that are in the process of being lodged by the British, the French and the United States. I understand your meal will be served shortly, so unless your appetite has been spoiled, there is no need for anyone to leave. Thank you for your time.'

Ryder had been watching Ballantine's expression. In the space of a few minutes it had gone from annoyance to rage, to consternation and finally to panic. His normally florid face was drained of colour and he was stumbling so badly that he was having to be supported.

Latimer and Poitou were similarly shocked, although the American senator was still protesting, shouting ineffectually while the Frenchman seemed to be in danger of having a heart attack, sweating heavily and pleading for his handcuffs to be removed.

The room had been remarkably silent, but now the directors were being escorted away, the noise level was increasing and soon the place was in an uproar.

People were on their feet, some of them bewildered, some shocked and several hurrying to leave, only to be apprehended at the door.

Reporters were quick to exploit the disruption, clambering on to chairs and tables to get the best photographs, or holding microphones and cameras high above the heads of guests who'd begun swarming around the group of departing directors.

Ryder too was on the move, forcing his way to the front of the crowd until he was in position, ready to do what had to be done.

Poitou saw him first. The Frenchman stopped in his tracks, unable to conceal his disbelief, muttering stupidly to Latimer who spun round to find Ryder standing at his shoulder.

Like Latimer and Poitou, Ballantine was stunned, staring blankly at Ryder, refusing to walk any further, his mouth working but without producing any words.

'Markovic wasn't good enough,' Ryder said. 'Now it's your turn. How does it feel?'

Still speechless, Ballantine was choking now, blinking in the light of the flashbulbs, his face a mask, his hands shaking.

'I've come to make you a promise.' Ryder kept his voice level. 'You'll only be getting out of where you're going in a box, so on the day they slam the lid down on you, *fgore v ardu.*'

He turned his back on the three men, fighting the impulse to say more – to do more – not trusting himself to leave things as they were, but knowing that, whether he liked it or not, the time had come to finally let go.

This wasn't justice. But what else was there? Not a broken neck or a .44 through the chest, but the only compensation there would ever be for the lives that had been twisted and cut short by men who, until tonight, had thought themselves beyond the law, yet who would still not suffer as they deserved to suffer.

He returned to the table and sat down, unsettled and feeling even more out of place than he had done before.

Santos, by comparison, had a different perspective on the evening. He was delighted, clearly pleased that the last stage of the Mars-96 project had been completed and evidently preparing to celebrate in style. 'You have something nice to say to Sir Richard?' he enquired.

'Same thing I told Markovic.'

'I am permitted to know what?'

'I told him to burn in hell. I'll take him there myself if I'm still around.'

'I think it is better we first make a toast to Alexei, and then have many more drinks together until you forget Markovic and these men who hired him.'

Ryder needed a drink, but he didn't want to have one here. He wanted to be by himself, to be somewhere quiet, either out in the fresh air or maybe alone in his hotel room where he could unwind in his own time.

'I'm not staying,' he said. 'You don't need me hanging around.' He smiled at Carlotta Santos. 'Have a nice dinner and a great holiday. If I get into trouble again, I might have to give your husband a call. Is that OK?'

'Of course. He has instructions from Señor Corrales to give any assistance you require.' Reaching into her handbag, she produced a small package. 'If you are going now, you must take this. It comes from the *señorita*.'

'What is it?'

'I am asked only to give it to you. A present perhaps.'

It wasn't a present. It was another damn video tape. He could tell by the weight and size. But he could no more guess why Isabel had sent it than he could imagine what might be on it.

He said goodbye to Santos and his wife, took a quick look around the banquet hall, then threaded his way through the people and headed for the door where the police were checking for identification before letting anyone out on to the street.

Ryder showed his invitation, wondering what he'd do if the name Schneider was to backfire.

It didn't. The young officer who inspected the card gave it barely a glance, wishing Ryder good evening in German and holding the door open politely for him.

Outside on the Rue de la Terrassière there was little activity now. There were no photographers, no police and no sign that Ballantine, Latimer and Poitou had ever been here. Like the cars that had taken them away, they were gone, and with them had gone Ryder's reason for being here as well.

He was glad he'd come nevertheless. Though his evening could have been better spent, the journey from Scotland had been worthwhile if only to bring finality to the mission he'd begun all those weeks ago in Canada when his excuse for travelling to South America had revolved more around Isabel than it had around any idea of killing off the PAF.

The irony was that by starting out on one thing he had accomplished something else, Ryder thought, a success rate of fifty per cent, but only if he ignored the cost and only if the dreams were going to stop one day.

He walked back slowly to the lakefront, enjoying the night air, reluctant to return to his hotel, because if he did that he'd have to play the tape, and then the need for a drink would become more pressing than it was already.

In the half an hour it had taken him to get a VCR delivered to his room, Ryder had not achieved a great deal. He'd consumed four miniature bottles of Scotch from his mini-bar, opened the package from Isabel and deposited the contents on the bed where they'd remained ever since.

In Grace's flat three days ago in London he'd been presented with an identical set of items. But the envelopes from Corrales hadn't been perfumed and the video tape had not borne a label. This one did – a white, adhesive label on which the word SUN-DANCE had been written in large letters.

Leaving the envelope unopened, Ryder switched on the television and loaded the cassette, waiting to see if this tape would be as intriguing as the other one.

The opening scene caught him off guard – a panorama of the Altiplano, taken at the airstrip on the morning of their fourth day there. The next shot was of Alexei emerging from the underside of the PC-6 where he'd been searching for the fuel leak. Smothered from head to foot in dust, he was unshaven and dirty, turning his back on Isabel and swearing at her in Russian whenever she tried to get a close-up of him.

Ryder hadn't realized she'd managed to save the tape, assuming it had been lost along with the camera on the night they'd abandoned the hut. But it hadn't been lost. There was more to come – shots of the hut itself, of the little sheds behind it and of

251

the runway shrouded in morning mist as the sun came up.

In the third sequence, Ryder was standing alone by the rim of a dust-bowl on the afternoon they'd dug up the last of the canisters. He too was filthy and unshaven, wearing a dead man's jacket, grinning like an idiot while he brandished the Winchester at the camera.

Wild though the Altiplano was, on video tape it appeared to be even more desolate than the empty, high-altitude tablelands that Corrales called the white desert.

Ryder could smell the sulphur, feel the cold and hear the wind moaning through the louvres in the hut – but not for long. Already the scene had changed from the bleakness of the desert to the colourful, sunlit city of Popayán – a brief two or three minutes of tape showing him walking along a street outside one of the churches they'd visited there.

So sudden was the jump that the tape had come to an end before he noticed. He let it run, more interested in opening the envelope than he had been, guessing it held copies of the still photographs Isabel had taken in Bolivia.

He was wrong again. The envelope contained a note and a handful of what looked like coarse, irregularly shaped confetti. Ryder knew what it had been made from – photographs, but not of the Altiplano or Popayán. The confetti was all that remained of the pictures the PAF had given her, the photos of his first assignment in Medellín, none of the pieces larger than a fingernail, but as easy to recognize as it was difficult to understand her purpose in sending them to him.

Her note was equally ambiguous:

```
I shall always remember you.
        All my love,
        Isabel. xx
```

Unlike the handwritten letters he'd received from her uncle, this had been typed on a computer, an impersonal message that, despite its sentiment, did little to make things clearer.

Were the torn up photos supposed to tell him something,

Ryder wondered? Were they intended to show him that the past no longer mattered to her? Or simply a means to rid herself of guilt so that, like him, she could start her life afresh?

He was no closer to making up his mind when the phone rang.

The call was from a woman in reception who apologized for disturbing him so late.

'What can I do for you?' Ryder asked.

'A Señor Santos is here to see you. He says he has some news.'

After an evening out at the dinner, the last thing Ryder wanted was more company. Whatever the news was, it would keep until tomorrow. On the other hand, he didn't want Santos to think him rude or ungrateful.

'OK,' he said. 'Ask him to come up.'

He switched off the TV and the VCR, then swept the confetti into a waste-paper basket and crumpled up Isabel's note, pleased that she'd sent it even though she'd only written three short lines. He could ask Santos how she was and what she was doing with herself, he decided, assuming the Colombian was sober and willing to discuss the personal affairs of his employer's niece.

Ryder was still gathering up bits of stray confetti when a tap on the door told him that his visitor had arrived.

'Come on in,' he called. 'It's not locked.'

The door swung open, but it wasn't Santos standing in the corridor: it was Isabel, smiling self-consciously, but becoming more confident now she'd seen the expression on Ryder's face.

Lightheaded from the Scotch, for a moment or two he refused to believe it could be her, too disconcerted to say anything and dazzled by her appearance.

She was wearing a knee-length yellow skirt, a white, cutaway halter shirt and flat-heeled shoes – plain, ordinary clothes making her so achingly beautiful that he couldn't take his eyes off her.

He was confused, distrusting his instincts for the second time tonight, half-expecting her to vanish in a puff of smoke.

'I haven't got things wrong, have I?' she said.

He shook his head.

'That's all right then.' She entered the room, closed the door behind her and started taking off her ear-rings. 'I couldn't stop thinking about you,' she said, 'you know – about us. It got worse and worse – every day and every night – so I had a long talk with Aunt Christíana. She guessed you'd be here and said I'd be crazy if I didn't come to say hello.' She paused awkwardly. 'So here I am. You don't mind, do you?'

'No.' Ryder didn't mind. 'You look wonderful.'

'Well, *muchas gracias.*' She came to stand in front of him and held out her wrists. 'No scars. My leg's all right too. Do you want to see?'

An answer was unnecessary.

To show him the bullet wound this time, instead of lifting her skirt, she took it off completely. Then she stepped out of her shoes and slowly removed her shirt.

'You're not like anyone I've ever met,' she whispered. 'And in my whole life I've never wanted anything as much as I want you. So, unless you've got a better idea, I thought we could carry on from where we left off after we'd been to Popayán. You remember that, don't you?'

Ryder didn't think he'd forgotten anything. But he had. No sooner had he kissed her than he realized how much. He'd forgotten the taste of her lips, the touch of her hair against his face and he'd forgotten how heady the feeling of anticipation could really be.

Because their last kiss had been as tentative as it had been short-lived, this one was going to make up for it. Now she was in his arms she was pressing against him, eyes shut, her mouth fastened on his mouth, her tongue flickering over his, offering herself to him while she pulled off his shirt and fumbled to unbuckle his belt.

He had the presence of mind to make things easier. Gathering her up in his arms, he carried her into the other room and lowered her on to the bed where he removed the remainder of his clothes and helped her strip off the rest of hers.

Now she was naked she was squirming, her skin on fire, incapable of curbing her demands, thrusting her breasts up hard into his palms and immediately spreading her legs when he slid his hands down over the taut, flat muscles of her stomach to touch and caress her between her thighs.

For Ryder, adrift in a haze of perfume and desire, unable to think of anything except the need to possess her, this was the culmination of what he too had wanted for so long – not the imagined, false reward that had spoiled their evening in Cali – not compensation for the hurt that had gone before, but a shared reparation for all the wrongs, and justification at last for all the years it had taken them to find each other.

Although she was guiding him urgently with her hands, he tried to prolong the moment by entering her slowly, only pushing when she arched her back to receive him and waiting until she was fully penetrated before he lifted his face away from hers to look down at her.

She was struggling to catch her breath, wide-eyed and eager for him to continue. 'Go on,' she whispered. 'Please.'

Lingering was not an option. The instant he kissed her again she started to move beneath him, holding him to her and murmuring his name as together they embarked on an intoxicating ride towards a climax of such exquisite and hedonistic pleasure that it left her gasping and Ryder's heart pounding like a hammer against his injured rib.

The pain was his reminder – a reminder of the extraordinary events that had brought her to him on this warm, summer night in Geneva where she alone would now begin to drive away the dreams and provide the peace that without her he had once thought he would never find.

She lay beside him quietly on the bed, content, holding his hand as if to preserve her claim on him, already half-asleep, not even opening her eyes when he pulled her hair away from her face and drew his finger gently across her lips.

He had things to say, but it seemed a shame to disturb her.

He wouldn't mention the big trout until he'd got her back to Scotland with him, he decided, although it might still be worth waking her up so he could tell her where they were going, and so she'd understand why there would never again be the need for him to resharpen the little cedar pencil at the cottage.

Author's Note

Although this book is a work of fiction, parts of it are based on fact. The ill-fated Mars-96 space probe was indeed launched shortly after midnight on Saturday, 16 November from the Russian Baikonur Cosmodrome in Kazakhstan.

Eyewitness accounts of the probe's re-entry are authentic and well documented, as are the statements describing the likely area over which the wreckage is scattered. To date, no searches have been mounted for the plutonium canisters. Consequently, they lie waiting to be discovered by anyone who cares to look for them.

The small hut which serves as Bolivia's farthest-flung meteorological station is, however, not recommended accommodation for that part of the country.

C.D.P.